Ulysses's Ultimatum

Love in Mission City Book 7

Gabbi Grey

Finn

Ulysses MacDonald left my bed after earth-shattering sex, but he certainly hasn't left my mind. When he turns up as the Mission City Gazette's new editor, I'm intrigued. Then he starts poking around my fire hall, sneaking and spying. He won't tell me what he's doing there, and he keeps dodging my attempts to get close. I don't trust him, but Ulysses is hot as hell, and I hate realizing I still want him.

Ulysses

Sleeping with Finnegan O'Sullivan should've felt like a mistake—but it doesn't. I'm still attracted to the firefighter's quick wit and willingness to put his body on the line to save total strangers. But an anonymous tip has led me to illegal activities in Fire Hall One, and I'm a reporter before anything else. I'm not going to back off or get distracted, just because Finn is around. My first job now is to figure out if Finn is involved in the crimes, or just an oblivious bystander. If I'm wrong, I might ruin a good man's reputation. Oh, and I might also get us both killed.

Ulysses's Ultimatum is an interracial, age-gap, grumpy/sunshine, small-town, gay romantic suspense novel with a valiant firefighter, an investigative reporter with a dubious past, and the secret that might destroy them both.

This is a work of fiction. Names, characters, places and incidents are either the products of the author's imagination, or are used fictitiously.

References to real people, events, organizations, establishments or locations are intended to provide a sense of authenticity and are used fictitiously. Any resemblance to actual events, locations, organizations, or persons living or dead is entirely coincidental.

Edits by ELF

Cover by Jo Clement

Dedication

Danika

Marilyn

Rossco

Martyn

Shawn

Kaje

Renae

ELF

Wendy

Contents

Chapter One

Ulysses

I didn't expect the next time I'd run into Finn O'Sullivan would be in a gay bar.

I *should* have.

But I hadn't.

The man was the same cool drink of iced tea on a hot day that he'd been months ago when I'd snuck out of his bed in the middle of the night and ridden away on my motorcycle.

Now, I sat at the bar and he stood in the doorway.

Our gazes locked.

I refused to admit that my breath caught and my heart sped up. This wasn't a cheesy romance movie.

He arched an eyebrow.

I gestured with my beer bottle to the seat beside me. As a rule, I didn't drink alcohol. Today, though, I was already making an exception.

With the grace of a cat, he slid onto the stool next to me.

"Hey, sugar." The server appeared out of nowhere. "How's it going, Finn?"

"Doing well, Marc, thanks. Just a root beer. I'm driving tonight."

"Fair enough. Coming right up."

Marc was one handsome man and, for just a moment, I wondered if he and Finn had ever slid between the sheets together.

None of your fucking business.

Nope, it truly wasn't.

My gaze cut to Finn. Same spiky red hair. Same trim figure with just the right amount of muscles under that jacket—very necessary for hauling around all that firefighter gear. Same solid thighs he'd wrapped around my waist as I'd fucked him into the mattress. Same stunning dark-blue eyes that assessed me thoroughly.

What does he see?

A man who felt washed up at forty—especially sitting across from the spry guy who was twenty-six. Or twenty-seven now? We'd parted ways nearly four months ago. A guy could pass a milestone in that time.

Did he see the horny, shaven-headed Black man who'd fucked him into the mattress with a great deal of pleasure?"

Or did he see the man who was likely to betray him? To cost him his job? To perhaps even get him arrested and thrown in prison?

I just didn't know.

"Fancy meeting you here." His voice was as light and melodic as I remembered—so different from my own deep baritone.

"Well, there's only one gay bar in Cedar Valley. We're both gay—" I gestured between the two of us.

His smile didn't dazzle, as it had in the summer. This time, he appeared more reserved.

I didn't blame him.

He shrugged. "I tend to go down to Davie Street in Vancouver."

"One root beer." Marc placed the glass before Finn.

Finn offered the dazzling smile from my memories. "You're awesome."

Marc fluttered his eyelashes. "Enough for a repeat?"

After a moment, Finn cut a furtive glance at me.

I shrugged. *I don't have a claim on you. I was the one who abandoned you. I was the one who chose to walk away rather than risk discovery.* I wouldn't have cared if someone had revealed I was gay—I didn't hide that fact. Being found in the bed of a potential suspect? That I couldn't keep doing. I wasn't a cop, but I still had ethical standards in my profession that I took seriously.

Finn turned his attention back to Marc. "I've got an early start."

Marc pouted.

"Maybe—" Another glance my way. "—some other time."

"I'll hold you to that." Marc sashayed away.

I'd only just met the man—but I wasn't predisposed to like him.

Jealousy doesn't suit you—especially when you don't have a claim on the man next to you. "You're on duty tomorrow?"

Finn arched a perfectly sculpted eyebrow. As elegant as a woman's—except he was all man. "Yes. I'm going in early because Albert has to take his kid to school."

"His wife can't?" Not that shuttling kids to school had to be a woman's job—

"Bed rest. The pregnancy isn't going well, and you did *not* hear that from me. Off the record. Oh, am I supposed to say that *before* we talk? Or before we fuck?"

My eyes widened. *Well, you'd wondered if he was going to go there—now you know.* "Will there be fucking?"

He sipped his root beer. "Never say never, right?" He feathered his fingers through his hair. "You were a good lay."

"High praise from a guy who runs down to Davie Street on a regular basis."

"You don't spend much time there?" His stare pinned me to the wall like a specimen of butterfly being examined.

"I didn't say that. But, discretion—"

Finn barked a laugh. "What do you know about discretion?"

"I never told anyone about you."

He stilled. "Not even Spring Dixon?"

This time, my eyebrows shot up. Spring had a good nose for a story. I wouldn't have employed her at my newspaper otherwise. But she had nothing to do with Finn and the mess last summer. "My reporter?"

"Your best reporter."

"She's still young."

"But not naïve. One doesn't have seven sisters and a cop for an ex-brother-in-law and get to claim naïveté." His blue eyes penetrated. Dared me to speak.

"I'm not going to touch that one with a ten-foot pole."

"So you've met Corporal Colton Pritchard? The venerable RCMP Officer?"

"Is there a right way to answer that question?"

"Truthfully." He sipped again. "Because if you're half as sneaky with the RCMP as you were with me, then I suspect you're in for a world of hurt."

The Royal Canadian Mounted Police and I only ever crossed paths when a story came up and I needed to get the scoop on any investigations or arrests. Generally, I kept my nose clean and avoided cops whenever possible. "I won't step out of line—I promise."

He chuckled. "You took off. You never contacted me."

I winced. "Yeah, about that—" And yet words wouldn't come. As a man who relied on them for everything, these words wouldn't come. I took a breath and tried again. "Yeah." Nope. That was all I was good for.

"So, you gonna contact me now? Gonna ask me for a date?"

Easy one. "No. Just...not a good time."

"Too bad." He sipped his soda.

"Yeah?"

"Well, I only fuck after the first date." He gestured to his body. "You're missing out on this."

I swallowed. *Yes, I know exactly what I'm missing. Still not enough to agree...* "You brought me home that night." *Yeah, like bringing up that night is somehow going to get you back in his good graces.* Except...why did I feel the need to be in his good books? We were nothing to each other.

Or so you tell yourself.

"Well, exceptions can be made when the guy I invite into my house has just had a near-miss. That's a life-altering experience, right? Your life flashing before your eyes as you contemplate death?"

"I wouldn't put it quite so dramatically." My tone was as dry as the Sahara. "My only thought in that moment was not getting hit by the minivan running the red light."

"Huh. I always figured you would have a fraction of a second to reflect on your life. What you regret. What you rejoice. That's how I envision it for me." Another sip.

"You must see people who barely escape death all the time. Do you ever ask them?"

He shook his head. "That would be inappropriate. And I don't ask the kids on the cancer ward either."

Oh God, help me now. "You visit kids on the cancer ward? In the hospital?"

"Yep. Every other week or so. My schedule's erratic, but I'm always welcome because there are always kids with cancer. Super sad. My friend Quinton, who's a nurse, suggested I go. I wear my fire helmet, department T-shirt, and I tell them exciting stories. A couple of them want to grow up to be firefighters. I hope to fuck they have that chance."

"Sounds brutal." *Jesus.*

He shrugged. "My mom's been a nurse for like, thirty years."

The woman who'd given him the cabin he lived in. For whom he kept a room decorated. Someone he was clearly dedicated to. As a good son should be—for a deserving mother.

Something I knew nothing about. "You're a fine man, Finnegan O'Sullivan."

He cocked his head. "And how exactly do you know my last name? I damn sure didn't give it to you—Ulysses MacDonald."

Since my name was in the weekly newspaper, I hardly needed to question how he knew. "Touché."

"I went to school with Spring Dixon."

Oh shit. "I didn't realize that. She's...a very good reporter."

"You mean she's nosy, a pain in the ass, and a skilled investigator." He smiled. "I'm certain you know she's the one who uncovered RD Watts's true identity."

The fantasy writer of the incredibly successful and renowned Zaragoza trilogy. Also known as Professor Raven Duhamel. Serious academic identified as one of Mission City's most famous authors.

I pointed out, "I don't think the professor wanted the world to know who she was." Spring's reveal of the woman made me very wary of my cub reporter. She might be new—but she was also aggressive and of the *take no prisoners* and *revealing secrets is just fine* variety. One day that ethos was likely to bite her in the ass. Sadly, she wasn't taking advice from me.

Finn shrugged. "Linguistic analysis by AI wasn't as big a few years ago. Matching the name to the books was impressive work on Spring's part."

"Yes, Spring had to beg for time on the university computer. Today, she could do the comparison in the comfort of her living room."

"Right. So we all need to be careful." His blue eyes sparkled.

Oh shit. Does he know? He can't possibly know. No one knows. Absolutely no one. If they did, it would've come out during the clusterfuck.

The clusterfuck I categorically didn't want to be thinking about right now.

I took a long pull of my beer. I was only drinking the one, so I wasn't worried about driving home.

Finn waved to someone who'd just entered, and I pivoted my gaze that way.

Two couples had just stepped inside. The men, holding hands, were a study in contrasts. One was blond with blue eyes. His boyish grin was just adorable. The brunet who stood next to him appeared a little...leery.

The blonde woman who stood next to the blond guy, resembled him in many ways—including those stunning blue eyes.

Siblings?

A shorter woman with fiery red hair and green eyes clung to the blonde. She smiled, although more tentatively. And her facial features resembled the dark-haired guy's.

More siblings?

Kind of took me a moment.

Finn beckoned the group over as he leaned into me. “Yes, two sets of siblings paired up. Roll with it.”

Okay. I wasn’t certain how this affected me, but I was willing to play along—if only to get the backstory of these interesting couples.

The blonde woman was the first to greet Finn. And greet she did—she threw her arms around his neck and kissed him full on the lips.

Finn held her tight to him and, as the kiss ended, he wrapped her in his embrace.

An embrace I was well-familiar with.

“Hey, Stephanie. Oh God, your smile…” He gently touched her nose. “Married life suits you.”

Stephanie stepped back and into the arms of the redhead. Her wife? Which made her greeting to Finn just…friendly.

Finn held out his hand. “Great to see you, Taryn”

“Oh, I do hugs now—all Steph’s doing.” The redhead stepped into Finn’s arms. She was shorter than her wife by a few inches and way shorter than Finn. Still, they held on tight.

“Hey! What about my turn?” The blond man ran his hand through his hair. “After all, I’m the one who has a history with Finn.”

The brunet, who I took to be the man’s boyfriend or husband, scowled.

“Oh God, Lachlan, your face.” The blond guy kissed Lachlan on the mouth. Then gently eased Taryn from Finn’s embrace and stepped into it. He was mere inches shorter than Finn, so when he grasped the back of Finn’s neck and dragged him into a kiss, Finn didn’t have far to go.

And what a kiss. At least with Stephanie, there hadn’t been any tongues involved.

Not so between this guy and Finn. This was full-on French-tongue, ass-grabbing grinding.

Stephanie looped her arm through Lachlan's. "Just a fling. They weren't...compatible."

Ah. Does that mean the blond is a bottom?

Like that really mattered.

Like I had any claim on Finn.

Like I had a right to be jealous.

The man finally untangled himself from Finn's embrace. "Great to see you!"

Finn chuckled. "Hello, Cooper. How's it going?"

Lachlan nudged Cooper—none too gently—out of the way. He held out his hand. "Great to see you, Finn."

The firefighter yanked him in for a hug.

The clearly stunned Lachlan caught my gaze. He quirked an eyebrow even as Finn gripped him.

Ah. So he sees what I'm seeing...Finn trying to make me jealous. Or at least to catch my attention. Well-done, Finn. Because I'm jealous as hell...

Finn gestured to an empty booth. "May I join you? Oh, I meant we." He pivoted to me. "This is Ulysses. Ulysses, this is—"

I waved him off. "I think I've got it figured out."

Marc sidled up to the group. "For six?"

Finn nodded enthusiastically. "That booth. Thanks!" Then he shepherded everyone in.

I snagged his arm and whispered, "What if they didn't want you to join them? How do I know they want me to—"

"Finn, get over here." Cooper patted the bench next to him. "And Ulysses as well. Cool name. I want to hear all about it."

"Yes, Finn. Please join us. And your friend." Taryn's green eyes sparkled with pure joy.

Like I was going to turn down this offer. More people to meet—possibly from Mission City. Catnip for the editor of the local paper. And if they knew Finn, they might know some of his secrets.

Chapter Two

Finn

Yeah, okay. So railroading the Gander and Briggs siblings into accepting me as a fifth was bad enough. Shoving Ulysses between Cooper and me was either going to prove to be brilliant or a big mistake.

Cooper was a hoot. Hooking up with him had been great. Discovering we weren't compatible because we both *really* liked taking it up the ass had been a disappointment. Seeing him marry stuffy Lachlan Briggs made me happy because I'd never seen Cooper light up like he did when he was with his husband. And that said something since Coop was a firecracker and beacon of light on the darkest winter days, even without Lachlan.

"Hey, what did you all settle on for last names?" I nudged Ulysses's shoulder with mine. "Taryn and Lachlan are brother and sister. Cooper and Stephanie are brother and sister. Taryn and Stephanie got married and—" I gestured between the two men. "—I thought you were antagonistic to each other right up until you got married."

Lachlan cleared his throat while a rosy blush stole across his cheeks.

Cooper flung an arm around his husband. "Yeah. I'd love to say we had the world fooled—but I really couldn't stand this guy. All stuffed shirt and no sense of humor."

"Hey!" Lachlan pushed out the word, but without much heat behind it. He cleared his throat. "I just saw a different side of Cooper. During the wedding preparations and, uh, during the actual ceremony."

"Oh!" Cooper reached into his back pocket to retrieve his phone. He tapped, swiped, and then showed it to a very surprised Ulysses. "Finn's seen these wedding photos."

"I don't mind looking again." *Especially if it means I can get up close and personal with this enigmatic man.* So I leaned over and pressed myself against Ulysses. And, of course, had to put my arm around his shoulder to get even closer.

The first photo again had me burst out laughing.

In a good way.

Stephanie in a light-blue-and-white-checked dress with black boots.

Taryn in an elaborate crushed-velvet outfit.

Cooper wearing a red-and-black patterned dress as well as a crown.

Lachlan wearing bunny ears, a white face, and a matching suit.

"Uh—" Ulysses scratched his nose. "Alice in Wonderland?"

Cooper grinned and pressed his hand to Ulysses's thigh.

The man startled.

My protective instincts kicked in. Ulysses hadn't given Cooper permission to be so informal. To take liberties.

Right, and you sought permission to sling an arm over his shoulder and ensure your thighs are pressed together? Well, when put like that?

The answer was a hard no. I could use the excuse we'd been intimate before. Or point out familiarity in a gay bar was more acceptable.

Neither reasoning stood up to scrutiny.

Cooper continued to swipe.

I tried to subtly pull away from Ulysses.

He grasped my thigh—presumably to hold me in place.

And since I didn't want to move, I placed my hand over his.

After about twenty photos, Cooper re-pocketed his phone. "This was all Stephanie's idea, but I love that Taryn went along with it. She made a great Mad Hatter."

"Also that Cooper and Lachlan were game." Taryn beamed. "Cooper as the Queen of Hearts? Perfection in that dress and those heels."

"Wearing heeled boots is always easier than stilettos." Cooper winked.

I was intensely curious about when Cooper had worn stilettos—but now wasn't the time to ask.

"Lachlan as the White Rabbit was special." Stephanie offered a massive grin.

Despite her sunshine, she was, ironically, the dark horse of this group. She'd come out at twenty-two—a mere three years ago. She and Taryn met shortly after, and love had followed.

I corrected myself. Lachlan was an even darker horse. He was in his late-thirties and had shown no sign of being gay. Had even been photographed with famous women for his job back in Toronto. I cocked my head and directed my question to him. "How is it being back in small-town British Columbia? After being a famous attorney in Toronto?"

Ulysses cut me an indecipherable look—then immediately refocused his attention to Lachlan.

Who gave me *that* look as he arched an eyebrow. "I wasn't famous. My clients are." He met Ulysses's gaze. "Entertainment lawyer. I gave up my place in the practice back in Toronto to move to Mission City so I could be with the love of my life."

Cooper pressed a hand to his chest and blinked.

Lachlan pressed a kiss to his husband's temple before continuing. "I have a few clients who jumped ship and have joined my fledgling practice in Mission City. The good news is I work a lot on referrals and Vancouver is full of entertainment types. I have several private clients and a lead on a job at a studio. That might mean commuting from Mission City to North Vancouver a couple of times a week, but the opportunity is too great to turn down—if it comes."

I blinked. Our small town to North Van was a hell of a drive. "Oh. Would you drive or take the West Coast Express?" Our commuter train ran from Mission City to Vancouver.

"Depends on the day. The last train runs at about half past six. There's a bus later, but it's a pain to catch. Or I can just drive. If I leave early enough in the morning, I should be okay. For the afternoon, I'd either have to leave very early or much later."

"Vancouver rush hour." Ulysses rolled his eyes.

Interesting. When I first met him, I'd known he wasn't from Mission City—but I hadn't been certain if he was from Vancouver or elsewhere. At the time, without having a last name, searching him on the internet had been virtually impossible.

Okay...I'd tried. But with just a first name, and the fact he rode a motorcycle, I didn't really have much to go by. So all that hadn't helped. I'd even considered hiring a private detective—we had a new one in town. Rayne Williams appeared quite competent, but I figured even he'd struggle with what little I could give him. Then my mystery man'd appeared as the editor of the Mission City Gazette.

Did I think I might run into Ulysses here? In the only gay bar in Cedar Valley? Nope. Was I still irritated with him for bailing on me? Yes. Finally...was I curious why he often sent Spring Dixon, his staff reporter, out to cover fires and accidents and anything else where the fire department—and therefore me—might respond? Hell fucking yes to that as well.

"Eh, Finn?"

I blinked. "Uh, sure, whatever."

The entire table burst into laughter—including Ulysses. Although his was more of a reserved chuckle.

Brazen it out. "Well, I suppose it's okay."

Stephanie blew a raspberry. "It's so *not* okay. If you and Coop had become serious after your ill-fated hookup then he wouldn't have been available when he got together with Lachlan."

Heat crept into my cheeks. "When put like that—"

"Honey, we were *so* not meant to be together." Cooper winked.

Yeah, that heat intensified. I worried my cheeks might look like Rudolph's nose. "That's probably true—"

"It's actually quite remarkable Cooper was single when our sisters married." Lachlan rolled his eyes.

"Hey." Cooper shrugged. "I like dating. I prefer being married to the love of my life, though."

Lachlan ducked his head.

Cooper snagged his jaw and guided him up so their gazes met.

My breath caught. I'd known Cooper had fallen hard for Lachlan. A real-life *opposites attract* romance. Along with the substantial age gap, they didn't really have much in common. Cooper worked in an advertising agency. Lachlan was an entertainment attorney.

That said, Taryn the tow truck driver and Stephanie the retail specialist at a fashion boutique in Mission City weren't exactly the couple most predicted either.

The palpable love at this table overwhelmed me. In a good way.

Marc arrived just in time. "Drinks?"

Taryn, Ulysses and I opted for soda since we'd abandoned our drinks at the bar. Stephanie and Cooper chose cosmos while Lachlan opted for a vodka tonic.

Taryn laughed. "You can tell who the DD is tonight."

"Whatever keeps the roads safe." I winced. "I see way too many drunk-driving crashes. Things are better than they used to be, but people are still fucking idiots."

"Yes." Ulysses said the words quietly. "Idiots."

"Oh my God, I love this song! Move!" Cooper nudged Ulysses.

Out of self-preservation, I scooted out of the booth as well.

Where I expected Cooper to coax Lachlan to join him, he grabbed Ulysses's hand and dragged him over to the surprisingly full dance floor.

For a moment, I just stared.

Cooper wrapped his arms around Ulysses's neck.

Ulysses met my gaze, held it for a moment, gave an almost imperceptible nod, then focused his attention back to the bubbly blond.

Well, okay then. I slid back into the booth.

Stephanie winked. Lots of Gander siblings winking tonight. "He'll be fine. I mean, I assume he'll say something if he's not comfortable."

I nodded. I might not know much about the enigma that was Ulysses—but I was certain he could extricate himself without making a scene if he wanted to. I pressed against Lachlan. "You okay with this?" I gestured to Ulysses and Cooper.

Lachlan burst out laughing—something I'd never heard him do before. We were more than ten years apart, so I supposed we hadn't interacted much.

"I'm damn secure in my marriage. I can't—" Lachlan scratched his stubbled jaw. "I mean, maybe it's crazy. But Cooper...he's a one-man guy. Yes, he dated plenty before he met me. But we just...clicked."

I smiled hard. "That's so amazing."

Stephanie reached across the table to grasp my hand. "You'll find that too, Finn."

I waved her off with the hand she wasn't clutching. "I'm young. I'm sowing my wild oats. Or some shit like that. I love my life." I wasn't lying either. That said, I might've snuck a peek over at Ulysses as he danced with Cooper.

Stephanie squeezed my hand. "Do you want to dance with Lachlan, Taryn, or me?" Note that not dancing wasn't an option.

"Who wants to dance with me is the better question."

She offered me a megawatt smile. "All of us, of course."

Taryn nodded enthusiastically. I remembered her as being shyer. Being with Stephanie had really drawn her out of her shell.

Lachlan nudged me. "If we dance, then it's easier to swap partners. Is he your date?"

"Uh...something like that?" I certainly wasn't going to say that Ulysses had been my half-a-night stand.

"Great." Lachlan nudged me. A lot of that going on tonight. Everybody was all very familiar. Truthfully, I enjoyed it. I was an easygoing kind of guy who loved being around people.

From the little I'd seen, I didn't peg Ulysses as such.

I scooted out of the booth and allowed Lachlan to grab my hand. We made our way to the dance floor as another slow song started. "Is this Jann Arden?"

Lachlan shrugged as he pulled me flush against him. "I don't see how *I Would Die for You* is necessarily romantic, but I do remember it. Well, sort of. And yeah, I love Jann Arden."

"Okay," I wrapped my arms around his neck and ducked a little to rest my head against his shoulder. He was familiar and unfamiliar at the same time. I'd danced with tons of guys over the years. So generically familiar. Lachlan was an unknown person to me in this way. Definitely unfamiliar.

Every time we made a rotation, I caught sight of Ulysses and Cooper. They weren't plastered together. *That's likely Ulysses's doing—I can totally see Cooper leaving no space between the two of them to make me jealous. More fool him.*

Yeah.

Except I was kind of jealous. I did want to be back in Ulysses' arms. To have him holding me tight. Something about that made my heart accelerate.

"We can trade partners anytime." Lachlan chuckled.

Even as he said the words, Cooper and Ulysses stepped back from each other. With Cooper holding Ulysses's hand, they made their way over to me. Cooper tapped my back. "I miss my husband." He said the words in a very whiny tone.

Lachlan chuckled again. "My husband is quite a character." He pecked my cheek. "Good luck." He whispered words into my ear as he released me and stepped into Cooper's arms. They sort of floated away.

Ulysses eyed me. "I don't particularly like to be manipulated."

I smiled as I grasped his hand and tugged him into my arms.

He came more or less willingly.

More or less.

Quickly, though, he wrapped me in *his* arms. Clearly he wasn't going to be led anywhere.

To my surprise, another ballad played. Jeff Healey. Damn, I wasn't going to cry. He'd been one of my favorites growing up, and *Angel Eyes* was the ultimate song. No way anyone could know this about me, of course. Just some random choice. Especially since it was a very het song.

That said, I replaced *girl* with guy and thought about Ulysses. And although the song was about love, there was also the element of why he chose me. When he'd pulled up beside me at that intersection, how had he known that I was gay? That I was interested? And if he'd kept going instead of nearly being in an accident, what would that have meant? As the editor of the paper, we should be encountering each other regularly.

Which led me to the question of why he was clearly involved in other aspects of the community but never any time he might encounter me over the last three months. *Because he's not looking for a repeat.* Yet even as I had the thought, his very erect cock brushed my hip.

Well okay, then. Maybe things are going to change.

Yeah...but don't make it too easy for him.

Right. I wouldn't. Bruised ego and all that. I was going to make him work for it.

Chapter Three

Ulysses

Telling myself not to get hard there on the dance floor and actually succeeding were, apparently, two very different things. I didn't want Finn to think this nebulous connection was all about sex for me. I would need to woo him, I suspected, to gain his trust. He wasn't angry—but he clearly wasn't happy either.

"Relax, baby. I got you." He whispered the words in my ear as he ran his left hand down my right flank, then meandered it down to my ass where he squeezed.

Squeezed.

"Baby?" A little gruffer than I wanted. I cleared my throat. "Baby? Seriously?"

He chuckled, pressing his cheek against mine so he could again whisper in my ear. "That's what you called me when you fucked me. I think a little reversal is fair play."

Did I? I wracked my brain. *Holy shit. Yes, I did.* I couldn't remember another time I'd done that with a guy. I wasn't into that level of intimacy—with anyone. So the fact I'd gone there so quick with this man—in the throes of passion, obviously, meant my subconscious had been at work all those months ago. Apparently, it knew more about me than I did. *Well, it is* your *subconscious.*

Sometimes I hated my inner voice.

"Did you like it when I called you *baby*?" Because now I needed to know. If he saw it as a denigration then I'd never—

He rubbed his crotch against mine, bushing our cocks. His hands trailed down my back and cupped my ass. Again, he pressed against me. "Oh yeah, I liked it. But we can't call each other *baby*." He nipped my earlobe.

I nearly came right there—on the fucking dance floor. "I like...something..." *You expect me to think at a moment like this?* Yet this was completely unlike me. I always had my shit together. I was always the aggressor.

Always implied I did this often. I did *not* do this often. Or at least not often enough.

Yet I'd been celibate for the entire time since I'd fucked Finn. Not my longest dry spell, by any means—but getting up there. Again, I cleared my throat. "What would you like to call me?"

He laughed, his breath ghosting across my neck. "Well, I don't reckon you'd take to sugar."

"No." Easy to reject that.

"How about sweetheart?"

I tried to pull back—to gaze into his eyes—but he held me firm.

"Don't like that?"

For the third time, I cleared my throat. Like I was getting a fucking cold or something. "*Sweetheart* implies a level of intimacy we don't, I think, at this moment possess."

"Would you want to?"

"Want to...?"

"Possess that level of intimacy." He brushed our cocks together again.

This was downright obscene. I comforted myself that no one under nineteen was going to see us—the legal drinking age in Canada—and if they came here, they likely were expecting some level of raunchiness.

Tell yourself that—if it brings you comfort.

Right.

I brushed my cheek against his. "So if I invited myself back to your cabin, then we could continue our journey back to intimacy?" *Jesus fucking Christ, you're out of your mind. You still don't know if he's a good guy or not. He could be up to his neck—*

Finn chuckled, just as the music changed.

Wham. *Wake Me Up Before You Go-Go.* Personally, I preferred *Careless Whisper*. And not just because I wanted to continue holding him close.

"I never put out on the first date." He yelled the words, and then was promptly dragged away by Stephanie and Cooper, who began bopping to the beat.

Lachlan and Taryn sat at the table, tapping out the rhythm.

Since I'd finished my drink—and therefore had no reason to go back to the table—I left. Well, I had a jacket to retrieve from coat check, because riding a motorcycle without a jacket was true lunacy. Coat in hand, I stepped out into the cool, dark night. Because of the light pollution, I couldn't see the stars. They were out there, though, on this cool, clear night. I avoided driving the bike in the pouring rain or during snow. That hadn't been a problem since arriving in Mission City, but it would soon be. Southwestern British Columbia's snowfall varied from year to year. In Vancouver, I was able to use transit to get just about anywhere I wanted to get when weather grounded my bike. Plus, after I'd done my time as cub reporter, I'd moved to the investigative desk. I'd spent more time chasing down leads from my desk than running around the city.

Yeah. How'd that work out for you?

I mounted my bike, put on my helmet, and started the engine.

Riding a bike with a hard-on sucked. Fortunately, my boner had pretty much deflated and no way was I going to think about Finnegan O'Sullivan's ass while I drove home.

I had two choices. Either Golden Ears bridge, Maple Ridge, and then Mission City. Otherwise, I could take the TransCanada highway to Abbotsford, through that town, and then over the Mission-Abby bridge. About equidistant, but I didn't want to do the big highway at this time of night. People sped everywhere, but someone was clocked at nearly two hundred klicks last week. Stupid teenager with just a learner's permit and his mother's red Ferrari. *Doubt he'll be behind the wheel legally anytime soon.* Also, I'd done a story about the son of a bigwig business guy in Vancouver. The son had crashed a Lambo.

I headed toward Golden Ears.

Interestingly, I'd done a follow-up on the son. Kellan something. He'd turned his life around—enrolled in the University of British Columbia as a psych major. Moved in with his boyfriend. Some scientist he'd met after the Lambo debacle. A real phoenix rising out of the ashes, that kid. That said, his bigoted father had rejected him.

I'd delved into that and found the father had been involved with some shady shit. Felt good to bring that asshole down a peg or two and get the tax authorities interested in him.

I watched my speed carefully as I navigated the sparse traffic I found on the bridge. Soon I took the off-ramp and cut my speed as I headed down the Lougheed highway. Businesses and trailer parks guided me until the Haney Bypass.

Still not thinking about the fact I'm going to fly past the turnoff to the street that leads to Finn's cabin. I'd only been there once, but the memory of how to get there burned bright in my memory. Something I'd never forget.

One of my greatest regrets.

And I had more than a few—so that was saying something.

I catalogued all the things I had to do as I headed toward downtown Mission City. Yesterday's paper had gone out without a hitch. My reporter Spring was covering the hockey tournament this weekend. Pretty much the most exciting thing in town. Next weekend was the turkey dinner for the homeless. Which reminded me—I hadn't made a donation yet. I wasn't flush with cash, but I could contribute to a Thanksgiving dinner for those less fortunate.

I hit the remote and drove into the underground parking of my condo building. Selling my beautiful place in Vancouver so I could buy something in Mission City hadn't been easy. From soaring concrete in the sky—seventeenth floor looking over Coal Harbor—to a fourth floor looking out over Cedar Valley and beyond. Not quite the same. Still, I'd done so well with selling my little piece of heaven—emphasis on *little*—that I was mortgage free in Mission City. At first, I'd resisted. I wasn't staying, after all. This was just a blip before I made it back to a big-city paper. Now I'd come to see I'd run out of options. Going back to Vancouver wasn't likely. And that hurt.

I parked in my spot and dismounted. I pursed my lips. Buying here was an acknowledgement that I likely wouldn't earn in income what the appreciation on this place would be and, more importantly, I wouldn't be paying rent to some random landlord. I owned my place. That had to be good enough.

Still, this was a step down.

The elevator took me to my floor, and I slipped into 412. I liked my neighbors. Well, what little I saw of them. Many had dogs since the building allowed two pets per unit, and the pooches could be any size.

I could get a dog. God knows, I mostly work from home and I could certainly take the dog into the office when I go. Spring would lose her mind. She was always carrying on about the therapy dog, Tiffany, at her sister's ranch, Healing Horses.

At first, I'd thought they rehabilitated horses.

Nope. The horses were therapy horses. The dog was a therapy dog. The patients were humans in need of help. Out of curiosity, I'd checked their website. Notable testimonials. Those could be faked, of course. Still…I'd been impressed.

Then my intrepid junior reporter would carry on about her other sister, the dog trainer, and how successful she was.

Again, I'd dug up the website for Torah Dixon and her training business. These testimonials came with pictures of dogs and their owners. So that'd felt more plausible.

I shucked my jacket, hung it up, and headed for the kitchen. A realization hit me right between the eyes.

Goddamnit.

Jesus.

I hadn't paid for my fucking drink. I'd been running a tab because, after my beer, I'd planned on switching to ginger ale.

I closed my eyes. The last thing I wanted to do was drive the forty-five minutes back to Langley to pay ten bucks for a beer. Plus, a tip. I yanked out my phone, located the number for the bar, and dialed.

The phone rang for a long time before someone answered. "Hello." A clipped female voice answered.

"Uh…is this…?" I scrambled to check the bar's name.

"Yep, that's us. How can I help you?" The woman sounded positively frazzled.

"I forgot to pay for my beer."

"Tall, dark, motorcycle?"

"Uh...yeah...?"

"Finn paid your tab. Gotta go." The line disconnected.

Fucking hell. That was almost worse than having to drive back to the bar. Because I didn't want to owe Finnegan anything. I'd already snuck out of his bed without a word. I'd already spent several months avoiding him at all costs. *Yeah, but you were sort of hoping to run into him tonight.* Long shot at best. He could've as likely have gone to Davie Street in downtown Vancouver. Just because I happened to know tonight had been his first night off since his last four days of night shifts...

I yanked off my T-shirt. The pure white contrasted with my dark skin, and I wore it a little tight to show off my muscles. Yes, I might be forty—and way too old for the twenty-six-year-old Finn—but I wasn't going into middle age without a fight. This building had decent gym equipment that I made good use of in the mornings before most of the world was awake. I was of the *early bird gets the worm* persuasion. Tonight, I was out way past my bedtime.

Spring, thank God, was a night owl. Between the two of us, we kept Mission City news covered.

Only as I was removing my jeans did I realize my blinds were still up. Doubtful anyone could see in, but I wasn't an exhibitionist. During the day, I kept the curtains open to get as much light as possible.

Tonight, I shut the blinds, and the light pollution lessened. I eyed my blackout curtains and decided to leave them open. Bad for sleep hygiene, but I needed a connection to the outside world.

After finishing stripping, I hopped into the shower. I bent my head so the hot water ran down the sides of my face as well as my back.

As if I could wipe tonight from my mind.

I never put out on the first date.

What did that mean? I rubbed my face. He'd *put out* the first time after my near miss with a joyriding teenager in his mother's stolen minivan. Had that been adrenaline or had he not seen it as a date? Which was true—that fuck really hadn't been a date. One shag didn't make a relationship. Especially when one party snuck out in the middle of the night without leaving a note.

No putting a rose smell on that shitty act.

I grabbed my vanilla body wash and coated myself. Like I could wipe away Finn's scent from where it lingered in my mind where he'd pressed up against me. Old Spice? Light, for certain. So, soap? Or just that the scent had mostly worn off after a long day?

My skin tingled at the thought of him touching me—even if it'd been over my henley and jeans.

Fuck, I wanted him.

All of him.

Because the more I got to know him—through other people's stories, admittedly—the more I liked. Well, as long as he was the goddamn boy scout he appeared to be. Earnest, helpful, generous, kind, and a bunch of other stuff. No one had a negative word about him. He was, according to everyone, just a great guy.

Great guys are often hiding the biggest secrets.

Which was why I'd kept my distance. I just didn't know. And I couldn't risk getting involved with him as long as I didn't have answers.

My cock stirred at the memory of brushing against him, but I ignored it. I needed sleep—not to unsatisfactorily jerk off to the long-distant memory of his beautiful ass.

Long-distant? Like, three months ago.

Or a lifetime—depending on one's perspective.

After the water sluiced off the last of the body wash, I hopped out of the shower. My centimeter of hair took ten seconds to dry. I kept the buzz cut because otherwise the curls went everywhere. I didn't mind the natural look for some guys. For me? It just didn't work.

The mirror didn't lie about my age, with the first white hairs in my beard. Neatly trimmed to accentuate the shape of my face. Or so my last barber had told me. Also easy to maintain. I was not, however, going to trim now. Right at this moment, I was ready to drop in bed and crash. Then sleep for a month.

Yeah...but what if you'd met someone tonight? What if Finn invited you for a repeat?

Then likely I'd have perked up—both my brain and my cock. Because the idea of doing anything again with Finnegan was worthy of rousing. Cup of black coffee or a cola would've helped.

Instead, I crawled into bed naked, shut off the light, and let myself go.

Chapter Four

Finn

Giancarlo eyed me. "You didn't get laid on the weekend, did you?"

I glared.

He grinned. "Hey, you're so easy to read. You went to Langley on Friday night hoping to score. This hangdog Monday morning look tells me you did not."

Pursing my lips, I considered his words.

Giancarlo brushed his overlong hair to the side. When he wore his mask, his hair was always pushed back. His midnight-black locks always had a glean to them. With his tanned skin, perfect teeth, and jovial nature, Giancarlo was the perfect package.

For women.

I sighed. He would totally be someone I was into.

Except for that little *straight* thing. Not even a slight bend. Ever.

But he was always game to be my wingman, so that was awesome. And in turn, I'd talk him up to interested ladies.

"Uh, where's Marlon?" I scanned the truck bays, trying to find our shiftmate.

"Asleep." Giancarlo buffed a tire on one of the engines.

I hadn't seen a scuff. He was always far better at keeping things pristine. I lived in a rustic cabin in the woods. Dirt and muck were a way of life. At least I always made my bed. Mostly because I never knew when Mom might drop by. "Asleep again? It's the middle of the day."

"Well, you know he needs his beauty sleep. You want to work out or something?"

"Or something?" I grasped his biceps. I might be ripped, but he was pretty buff too. I took pride in my looks. We needed to be in tiptop shape for this job. Some guys, after they made the team full time, didn't put in as much effort. I was never going to do that. I was never going to let anyone down.

Miriam emerged from the kitchen. "Either of you two hungry? I made way too much spaghetti."

"Never going to turn that down." Giancarlo bounded into the kitchen.

"He's in good spirits." Miriam held my gaze.

"Yeah, today's a good day." He'd had more than a few bad ones since the fire in February that killed a young woman. Giancarlo had been responsible for checking the room we later found her in. He still carried a damn heap of guilt. The fact he'd been injured trying to save her didn't mitigate his feelings. He'd seen a psychologist to work through the intensity of his emotions. I tried not to notice how often he still was down because I felt almost as guilty. We'd found the victim and gotten her out of the building, but she'd been badly burned and, blessedly, had never woken up. Her life would've been an ongoing nightmare. Sometimes death was a better outcome. A philosophy I hated, but I'd met enough burn victims to know resiliency only went so far. "Spaghetti, eh?"

"Yep. And you know—"

The alarm sounded.

Giancarlo strode out of the kitchen while stuffing a piece of garlic bread into his mouth.

Dispatch let us know this was a medical emergency on 12th Avenue.

We were ready to go, but Marlon still hadn't appeared.

Miriam, the driver today, laid on the horn.

Fuck. I don't have time to run upstairs. "We go without him." I shouted the words even as Miriam put the truck in gear and we headed out. The drive wasn't far and a stout man at the end of a driveway was our first clue we'd found the place. I was out of the rig in a flash. I grabbed my medical gear and made my way over to him.

"My daughter." He pressed a hand to his chest. "She no wake up."

Since the guy couldn't have been older than about sixty, I tried to recalibrate my expectations. We hadn't been given an age of the patient—everyone had been too distraught to answer questions. So we'd raced up here and figured we'd get this sorted once we arrived.

Giancarlo and I followed the man into the house and up a staircase.

The daughter—no more than twenty-five—lay on the floor. The foaming at her mouth and her grayish-tinged skin worried me. Still, I got down to doing the basics—figuring out if she was breathing, if she was bleeding, and if she still had circulation. Unfortunately, the answer to all was no. Well, no bleeding wasn't a bad thing—but the rest was.

Still, I had to try. I donned gloves and attempted resuscitation with Giancarlo's help.

The paramedics arrived and immediately took over, but clearly we were fighting a losing battle.

Likely drugs.

Either an overdose or intentional.

Not going to make it.

Dejectedly, I made my way back to the rig.

Marlon stood next to Miriam grinning as though he'd teleported out of thin air.

She was *pissed*.

I offered her a grimace that attempted to convey both the fact our patient wasn't going to make it, and that I felt badly she'd been stuck with Marlon.

The paramedics, with Giancarlo's assistance, loaded the patient into the ambulance.

We all stood still until the sirens disappeared.

The older gentleman emerged from the house, trying to put on a coat.

Giancarlo stepped toward him. "Slowly, okay? Let's get you into your jacket. Where are your keys?"

Even as Giancarlo said the words, the man pivoted and headed back into the house.

Marlon snickered.

Miriam whacked him.

Hard.

The man reemerged and Giancarlo helped him get into the car, urging him to drive slow and be safe.

We probably shouldn't have let him drive, but we didn't have the ability to take away his keys. At the moment, he had hope. The hard part would be when the doctors at the ER called time of death.

"Let's go." Miriam glared at Maron who shrugged.

I cocked an eyebrow. "How did you get here?"

"Dad gave me a ride." He puffed his chest as if getting a ride from his father was a good thing.

Since I didn't spot Chief now, that meant we'd be taking Marlon back to base on the rig.

He sat in the back and was on his phone the entire time—the phone that was supposed to be back at the station.

Once we had the truck backed in, I started—with Giancarlo and Miriam—to restock what equipment we'd used.

Miriam sighed. "Another one."

I double-checked our bandages—even though we hadn't used any. "Part of the job."

"The part I hate."

"Addiction sucks." I couldn't fault Miriam. We all struggled with the opioid crisis.

Miriam wanted legal answers.

Maybe because my mother was a nurse, I looked at the problem through the medical lens, as a disease.

In the end, though it made no difference. Our neighbors were dying of the scourge, and we hadn't found an effective way of dealing with the problem or the victims.

"I'm hungry." Giancarlo offered a measured smile. Likely uncertain of what to say.

"Yeah." Miriam offered a smile. "All good." Then, as if shaking off her mood, she strode over to the breakroom.

Giancarlo gave me *that* look.

"You fucking asshole!" Miriam's cry rang through the fire hall.

I sprinted over—Giancarlo fast on my heels.

We arrived to find Miriam pointing to her pot of pasta and Marlon digging into a mountain of pasta on his plate.

Jesus. Not just incredibly rude...but with no sense of self-preservation. Everyone knew spaghetti was Miriam's favorite meal, and we never took any unless she offered—which she often did. Just not to Marlon.

None of us shared with Marlon.

One might think he'd take the hint.

He never did.

"What?" He actually said the word with his mouth full of food.

"Dude, that's so gross." I tossed him a cloth napkin. "Cover your mouth if you speak with your mouth full."

"Or better, don't speak at all." Giancarlo's glare matched Miriam's.

Marlon swallowed. "I didn't see a name on it."

I rolled my eyes. He'd have been better off keeping his fucking mouth shut.

"Because we were out on a call. A call you were late to. You should get written up." She had her hands on her hips and was spitting mad.

I didn't blame her. We also knew he'd never be written up—what with his daddy being the fire chief and all.

Glad to see nepotism is still alive and well. I walked over to the pot of spaghetti on the stove. "Plenty for you, Miriam. Since you made it."

"I made enough to share."

"See? So why's everyone upset I'm having some?" Marlon said with a shit-eating grin.

"Because I made enough for Giancarlo and Finn." Miriam gazed into the pot. "There's barely enough for me—let alone the guys."

"I was thinking a burger anyway." Giancarlo rubbed his belly. "Isn't it great we can get anything we want delivered?" He grabbed the fast-food menus we'd accumulated. "I'm thinking A&W. Gotta love the onion rings. You with me, Finn? I'll pay."

Ever the peacemaker.

Now I could smell the tomato sauce, however, I really wanted pasta. I could get some from Boston Pizza—but A&W would be faster. And my stomach was growling. "Sure. Sounds great. I'll pay the next time."

"Fantastic." Giancarlo went in search of his cell phone.

I eyed Marlon. "Dick move. Maybe clear out so Miriam can eat her food in peace?"

"Nothing wrong with me hanging around here." He gestured expansively "The room's for everyone. The bitch—" He pretended to wince. "—sorry, the lady, is welcome here. Even though she shouldn't be." He scowled. "In fact, I'm outta here."

He took his plate with him—which meant we'd find it abandoned somewhere later with a crusty layer of red sauce on it.

"Gross." Miriam poked the wooden spoon into the pot. "Do you suppose he spit in it?"

I winced. "I wouldn't think so—since he might've planned to steal more later."

My response should've been a hard *no*. Except Marlon really had a bug up his ass about Miriam. DEI hire and all that bullshit. The truth was she was a hundred times better than him. Partly because she had to prove herself over and over and mostly because she worked so damn hard.

Nepo baby was just a jackass who barely completed his required training, and who never put effort into anything.

"Food's ordered." Giancarlo popped his head back in. And I got extra fries." He grinned.

For Miriam. Because that was the kind of guy he was.

The bell went off, and dispatch's voice rang through.

Miriam tossed her pot into the sink with a muttered curse.

I said thanks to the powers that be we'd have an admin person here to sign for the food delivery and a microwave to heat it up later.

Then we were off.

Chapter Five

Ulysses

"Please tell me you weren't here all night." Spring Dixon sauntered into our newsroom—if it could be called that—at five minutes after nine. As always, her long black hair swung loose and her pale-blue eyes sparkled. Not the palest of the eight Dixon sisters—that was Rainbow. Still, nearly translucent. She wore a huge grin and carried a takeout bag and drink tray from Tim Hortons. My cub reporter dropped the bag on her desk. She handed me an extra-large black coffee and put her double-double on her desk.

I couldn't abide either milk or sugar in my coffee. She liked two of each.

Gross.

Then she tossed me a bran muffin.

My appreciated treat. I'd buy lunch today for the two of us. Fridays were always office days. The paper came out Thursdays, and we strategized our upcoming week and celebrated the arrival of the weekend—even if we both usually had things to do. Underfunded community papers kept dedicated reporters stretched thin with too many stories to tell and not enough resources to get it done.

I removed the wrapper from the muffin. "Another fire last night."

"No shit." She plopped into her chair. "I can't even keep track. Surely this isn't normal."

"Chief McInerny told me the same thing he has been saying since I arrived in town—long, dry summer. No rain. Last night, he pointed out we were in the first week of October and still haven't had any decent rain."

"Yes, but there's a nip in the air. That should help with the tinder-dry conditions, right?" She sipped her coffee. Then sighed.

"Something to investigate, I guess. Last night was the second fire this week."

"Sheesh. Which firefighters worked it?" She yanked her laptop out of her messenger bag and hooked it up to her docking station.

"I didn't get a chance to ask. Seth held me back."

"Good old Seth." Spring chuckled.

Seth Jacobs was an RCMP officer working out of the Mission City detachment of the Royal Canadian Mounted Police. "Yeah, he's a good guy."

"Better than Colton." Spring shivered.

Colton Pritchard. Corporal with the Mission City detachment. Also, Spring's ex-brother-in-law.

She'd never been entirely clear why she held such animosity toward the man—just that she did.

I knew better than to pry. "Colton doesn't work the streets, right?" I already knew the answer, but hoped this time she might elucidate.

"Nope." She stared at her computer screen. "Great for the average citizens of Mission City. Not so good for the accused criminals."

"I thought catching criminals was a good thing." I bit into my muffin.

"I said *accused* and in custody. He can be...tough. If the person turns out to be innocent, he in no way apologizes." She eyed her breakfast sandwich.

There's a story there...I just don't know what it is. Something I should research? I couldn't be certain if I'd be going down a useless rabbit hole or ferreting out important information. "That smells good."

She arched an eyebrow. "You know I'll bring you one." She gestured to my bran muffin with her chin. "Because really..."

A common refrain from her.

Alas, I wasn't twenty-five anymore. "I had my poached eggs this morning."

"With whole wheat toast and a dab of peanut butter." She wrinkled her nose. After three months, we knew each other well. A few times, she'd been over to my place first thing in the morning. Or, in at least one case, last thing at night. Depended on one's view of six a.m. after a long night. She pursed her lips. "Back to the topic at hand."

"I didn't know we had a topic." I took another sip of coffee. Nectar of the gods.

"The fires." She pulled a strip of bacon out of her sandwich.

My salivary glands kicked into high gear.

She waved it around. "Chief made excuses again?"

I nodded. *Please don't pursue this. I don't need your help.* I had enough with my investigation—I wasn't ready to share my theories at this point. "I believe him—for what it's worth."

"He's...weird." She ate the bacon.

"I probably shouldn't ask—"

"Just...I don't know. He's been around as long as I can remember."

"That's normal. It's not like there's a higher position in Mission City. I suppose he could try to move somewhere with a bigger department. I suppose that might bring a higher salary. Or he stays here because he likes his fiefdom."

"Harrumph." She sipped her coffee again. "I just don't see it. But then maybe I wasn't meant to. Being just content with that?"

"You came home to your small town after finishing your degree. You certainly could've gone to a major city."

She shook her head. "Have you met my sisters? You think they wouldn't have hounded me to death about coming home?"

"Oh, I don't know. You're pretty formidable yourself. I can see you holding out—despite any pressure seven other women might apply." I sipped my coffee.

One eye closed. She did this when she concentrated really hard. "Maybe. Possibly because Autumn, Zephyra, and Rainbow wouldn't nag."

The college student, the veterinarian, and the ranch manager.

"That's fair. I don't see Kennedy nagging." The eldest of the Dixon sisters. She founded Healing Horses Ranch, a therapy and counseling center. As a psychologist, she ran the place with adroitness.

"Well, Kennedy might not nag. She would just make pointed comments about how much I'm missed." Spring yanked out another strip of bacon. "I really wouldn't want to disappoint her." She flapped the bacon around. "Although Torah would probably be understanding and Summer's pretty self-absorbed."

The dog trainer and another college student—twin to Autumn.

I did the math in my head. "That just leaves Sunshine."

Spring sighed dramatically. "The nagger-in-chief. She'd never let me alone."

"Isn't she Colton's ex-wife?"

"Yep. What's your point?"

"Well...I suppose you could bring him up with her whenever the conversation got weird." Even as I said the words, I regretted them. I had no idea what had gone on in that marriage. For all I knew, he might've been abusive toward Sunshine. The woman's disposition absolutely matched her name. And she was also a clerk in the local bookstore which was, likely with her assistance, the hotbed of Mission City gossip.

"Mentioning Colton around Sunshine is never a good idea. She gets...oddly concerned. I mean, the guy's a jackass. And she was right to divorce him...but she just feels like she needs to defend him."

"Unlike the rest of you."

"Well, Kennedy and Autumn would never say anything bad about anyone—Colton included. Torah would never, under any circumstances, hold her tongue."

My head spun. *You asked for this*. "Okay, so don't mention Colton. For that matter, stay in Mission City—you're my best reporter."

"I'm your only reporter."

"Well, there is that." I grinned.

She arched an eyebrow. Then she took an inelegant bite of her sandwich.

"I was just about to ask about your plans for the next few days." I tapped my desk with my finger.

She motioned for me to go first.

"The pediatric oncology department at the Abbotsford Hospital just got a huge donation. From an anonymous donor. They want to show their appreciation by getting some publicity."

Spring swallowed. "In hopes of getting more donations?"

"Possibly."

"Someone knows who the donor is. There's paperwork. Tax receipts. Someone knows. I mean, unless someone dropped a bag of cash at the door."

"Surveillance cameras." I tapped my blotter with my finger. "And one wouldn't just carry around ten million dollars."

She wiped her mouth with a napkin. "Holy shit."

"Right? So they would appreciate an article. Of course, we won't publish the name if there's not something underhanded about where the money comes from."

"Why Mission City?"

"That was my question. Why not the Abbotsford paper?"

"And?"

"Best I could figure—and this was reading between the lines—the donor is believed to have come from Mission City. Abbotsford's newspaper will do a follow-up story later."

"So a bit of a scoop." She took another sip of coffee.

I nodded.

"You going or do you want me to?"

"You're doing the profile on the figure skater, right? The one who hopes to make the national competition this year?"

Spring nodded. "Yeah. The kid's visiting home from Toronto where he's been training. I managed to get him to agree to an interview. He's so damn shy. I pointed out he needed to get used to the attention if he was going to be on the team and why not start easy with the hometown paper?"

"No manipulation whatsoever." I smiled.

"None." She took another bite of sandwich.

"That's a good story. I'll take the hospital one."

"You need to hire another reporter." She examined the last bite of her sandwich—clearly debating.

I snagged it from her and shoved it in my mouth.

Her cry of indignation was half-hearted at best.

I swallowed. “I can’t afford another reporter. And if the paper didn’t have to cover our ad guy and all the folks it took to pick up and deliver to shops and front doors…” I winced. “We have five free-lancers.”

“Three of whom haven’t come up with a good story in weeks.”

“So put out feelers. You know this town.”

She scowled. “You’ve been here three months.”

“The Dixons have been in Mission City for how many generations?” I checked my phone. “I have an hour before I have to be at the hospital.”

“Anything else you need from me?”

I shook my head. “Not that I can think of. Will you take the city council meeting on Monday?”

She rolled her eyes. “Seriously?”

“I’m covering the weekend—it’s only fair I get Monday off.”

“Again, if we had another reporter…” She twirled her finger in the air.

“I’d get more time off?”

“We’d have someone else to send to city council meetings.” Her grin lit the room. All bright white teeth and a hint of mischievousness.

Or was that deviousness?

“You’re up to something.”

“I am not.” She gave me a mock scowl. Faux indignation.

I laughed.

She tossed the paper bag at me.

I caught it easily, tossed it into the recycling bin, grabbed my coffee, and stood. “I’ll have my phone if you need anything.”

“Hey, it’s your turn to buy lunch.”

"Right." I glanced toward the ceiling—making some calculations. "I should be done by noon. Say Fifties at twelve-thirty?"

"Done." The megawatt smile was back. "You on the bike today?"

I shook my head. "Nah. There's a chance of rain and the roads will be extra-slick after such a prolonged drought. Plus, cars will have forgotten how to drive in the rain."

"I don't think *cars* forget." She waggled her eyebrows.

I rolled my eyes. "You get the point."

She nodded. "I'll be extra-careful."

"See that you do." I saluted her with my coffee and headed out.

Chapter Six

Finn

I'd forgotten the big announcement of the donation to the children's oncology department was being made today.

Kiana gazed at me as she sat in her wheelchair. She'd been positioned between her father and the president of the hospital foundation. They'd tasked the girl to *receive* the check.

I worried about how she'd handle all the activity, but she thrived in a way I'd never seen. Apparently being the center of attention was clearly her happy place—which surprised me. I'd only ever spent time with her in her room and reading her fantasy dragon young-adult novels written by a local author. I treasured those moments. For now, Kiana was smiling wider than any quiet moment we shared.

Maybe we need to get her out more often. Infection was always a risk when the kids went beyond their ward. With a KN-95 mask, though, she would be at least a bit protected.

"This is a wonderful day for our foundation and the children of Abbotsford and beyond who come here for treatment. This money will enable the purchase of the latest equipment and—" The president, a lovely woman named Catherine—continued on with her speech as I scanned the gathered crowd.

And spotted a familiar face.

Huh.

Ulysses is a reporter. This is a news story. Kids from Mission City come here for treatments as well. In fact, Kiana was from my hometown. She was lucky she only had to travel twenty minutes to get here. Her dad also worked in Abbotsford, so he came here every night after work.

The man looked exhausted. Dark circles under his eyes, more scruff than I'd seen him with for a while, and a mouth turned down—despite the huge check Kiana now gripped.

"I want to thank the generous donor." Kiana beamed a radiant smile. "I'm lucky to have such great doctors, nurses, and support staff. Thanks to them, I'm going to beat my cancer."

God, let that be true. She'd been diagnosed with a stage three hepatoblastoma a year ago and, with surgery and aggressive treatment, things were looking better. She wasn't in the clear yet, but slowly she was improving. Soon, she'd be able to leave the hospital and continue treatment on an outpatient basis. She looked forward to going back to school and seeing her friends. *Please let her be okay.*

Her father, Rhys, spoke next. Haltingly about how wonderful everyone had been. Although the words appeared rehearsed, his genuine appreciation couldn't be faked. He was a man who, unlike his daughter apparently, didn't enjoy the spotlight.

The audience applauded, Catherine took the check back from Kiana, and the group began to disband.

Ulysses approached Kiana.

I headed that way.

"—just a couple of words—" The reporter appeared on a mission.

"My daughter's very tired." Rhys—who appeared even more weary and wary.

Kiana gazed up at her father, then back at Ulysses. "Another time? I am kind of tired."

The man looked ready to argue. Then he caught sight of me and his expression changed. To what, I couldn't be certain, but he backed away and dug his wallet from his back pocket. "I would really love to sit down with you. Whatever time you can give me."

Rhys snatched the card before Kiana could. "We'll think about it. I need to see my daughter back to her room."

Kiana appeared ready to argue. Then she clearly saw something in her father's expression that had her reconsidering. "Thank you. Later?"

Ulysses nodded.

Father and daughter retreated toward the elevators that would take her back to the oncology department.

My one-night stand pivoted toward me. "What are you doing here?"

"I volunteer. Catherine asked me to appear today—to *fill out the ranks*. Since I was going to see Kiana anyway, this felt logical." I could always visit another day, and her book would always be waiting. The second in a trilogy—so much more material remained for me to read. Of course she was more than capable of reading on her own. To hear her say it, I was a better reader. I didn't know whether that was true or not, but sometimes she was too tired to hold her book. I'd offered to buy an audio version, but she said she fell asleep too easily.

"Yeah, you'd said that. Just in the oncology department or...?"

"Pediatric oncology. Kids are impressed when I show up wearing my Mission City Fire Department T-shirt. Or, better, uniform."

He arched an eyebrow.

"I save the uniform for a day when a kid is being discharged. We do a little ceremony—which is way more than you needed to know."

"I'd like to hear more about—"

My phone buzzed in my back pocket. I snatched it and read quickly. "I have to go."

He arched an eyebrow. "A fire?"

I nodded.

"You don't look like you're on duty."

"This is a big one. They might need me."

"But if you were out of the area—"

"Well, I'm not. Bye." I strode toward the exit and was out of the hospital in a flash. I hotfooted it to my truck and was out of the parking lot in a flash. Of course I didn't have lights and sirens—much as I wish I did. As I headed north toward Mission City, I said the prayer I always did—that no one got hurt.

That no one got killed.

Once I was past all the stoplights and on the highway, I increased my speed. The gray day was getting darker. *Might we get rain? Rain would be good.* Well, crappy to run a fire in, but good for life in general. We needed rain.

As I crested the bridge and got my first good look of Mission City, I spotted the plume of thick, dark smoke.

Shit.

I exited the bridge and followed the road to the industrial part of town. A tire warehouse was on fire—which carried all kinds of horrible environmental issues along with just the putrid smell of burning rubber.

Unsurprisingly, I came across a roadblock. Car were being turned around by Seth Jacobs—an RCMP officer.

Optimistically, I waved.

He frowned. Then gestured for me to turn back.

I held up my hands in question.

He shook his head and pointed behind me.

So I turned my truck around and parked on the side of the road. I got out, locked the truck, and headed back toward Seth.

"No way, Finn. Unless you're here on duty—"

"Jacobs, what the fuck? You know I might be able to help."

"I don't see turnout gear. I don't see a mask."

I pursed my lips.

He waved another car to turn around. "You'd think people would see the smoke and realize we're not letting anyone through. What the hell?"

I turned in time to see a nice silver SUV parking behind my pickup. I shouldn't have been surprised to find Ulysses MacDonald getting out—but I was. He must've been hard on my heels to have made it so quickly. *We're both lucky we didn't get speeding tickets.* The man headed my way with a look of determination—and a furrow in his brow.

Don't think that's super sexy. Don't fall for his concerned act again. Don't—

Yep, too late. All I could think about was how great of a lay he'd been all those months ago and how I liked the look of concern on his face.

Seth held up his hands. "No off-duty firefighters. No reporters. No questions. Just...move along."

I cocked my head. This wasn't like Seth. He was the easiest-going of all the Royal Canadian Mounted Police constables in town.

"Look." I had to try.

Seth shook his head. "Not this time, Finn."

"Okay." I ran through this in my mind.

Giancarlo was working today anyway. I'd get a debrief from him. I could've just driven up the hill to the fire hall, but I resisted the urge. Something told me to stay here.

I ignored Ulysses and sauntered over to my truck. I yanked my phone out of my back pocket, leaned against the truck, and began scrolling.

"Hey!" Seth's voice reached me easily.

I gazed up.

Ulyssess sauntered over and leaned indolently against my truck as well.

"I asked you guys to move on."

"So give us a ticket." I shrugged. In truth, this wasn't like me. But I didn't like being held back from a scene for no obvious reason.

"What he said." Ulysses deep voice carried with vague humor.

"I'll call Colton." Seth's voice carried more exasperation than menace.

"Go ahead. I'll ask how Mallory's doing." I kept scrolling. Mallory was Colton's younger sister. She'd been dating Darius lately—a local accountant—but, once upon a time, she'd been a bit of a hellion.

Ulysses moved closer. "There's a story there."

"Not one I'm sharing."

"Are you going to tell me why the cop won't let you through to the fire scene? Because I'd like a crack at it as well. I've got my photography equipment in the back of my SUV."

"You're not worried about it being stolen?"

"Under a tarp, vehicle alarm, and insured." He inched closer. "There've been a lot of fires lately."

"Long summer."

"Structural fires? Am I missing the connection?"

I sighed. "I don't pay attention to statistics." *Why are you lying to him? Because he might write a story about something that's vaguely bothering you?* Except none of the fires had been ruled arson. Just a pile of anomalous fires that no one could explain. And yeah, dry grass didn't provide some kind of justification.

"Ah. There's a story here."

The acrid smoke was seeping into my pores, and the longer I stood here without a mask, the more crap I inhaled. "Hey, Seth?"

He glared.

"You should be wearing a mask."

He waved me off.

Yeah, nearly as stubborn as me. Big surprise.

"Do you want to get out of here?" Ulysses gestured toward downtown Mission City.

"Like where?"

"A restaurant? You could answer some of my questions."

That'll never happen. Still, intriguing thoughts invaded my mind. I turned to face him. "What? You just want me to answer all your questions after you wouldn't even call me?"

His dark brown eyes widened. "Look—sorry about that. That was personal. And I admit I'm an ass. This is business."

I arched an eyebrow. "Right—so I'm business, then?"

"Yes." He held my gaze. Steady and strong. And I remembered the look in those eyes when he'd pinned me to the mattress—with both his body and his force of will and personality.

"You just want me to give you all the inside story without even buying me coffee?"

He blinked. "You want coffee?"

I nodded.

"Uh, why?"

"I thought informants got paid. You can buy me coffee."

Ulysses arched an eyebrow. "Fine. Coffee."

Did he say that through gritted teeth? I couldn't be certain—but a good part of me took perverse pleasure in riling him up. To what end, I wasn't certain. "Great. Follow me." Without waiting for a response, I opened the door to my truck and got in. As he made his way to his SUV, I rolled down my window and waved at Seth.

He shook his head—likely in exasperation—as I turned my pickup and headed to my favorite diner.

Fifties was very much as the name implied—built and opened in the fifties with very few additions over the years. The diner was a staple of life in Mission City, and I freaking loved it. Giancarlo and I often came here after work. To decompress. To hang out. To shoot the shit.

So he could flirt with Sarabeth.

I pulled into the parking lot, cut the engine, then hopped out. I was shutting the door and arming the alarm as Ulysses pulled into the spot next to me.

Even this far away from the fire—and over the railway tracks—the acrid smell was strong.

After he joined me, I grinned. "Let's go inside."

He followed me into the diner.

I smiled as Sarabeth approached. She winced. "I've got several empty tables. Smell's keeping people home."

"Probably a good thing." I gazed into the restaurant. "We'll take the two-seater at the back."

"Cool. Menus are on the table. Coffee?"

"You bet." I gestured to Ulysses with my chin. "He's with me."

"I'll take a coffee as well." He offered Sarabeth a smile. "Lovely to see you again."

"You too. I'll get right on that." She headed toward the coffee pot while I sauntered down the aisle to the last booth. I sat facing the dining area—with my back against the wall.

Ulysses hesitated for a moment before sliding in across from me.

I grinned. "You know, I've changed my mind. I want dinner." I grabbed the menu and made a show of opening it—even though I already knew what I wanted.

"You mean like a date?" Again with the arched eyebrow.

"No—a date is personal. You said business. I'm just business. You can buy me a steak." I flipped to the dinner part of the menu.

Fifties was open twenty-four hours a day. Three hundred and sixty-five days a year. I'd spent a few holidays in here when Mom was working. And since the diner was open all the time, most of the menu items were available all the time. My favorite was the pancakes—almost as good as Mom's. But today, I wanted to make a point.

"Business." Ulysses repeated the word slowly—almost like he was testing it out. "You're going to share?"

I shrugged. "Sure. Oh look, here comes Sarabeth with our coffees. Try to smile." I winked.

He growled.

Sarabeth brought our coffees and then proceeded to take our orders.

Chapter Seven

Ulysses

I had Finn here now. I intended to get him talking and to not let him stop. I'd texted Spring to bail on our planned lunch so she wouldn't show up. "You've noticed an uptake in fires? Small towns rarely see this many—"

Finn held his left index finger in the air—effectively cutting me off. "Food first. I'm starving. It's been hours since breakfast."

Despite the fact he wasn't wrong—we were well past noon—I wanted to argue. Since I was paying for this meal myself, I wanted answers. I would've loved to use my nearly nonexistent expense account, as I would've in Vancouver in a heartbeat, but the damn thing was well, nearly nonexistent. Saving those few dollars for a rainy day felt like a good idea. Plus, as a reporter, I didn't generally *pay* for tips. And after last year's clusterfuck, I was even less inclined to do so.

In the past. Nothing to see here. Don't rubberneck as you drive past the catastrophe that is my life...

Before I could come up with a coherent argument—like the fact I *was* paying—Sarabeth was back with our food.

Finn *had* ordered a steak along with a baked potato and a side of broccoli.

Pretty healthy compared to my deep-fried French toast with cream cheese and strawberry sauce. Just an explosion of sugar-and-fat goodness.

"So, what's life as a small-town reporter?" Finn asked—then proceeded to take a big bite of his steak.

I cut a piece of my French toast and dipped it in real Canadian maple syrup. "Same as being a reporter anywhere, I suppose." *Big fat liar.*

He swallowed. "So you've been a reporter elsewhere?"

I squinted. "I didn't just come into the world fully formed in July. Yes, I've had other jobs."

"As a reporter."

"As you say."

Finn waved his fork at me. "You're evading."

I shrugged. "You have a search engine. You know my full name—"

"I do now. Once I found out you were the new editor. Unlike in July."

I held his gaze. "Unlike July." The best and worst half-a-night-stand of my life.

"What if I said I didn't want to search you?"

The frown came quickly as I again regarded him. "Why would you not search me?" *Do you really want to be encouraging him? Nope. Probably not.* Still, I couldn't resist the urge to poke him. Sort of like poking the bear. God only knew what would happen. How he'd interpret the *official* story of what happened.

"Maybe I see you as a gift at Christmas. I want to savor the unwrapping rather than ripping all the paper off at once." The firefighter grinned.

"Something tells me, as a child, you ripped plenty of paper."

"That might or might not be true. Sometimes, though, I like to savor. Have things last more than a few hours."

Another jab at the fact I left him in the middle of the night and hadn't told him how to find me. I still didn't know the exact moment he'd discovered I was the new editor of the Mission City Gazette. I'd thought that might've brought him to my doorstep. If only in anger.

Even that news hadn't drawn him out. Nope. Took running into each other at a bar in Langley to finally bring on the confrontation I'd been expecting. "Sometimes a few hours is all we're capable of in that moment."

"Oh?" Finn sipped his coffee. "I think you can do better than that."

I wasn't convinced—but I also wasn't going to argue. "So...fires."

He gestured to his plate. "Not while I'm eating. I want to properly digest my food."

I held in the eye roll. Barely.

We ate in stiff silence for a while, Finn taking tiny slow bites, probably to be annoying, until...

"Finn! How's it going?"

A deep voice had me turning in my seat.

Two men stood just behind me. The Asian man was slender and had the cutest grin. The white man stood a few inches taller and was much broader.

I ran the couple through my memories.

Right. Dr. Leopold Rogers and his nurse husband, Quinton. Married just before the start of the school year. Leopold had two cute kids from a previous marriage. I knew all this because Quinton's mother paid for a huge picture of the men, the two children, and a dog to run in the paper shortly after the wedding ceremony. When someone dropped that kind of coin, I tended to remember. I stuck out my hand. "Ulysses MacDonald."

Quinton grasped it. "Quinton Rogers."

Ah, so he'd taken the doctor's name. Because of the kids?

I shook it firmly.

"This is my husband, Leo."

We shook hands.

"I'd invite you to join us—" Finn gestured to the very-small booth.

Quinton waved him off. "No worries. We're just having a quick bite before the kids get out of school. We're enjoying a rare weekday off."

Many medical staff worked crazy hours, so this made sense.

"Do you know anything about the fire?" Leo caught Finn's gaze. "I sort of thought you might be there."

"Day off." Finn shrugged. "I didn't get called in. Plus, I have this charming companion to keep out of trouble."

Quinton's eyebrows shot up.

Heat raced to my cheeks.

"He's a reporter." Finn chuckled. "If I wasn't here with him, then he'd be down at the fire inhaling all those noxious fumes."

Right. So you're doing this for my *benefit.* Since he hadn't answered a single question, I was beginning to doubt the veracity of his assertion we were here to *talk business.*

"You're new in town, right?" Quinton grinned at me. "So's Leo. Small-town living takes an adjustment. Oh, sorry, you're from Vancouver, right?"

Okay, someone knows how to use Google. Because I'd ensured there'd been no mention of any of my previous assignments when the announcement of my arrival had been made. “Yeah, Vancouver. I’m adjusting to small-town living. Definitely a different pace of life.”

Leo nodded. “Very true. I’m from Surrey—which was a hybrid of suburbia, but also connected to Vancouver. Hell, I used to work in New West, and that commute was bad enough.”

“Oh, the new bridge opened.” Anything to veer away from any topic that might touch me.

“About bloody time.” Leo frowned. “The Patullo was always such a disaster. I hated driving over it with the kids in the car."

“How are Melodie and Trevor?” Finn grinned. “So adorable.”

“In school and fully adjusted to living here.” Leo smiled back—although I would’ve said a little wistfully. “They love having two sets of parents. Always trying to see what they can get away with.”

Quinton laughed. “And yet we coordinate with Archer and Gideon so they don’t get away with anything.” He considered. “Well, much anyway.”

“Your kids are so fricking cute.” Finn sipped his now-cold coffee.

“We love them to death.” Quinton again smiled broadly.

I wracked my mind. *He’s the stepfather and...Archer was the other one?* Right. Gideon and Leo had been married. Apparently co-parenting was working. *Props to them.*

“We’ll leave you be before your meal gets cold.” Leo gestured to our food. “Truly lovely to see you, Finn.” He met my gaze. “I know you’re not *new* here, but welcome to Mission City. You’ll be so happy here that you won’t want to leave.”

A knot formed in the pit of my stomach. I saw this town as punishment for a transgression I hadn’t meant to make. As soon as I could get out of here—to anywhere—I was gone. “Thanks. Finn’s keeping me on my toes.” I turned to glare at him.

He smirked.

Quinton snorted. "Yep. That's Finn. Maybe you'll be the guy who can keep him out of trouble?" He linked hands with his husband and tugged him toward an empty booth.

I pivoted back to Finn. "*Out of trouble?* I thought you were a Boy Scout."

"I am." He puffed out his chest. "One of the scoutiest kids in town."

"That's not a word." *What's he getting at? For that matter, what did Quinton mean?*

"That's as good as it's going to get. Eat up."

Reluctantly, I dug back into my now-cold food. Still delicious, to be certain...but cold.

"Coffee refills?" Sarabeth held the pot.

Finn put his hand over his cup. "I'm good."

As much as I wanted another cup, I had the feeling we were almost finished here. I offered the vivacious blonde with the sparkling blue eyes a smile. "I'm good as well."

"You can pay up front when you're ready to go."

On those words, I took a quick look around. To my surprise, the diner was now full with a line of several couples waiting to get inside. "Yes, we'll get going."

"No rush." She said the words with a smile.

I believed her, but I also didn't want to hold the table longer than necessary. "We'll come and pay."

Finn pointed to me. "He's paying."

"And you're answering questions."

"Not until you've paid. You might back out of our deal."

"Deal?" Sarabeth grinned. "Another time, you'll have to tell me about it."

"Sure." Even as I said the word, though, I mentally crossed my fingers. No way was I sharing my queries with someone who clearly had the pulse of the heart of Mission City gossip. I wanted answers. From Finn.

After Sarabeth grabbed our empty plates, we followed her to the front of the restaurant. She deposited the dishes in a bin, turned, and entered our bill into a traditional cash register.

I honestly couldn't remember having seen one like it in probably a dozen years or more. Everything was scanners and computers these days. I sort of liked the throwback vibe this place held.

I paid, and then escorted Finn out of the diner. "Now?" I guided him away from the lineup.

He shook his head. "I'm not going to answer your questions in a public place."

I rolled my eyes. "You were the one who wanted a coffee. In public. And then you demanded dinner."

"Hey! I asked nicely."

You extorted me into it and I still have fucking zero answers. "Whatever. You want to go somewhere private?"

"Well, that was a nice date."

"That wasn't a date." It might've *felt* like a date—but if so, it was unlike any date I'd ever been on before. Frustrating was the first word to come to mind.

"You know, most of my dates come to my house, and then I get fucked for being such a good dinner companion."

I arched an eyebrow. Okay, things were *really* getting off the rails. "Can you repeat that?"

Finn smiled that boyish grin I found so difficult to refuse. "What if I make it a condition of me answering your questions? Will it make fucking me for a second time more palatable?"

I gaped. *Is he serious?*

From his expression, he was very serious—because lurking behind the mischief in his eyes was the desire I'd spotted that night. The night I'd almost died. The night he'd brought me to his bed. Still, I remained silent.

"Fine—fuck me and then ask me the questions." He sauntered over to his pickup, jiggling his butt in just *that* way.

Okay. This isn't normally how I get interviews.

I'm a goner.

Yeah, but what a way to go.

Chapter Eight

Finn

The rain started as I pulled out of the parking lot from Fifties and onto the main drag. I was sort of glad Ulysses wasn't riding his motorcycle. Well, sad I didn't get to see him in leather—although he looked mighty fine in khakis and a polo—but also glad because the roads were going to be slick and drivers were super stupid the first time it rained after months of drought. Like they'd forgotten how to drive.

Since I figured Ulysses remembered where I lived—although that might've been arrogant of me—I didn't wait for him as I headed up the Cedar Connector. I navigated the steep hills as if they were nothing. Which they sort of were—for me. This landscape had been part of me for my entire life. Even though the encroachment of houses farther and farther out of town was becoming a thing. The character of my town was changing. I wasn't a fan of either the sprawl or the taller condo buildings springing up under the new bylaws.

I checked my rearview mirror to find a silver SUV close behind me.

You're seriously thinking about city ordinances when the most gorgeous man ever is coming to your cabin to fuck you?

Yeah, I was. First, it kept my libido in check. Second, those new buildings meant new challenges for the older firefighters who'd only ever had to go up three stories before. Eight was something entirely different.

Our local fitness requirements weren't designed around charging up that many flights, and not all guys were up for the task.

I wasn't going to say guys *and* gals because Miriam, Dulcie, and Iris could handle that climb without breaking a sweat. And kick some serious ass of the guys lagging behind while they were at it.

I signaled to take the right turn onto my street.

Ulysses did the same thing.

Within a couple of minutes, I pulled onto my driveway and drove up to my cabin.

That evening, three months ago, flashed into my mind. The setting sun. The warm glow off Ulysses's dark skin. The frogs in the pond.

Nothing like the pouring rain today that made it hard to see out my windshield.

I hopped out of the truck and hotfooted it to the cabin. Once on the porch, and under the awning, I slowed my steps.

At the sound of a car door slamming, I turned and watched Ulysses striding toward me. *Those thighs. Those legs. Those arms.*

Memories assailed me. Of him in my bed. Of the expanse of his unmarred skin. Of the fun we had that night.

And of the feeling of waking up alone.

Well, you'll just have to boot him out while you're still conscious this time, so you don't have to deal with that awful feeling again.

I unlocked the door and gestured for him to enter.

He did.

I glanced down at his ass—which the khaki pants clung to nicely.

When I shut the door, he turned to face me.

I moved to turn on a lamp. "A little gloomy."

He raised an eyebrow.

I shrugged. "I want to see you."

A slow smile crossed his face.

"And you're wet."

"It's really coming down."

Even in the sprint from his SUV, he'd gotten soaked. "You want to throw your clothes in the dryer? Or will that ruin them?"

"Wash and wear. I'll survive if they're damp. If you're asking me to get naked, though, then I'm happy for you to put them in the dryer." He removed his keys, wallet, and cell phone from his pockets and put them on the bench. Then he sat next to his things and bent to untie his shoe laces.

I toed off my cowboy boots. I'd gone casual today—having forgotten that I would be witnessing the check-presenting ceremony. I removed my leather jacket, wiped off the wet, and hung it on the rack.

Ulysses, having removed his shoes, stood and removed his jacket as well.

"You look good."

He snorted. "What, when I'm not wearing my leathers?"

"I like you in your leathers. This way—the dryer is next to the bathroom. You remember where the bathroom is, right?" *Where you had a shower and then emerged gloriously naked? With a rivulet of water running down your chest and—*

"Yes, I remember." He followed me and, when I arrived, I pivoted back.

He had his shirt open and was fingering his pants button.

Yep. Great memory, Finnegan. He's exactly as hot as you remember. "You want a shower?"

He shook his head. "I was hoping we might head to your bedroom. The sooner I fuck you, the sooner I get answers." Even as he said the stark words, he had a little light in his eye.

Drat. I'd sort of hoped he'd forgotten about that. I'd hoped maybe he'd be...too overcome by passion to remember to ask me questions. Questions I likely didn't even have answers for anyway—but he didn't know that. I held out my hand.

He removed his shirt and handed it to me. Then he unbuttoned his pants and yanked them down as well.

I made a show of examining his boxer briefs for dampness.

With a sly smile, he slid them off as well. "Might as well have them nice and toasty warm."

"I like your thinking." I tossed all his clothes into the dryer. Then I removed my department T-shirt and chucked it in as well.

He eyed my jeans.

"Nah." I pressed the button to turn on the dryer and then gestured to the bathroom.

"Sure." He grinned as he sauntered in.

I was grateful he closed the door—I wasn't into listening to other guys piss. Had enough of that at work. Very little privacy in a fire hall. I strode back to the hallway lamp and shut it off. Then I pivoted and headed to my bedroom. Once there, I removed my jeans and underwear.

"Yum."

I spun to find Ulysses leaning against the doorjamb. His gorgeous cock stuck straight out.

Mine hadn't even begun to think about...what was to come. Part of me was wondering if this was actually a good idea. "Can I get you a glass of water?"

"You can do whatever you need to do and then let's get to it, eh?"

I cocked my head.

"I'm teasing you." He advanced toward me—clearly telegraphing his movements.

I stepped toward him.

We met somewhere in the middle.

He cupped my cheek. "I've been thinking about this for such a long time."

You knew where I was. You could've come. I wouldn't have turned you down. Well...probably not. I cleared my throat. "I don't know what to say."

"You don't have to say anything. I fucked up. I never should've left that night. Regrets? I've had a few. But I'm here now. In fact, you invited me." He grinned.

Something lurked in those luminous dark-brown eyes, though. Something I struggled to grasp. Something almost evasive. "So we're going to do this?" My cock was showing interest.

He moved closer. "Yeah, let's do this."

"Okay. Uh...I have to piss." I scooted past him and headed to the bathroom. Didn't want nature's call to interrupt...whatever this was.

I did my business, washed my hands, and headed to my bedroom.

Ulysses had yanked back the comforter and now lay in the middle of my bed.

Goosebumps ran up and down my arms—and not just from the chill in the air. We'd last been here in the dead of summer. Now autumn was upon us. "We might get cold." I moved to the nightstand to snag condom and lube.

He waggled his eyebrows. "I promise I'll heat you up." He held out his hand.

I snagged it and let him pull me in. I sort of landed on top of him, with my mouth inches away from his. A smile spread across my face. "Hello."

"Yeah, hi." Ulysses angled his neck so he could press a kiss to my lips. Then he pulled back. "What do you want? What would make you feel good?"

I pretended to consider. Then chuckled. "Uh...you promised to fuck me. Although blow jobs and hand jobs are just as acceptable."

"Pretty much anything to do with our cocks?"

"Yep." No sense beating around the bush. I was tired of games—his and mine. I wanted him. He appeared to want me. Well, if his erect cock was any indication. "You going to fuck me again? Because last time was...spectacular."

"True." He chuckled. Then he sobered. "I shouldn't have left."

"So you keep saying. How about we move on? I'm vers and fine with either, but my prostate feels neglected today."

"I can help with that."

"I thought you might. Do you want me to prep myself?" We were sort of going from zero to one hundred in ten seconds, but I didn't figure he'd mind that—I certainly didn't.

"Oh, I'm very happy to prep you." He grasped my hips to urge me off him.

I complied. He liked being in charge. I liked him in charge—at least for now. So I lay on my back in the middle of the bed as he snagged the bottle of lube.

He maneuvered between my spread thighs.

Our grins matched as he dribbled lube on his fingers.

I moved my cock and balls out of the way.

His gaze softened. "You really are stunning."

I didn't spend a lot of time before the mirror admiring myself. My mom had taught me about vanity. I also understood I had more options in the bedding-men department because of my looks. *Is he here just because I'm a pretty face?* Oof. *Nope, he's here because he thinks I have information.*

"Finn?"

"Yeah?" I blinked.

"You with me?"

"Oh hell, yes."

He nodded. Then he circled my hole with his fingers at a glacial pace.

As much as I wanted to beg him to go faster, I understood we were now on his schedule and we'd go as fast—or as slow—as he wanted. No speeding him up. That was for certain.

Slowly, he slid one finger inside.

And held my gaze.

I continued to grin. "You want me to tell you that feels good? Hell, yes. Will it feel better with your cock inside me? Hell yes to that as well."

"That's fair." He added a second finger.

I reveled in the sensation. Even just such a simple act had a profound impact. Possibly because I hadn't been with another guy in the three months since he'd snuck out of my bed.

Which I was so *not* going to admit to him. Because he might feel obliged to share where he'd been. Who he'd been with. I had no doubt the charismatic reporter hadn't spent all those nights alone.

He angled his wrist and brushed my prostate.

My cock, which had been getting more interested by the minute, now filled completely.

A drop of precum leaked.

He leaned forward to lick it up. Then he swirled his tongue around my crown.

I grasped the sheets in my hands. "Keep that up and I might just combust on the spot."

He pulled back. "Well, we certainly can't have that." He slid his fingers from inside me, wiped them, and snagged a condom wrapper.

I breathed faster, watching the dexterous movements of his hands as he ripped the packet and unrolled the condom down his length. More lube slathered on himself and he was moving into position above me. "Yeah?"

I pulled my lower lip through my teeth. "Hell fucking yes."

"As you wish."

"Ulysses?"

"Yes?"

"Don't go easy on me. I want to feel this for the entire weekend."

"You not working?"

"Even if I were, it wouldn't matter. I don't want to walk straight."

That appeared to give him pause as he frowned.

Fuck. "Whatever. Do whatever. Just...get inside me soon?"

"Sure." His smile didn't reach his eyes as he lined himself up. Within moments, he was pressing inside me.

His dark-brown eyes held an intensity that stole my breath as my body accepted him. In the dim light of this stormy afternoon, his pupils were so wide, I could barely see the irises. I was powerless to look away as he continued to slowly work his way inside me.

"You feel good?" His voice, although low and husky, hung in the air between us.

"Yes. Now fuck me already."

I'd never tire of that grin—probably because he didn't smile nearly enough.

"As you wish." He withdrew almost to the tip and then slammed into me.

My head hit the headboard with a resounding thud.

"Fuck." He grabbed a pillow and stuffed it behind my head. "Hang on."

"Yes. That." I grasped his biceps to pull him even closer.

He continued his thrusts—over and over.

He pushed me higher even as I tried to stave off the orgasm. I wanted to cling to this as long as possible and that meant thinking of anything except how he was nailing my prostate with every thrust. How I felt more alive than I had in the three months since he'd last been here. How I would be happy if he just never left again.

My mind stuttered on that because the thought made no sense. A world of difference lay between *he's a good lay* and *gee, wanna stay forever?*

"Finnegan." He said my name through gritted teeth.

God, he remembers? I told him that once...in passing. "Yes, Ulysses?" I tried for cheeky.

"Fucking come already. Because I'm on the verge of—" His voice hitched.

I grasped my cock and started tugging. *Sign of a generous man—he wants me to come first.* Or at least at the same time. And since simultaneous climaxes were a wonderful thing, I set my mind to matching his rhythm as I jerked myself.

Still, he held me captive with his luminous eyes.

"I'm coming." This time *I* spoke through gritted teeth.

"Thank fuck."

Even as the orgasm hit me and cum erupted from my cock, he arched his neck and let out an almighty growl.

Fuck, that's sexy.

Then all logic and reason left me as I flew up and over. Soaring above an ocean of turbulent seas.

The rain lashed against the window.

My vision narrowed—even as things became crystal clear.

I'm so falling for this man. This enigmatic stranger I barely know. A person who holds so many secrets. And yet, so did I. I just had to figure out which were mine to share and which I'd have to keep to myself.

Chapter Nine

Ulysses

I didn't get answers.

We had sex.

We showered.

Finn started to make dinner—ignoring the questions I tried to pepper him with.

Then his phone rang. A co-worker. Wanting to talk.

He gave me *that* look. Not an *I'm going to take this in private and could you wait* look. Nope, he delivered the *had fun, maybe again or never, there's the door don't let it hit your ass on the way out* look.

Never let it be said that I overstayed my welcome.

Still, as I drove home, I was a little miffed. *He promised answers. Yet he wouldn't even let me ask the questions. Is this payback? His way of putting us back on even ground? So...where does that leave us?*

As I returned to downtown Mission City, I contemplated the answer to that question. I nabbed takeout from A&W, and I chewed various scenarios over in my mind. As I drove into the parking garage of my condo, I had the vague notion I'd been had.

I locked my car, checked my bike under the tarp, and headed toward the elevator. Finnegan O'Sullivan was making me crazy. Somehow I'd avoided him for almost three months and now I'd seen him multiple times in a week. That need—that lust—was still unsated. I would've happily stayed the night if it meant we could go at it repeatedly. I needed to get him out of my system. Whether I meant once and for all or just for the time being was a question I wasn't willing to contemplate.

In my condo, I locked the door, tossed my keys on the counter, toed off my shoes, shucked my coat, and headed into the living room. I'd left the blinds open when I'd taken off this morning. Now, as dusk encroached, I spotted nothing but gray clouds hanging low. I couldn't see the bridge to Abbotsford—let alone the Sumas mountains or Mount Baker in the distance. On sunny days, I had a clear view of the dormant volcano in Washington State. So different than the cityscape view from my condo in Vancouver.

I put my soda on the side table and plopped onto the couch. Ater glancing at the wall clock—and seeing six o'clock neared, I turned on the television and selected the national news. Then I dug into the aromatic bag of hot food and removed the onion rings. *No worrying about onion breath tonight. Asshole.*

Whether I was referring to myself or Finn was entirely up for debate. I could've done better three months ago, and he could've done better tonight. If he'd gone into his room to take the call—or asked me to make myself scarce—I totally would've respected his privacy. Hell, I could've cooked dinner while he talked to his coworker.

I stopped, an onion ring suspended in midair as a thought hit. What if Finn had set up that call ahead of time? What if he'd asked a coworker to call about the time we'd be getting ready for dinner and—

What? He could've asked me to leave at any moment. He must've known I'd never overstay my welcome. I might've argued, at least a bit, but I would've left.

That left the call being genuine. So what did that mean? I eyed my phone. I hadn't gone back to the fire scene. Unlikely that Constable Seth was still there, but how much information I could've gotten at this point was debatable.

You could've tried to take pictures. Rainy, mucky pictures.

I wasn't averse to tough weather. God knew, I'd endured some pretty shitty conditions to meet sources or to, on occasion, take photographs.

After a moment, I shoved the onion ring into my mouth.

The newscast began.

I couldn't pay attention, though. My mind kept circling around to the fire. So I shoveled the mozza burger down with less grace than I would have if I'd had company, and then yanked out my laptop from my messenger bag. Within a moment, I was online.

First, the Mission City fire department.

No advisories or mentions of the fire. Not surprising—but worth checking

Next the Mission City detachment of the RCMP. Nothing.

Finally, I checked the town website. It rarely got updated, but—

Bingo.

Road-closure notice. Bridge Street was closed until further notice. No cause given and no ETA for reopening.

I pulled up a map of the industrial part of Mission City, since I wasn't overly familiar with it. Bridge Street was small and not an artery.

So this would be an annoyance for the businesses on that street, but was unlikely to have a broader impact on the town.

What does this mean? Is the fire out? Tire fires last for a long time...right?

I hadn't spotted smoke when I'd looked out the window when I came home, and I hadn't smelled smoke when I'd pulled up to the drive-through. But I hadn't been focused on those things. Just miffed at Finn and looking to appease my empty stomach after a bout of mind-blowing sex.

My phone rang.

Spring.

"Yep?"

"You're always so polite." She laughed.

"What do you want, Dixon?" Even as I asked the question, a sense of rightness permeated. She was down-to-earth and also easy to talk to. She didn't put on airs or ask me questions I didn't want to answer. Of course she'd done her research before I arrived as her new boss. She made a comment about *two sides to every story* and *welcome to the team*. That'd been it.

"Did you attend the fire?"

"Nope. Seth wouldn't let me near."

"You too, eh? I tried that as well and got turned away. He said he'd sent you on your way, but I thought maybe you'd snuck back—or gone in the other side."

"I considered it. Then Finn invited me to lunch, and I figured that stood me more likely to get answers."

"Did you get any?"

"Not a one."

"Did you do anything interesting?"

She's fishing. She knows nothing. "Yeah, a bill for a steak and—" I considered. "I'll try again."

"Right, because there's something fishy."

"Yep. How'd the interview go?" Because I did not want to talk about Finn and how I planned to convince him to talk to me in the future. Too much information for my cub reporter.

"The interview went well. I want to do a feature. I even got some good photos. Would be nice if we had a photographer..."

"You find me fifty new regular ad sponsors and we can talk about it. We're barely breaking even."

She huffed.

Right. That's how I feel. We were a dying business in some ways. Lots of storied community papers across Canada were shuttering. The Mission City Gazette held on—for now. Some of that success was from pivoting to more online content. But we still wanted an actual physical paper to come out once a week.

"Well, whatever." She sighed.

"What?"

"I heard something about a local business."

"Oh?" This wasn't a tone I'd heard from her before. Although, admittedly, three months wasn't a long acquaintance. "What's up?"

"Dog fighting."

I blinked. "I'm sorry, you'll have to repeat that. Did you say dog fighting? Like with, you know, dogs...fighting?" I wasn't naïve. Shit like that went on in big cities and small towns. But to envision people gathered in a circle and betting money on which dog would come out on top? That was unfathomable cruelty to me.

"Yep. Rumors."

"But often there's a kernel of truth behind the rumors."

"Yep."

"Okay...what are we going to do about it?"

"But I can't do anything."

"Huh?" I sat up, nearly dislodging the laptop.

"Because of my sister, Torah. If I go sniffing around this story and she gets wind then there'll be hell to pay that I didn't tell her."

"Oh. Uh...okay." I sighed as I woke the laptop up. "Tell that to me again?"

"Sheesh, Ulysses." Another dramatic sigh. "There's not much to go on. Pretty fucking thin."

"Still, give me as much detail as you can, and I'll try to run it down."

"Yeah, okay." So then she recounted what she'd heard a rumor about. *Just a rumor.*

Yeah...except some of my best stories had come from rumors, tips, and just shoe leather detective work. "This shouldn't be too hard to run down."

"So you'll let me know what you find?"

"Yeah. And we can share the byline if it proves to be true and we write a story. You're certain the cops aren't onto this?"

"Well, nothing's for certain. But this person said if the cops had been sniffing around that the ring would've disbanded. Or something."

"Like moving elsewhere or being put on hold." I'd had more than one Vancouver story evaporate when the subjects decided they'd be safer elsewhere.

"I guess."

"You don't sound certain about any of this."

"Because I'm not." Another sigh. "This is friend of a friend of some dude...but it smells plausible."

I trusted her nose for news. "Okay. Let me run it down tomorrow. Do you have a contact at the fire department?"

"I know Miriam. I did a feature on her when she joined the department as a full-time paid firefighter. Lots of bluster from people who said she couldn't do the job." Spring snorted in disgust. "Same sexist bullshit you'd expect."

"Glad to see certain of the good folks around here didn't miss out on their chance to be assholes."

"Yep. Vast majority of people either supported or didn't give a shit. I'll say this for council—they stood by the hiring. Miriam's also a super-sweet person who would be able to knock most of the men in this town on their asses."

"Is she the only woman?" I asked.

"Nope. Iris joined a year later, and Dulcie came on earlier this year. And we've got a female volunteer as well. There's a joke going around that at some point we might have an entire female shift."

"Times have changed."

"You're not *that* old, MacDonald."

"Old enough to know better. So can you give Miriam a call?" I rubbed my forehead.

"And ask about the fires?"

"Yeah."

"Why don't you just ask Finn?" She sounded baffled.

"Not a viable option right now."

"What does that even mean?" She chuckled. "You can charm the pants off him?"

"How do you know it's not the other way around?"

"Oh-ho." She snorted. "I figured two gay guys might be able to find a way to get together in this town."

I stilled. "What—"

"You think I didn't hear about my boss on the dance floor with the hottest firefighter in town? The one who happens to also be gay?"

I hadn't exactly come out and informed Spring I was gay. I hadn't had to because the article about me from Vancouver had done that. Damn thing had even implied my being gay had something to do with my discredited story. *As if.*

"I'm certain there are plenty of other gay men in Mission City."

"And single and hot and friendly?" A pause. "Well, okay—"

"What?" I tried to keep the exasperation out of my voice.

"We've had a lot of gay men getting married in the past few years and off the market. Hello, two of the psychologists who work at my sister's therapy ranch are gay. Wait, one sec. Cody's got his PhD and is single."

"Your point?"

"I should set you up with Cody. He's about Finn's age, super cute, and really grounded. Also like Finn."

"I don't need to be *set up* with anyone."

"It could be fun watching you flail around..." Her grin came through loud and clear.

"Dixon."

"MacDonald."

"No."

"You're no fun. And you still haven't explained what you and Finn were doing over at the gay bar in Langley if not hooking up."

I sighed. "How did you hear about that?"

"Cooper Gander is the biggest gossip ever."

Why does that not surprise me? Of the four people who'd joined us, I'd pegged Stephanie and Cooper as the two potential troublemakers.

"Dare I ask how you and Cooper got to talking about me?" *Right...like that's the biggest problem at the moment.* Still, knowing how the gossip mill worked in a small town was never a bad thing.

"We ran into each other at the grocery store. He's closer in age to Sunshine than he is to me, but he's always, uh, chatty."

"And you just happened to be chatting about me?"

"Well...funny you should say that."

"Funny how?"

"He asked how I liked my new boss and then the conversation just sort of continued from there."

"Was he fishing, or were you?"

"Uh...both?"

I sighed. "Personal-life boundaries, Dixon."

"He brought up seeing you in a gay bar first, and mentioned how you and Finn made a cute couple, but that he didn't see anything coming of it. And you've now pretty much confirmed there either was—or is, or both—a thing between you and Finn. I can see it, you know?"

"Because we're both gay?" I was happy to lay on the sarcasm.

Her laugh was full-throated. "Even I know there's more to relationships than just being gay."

"Oh?" I closed my laptop. I had the information she'd given me, and I'd look into it.

Tomorrow.

"Compatibility. Like how Justin the counselor has to be compatible with his husband, Stanley. Or, like, Stanley's ex-boyfriend has to be compatible with his husband Ravi." Another giggle. "And they all live on the same street, so apparently staying friends with your ex is a good thing as well."

"Do I want to know?"

"It's a cute story." She rustled something then let out a contented sigh. "You ready for the gossip?"

I leaned back. "Sure. Why not?"

Chapter Ten

Finn

Hearts and Paws Animal Shelter was both my favorite place in the world and the one that brought the most heartache.

Selah greeted me with a huge smile, though. "Finn! A rare Saturday off. So glad you could make it."

The adoption area of the shelter gleamed bright white while the concrete floors shone. The wood accents around the windows matched the counter and gave the place a homier feel. "I thought I'd walk the dogs today." I shrugged. "And then maybe spend an hour in the cat enclosure."

"Sure. The animals will love that. We got a surrender this week. A pittie mix. She's adorable."

"And might be harder to find a home for." Plenty of landlords and condo associations didn't allow bully breeds.

"True. But I'm certain she'll charm someone's socks off. Her name is Thelma. Want to come and meet her?"

"Sure."

When I'd first come here, I'd worried that I wouldn't be able to part with the animals at the end of my visit. Knowing I couldn't have a dog helped, though. My shifts at the station were too damn long, and I couldn't afford to either kennel the dog while I worked or pay to have someone come out and walk them. An alternative might've been building a doggie door and an enclosure for a dog, but I didn't like the idea of the animal being alone—even if protected by a strong fence.

Selah handed me the key to the kennels. "You know the routine. We haven't had any warnings, and there haven't been any issues, but you know—"

"I know. I'll be careful." Not just because I didn't want a dog bite—I didn't, of course—but because I wouldn't want to be the cause of a dog having to be put down.

I waved goodbye and headed to the dog area. As I passed each kennel, I said the dog's name. Some woofed. Some clawed at the glass. Some stayed at the far wall and didn't approach. Since I had the entire day free, I planned to walk everyone and then, of course, hang out with the cats. Generally, they appreciated my efforts less—but a couple of them liked scritches.

Thelma sat on her bed and, when she caught sight of me, made a beeline for her door.

The exact moment she realized I wasn't whoever she was expecting broke my heart as her smile literally vanished. "Oh, baby girl." I swallowed. "We're going to find a good home for you. I promise." I hadn't asked for the details of the surrender. Those stories often hit me in the gut as well. Especially when the issue was money. I had some. Not a ton, but Mom gifted me the cabin without a mortgage, and I made a good salary as a career firefighter. I donated both time and money—but I couldn't save everyone. Much as I wanted to—I just couldn't.

I took Thelma through the process of becoming acclimated to me so I could take her for a walk along the fence line of the shelter.

She was a bright dog who immediately settled beside me and walked without pulling. She kept glancing up at me as if to make certain I was still here. For fun, I took her through a series of tricks, each time giving her a piece of her kibble as a reward. She knew enough to show someone had worked with her in the past. When we'd made our way around twice, I guided her back to her kennel. "I'm so sorry, baby girl. I don't know why you're here—and I'm sure you think you've done something wrong. Well, you haven't. And we'll find you a new home. As soon as we can." I wanted to promise something better, but—judging by her behavior—she'd had a really good home.

Over the next two hours, I walked all the dogs. Some were older, and we took it slow. Some were energetic, and we ran to get the zoomies out. Old Walter was happy for me to carry him to his favorite spot in the grass. He needed a home sooner rather than later—although it would likely only be for a short time. Guy had a lot of years on him and, according to Dr. Zephyra, not that many more to go. But he wasn't suffering, so she didn't want to put him down. "Buddy, I would so love to take you home with me." I scratched him under his grizzled gray chin.

He closed his eyes in bliss.

"And that's Walter." Selah's voice carried to me.

I turned to face her and the person she was with. *Holy fuck. What are the odds?* Pretty good, apparently, because Ulysses walked next to the shelter employee.

"Walter's been here the longest?" Ulysses caught my gaze.

"Oh, not the longest. Sorry, I thought you meant the oldest. No, Poppin has been here the longest. She's being treated for a thyroid condition. She needs specialized care, and we're struggling to find a foster who can tend to her. Walter's owner died a couple of months ago, and so he's keeping us company. Both are available for either foster or adoption." She beamed. Many animals got adopted on her shifts—she could convince just about anyone to leave with a furry companion.

"I can certainly write about both dogs." Ulysses shifted his gaze from Saleh back to me. "Hello, Finn. Are you adopting?"

"Finn's one of our best volunteers. He spends time with all the dogs and then hangs out in the cat enclosure. He's sure a favorite with our fur babies. I keep hoping he'll rescue—"

"Day job." I offered a smile. "But happy to visit."

Ulysses pulled out his phone. "May I take a photograph?"

"Of me and the dog?" I blinked.

"Oh, that's a great idea!" Selah flapped her hands. "I suggested we do a calendar with all the hunky guys in town, but with how long printing takes, most of the rescues would be, well, rescued, before the thing ever reached the public. But if you could put the photo in this week's paper, maybe Walter can find his forever home." She was all grins.

I eyed Ulysses.

He was all grins. More of the lascivious kind, though. "For Walter," he crooned.

I managed not to roll my eyes. Barely. What I did do, though, was sit cross-legged and pull Walter into my lap. "This is your moment, Buddy. All smiles."

He licked my chin.

Selah laughed.

Even Ulysses chuckled. "Got that."

"Thank you." Selah gestured toward the kennels. "There are plenty more. Oh, maybe you could feature an animal a week?"

"That would be a lot of work for him, Selah." I rose, all the while holding Walter in my arms. "I'm certain he's got better things to do with his time."

"Than ensuring animals find forever homes?" Ulysses held my gaze. "If so, I can't think what."

Damn.

Selah gestured toward the kennels. "I can show you Poppin. She's a sweetheart."

"I can certainly take a picture of her as well."

Ulysses offered what I thought was a genuine smile. With him, though, sometimes differentiating between sincerity and nicety was a challenge. His demeanor could flip from grumpy to happy so quickly.

Unlike me. What one saw was what one got. I was happy with my life and wanted other people to be as well. With the exception of—

"Finn's not the only regular volunteer. We have a bunch of them. We rely on donations as well, obviously. We have four staff members, including me. Charging an adoption fee helps keep the place running, but we do have a benefactor who will cover the fee in cases of hardship." Selah opened the door back to the administrative area.

"But if a person can't afford the fee, how can they afford all the things that come with pet ownership? Food, vet bills, vaccinations..." Ulysses followed her while I veered off so I could return Walter to his kennel.

I sat with the little guy and let him lick my face repeatedly. Being here hadn't dulled his spirits and, if it were in my power, I'd bring him home and give him the perfect life. Alas, life didn't work like that. I gave him final scritches and secured the gate. Rubbing my concrete-numbed ass, I eyed the cat building and decided I'd see them next weekend. Rescuing a cat was a possibility—but I really liked my freedom. To go wherever I wanted whenever I wanted. To be able to just lock the cabin and go without worrying about a pet. *You do good work here. No one can ask for more.* Maybe...but I did.

In the office, I handed the keys back to Selah. "I might come in tomorrow as well. I didn't get to see the cats."

"You know you're always welcome. Meyer's working tomorrow, and he'll be happy to see you." She beamed.

"How did it go with the, uh, reporter?"

"He's going to come back another day to take a picture of Poppin. I'll try to sneak Thelma in as well." Her shrug caught me off guard.

"What?"

"I'm just thinking Thelma will probably be gone by the time he comes back."

"Oh, you have a lead?"

She nodded. "I think I know someone. We'll see."

"Thelma is truly wonderful. She deserves the best." They all did, of course, but I felt a special kinship with our new arrival. She really needed tons of love. "All right, have a good evening."

"Thanks for coming, Finn. Take care."

With that, I headed out. As I made my way across the parking lot, a familiar figure stood leaning against my pickup. "Okay, what now?"

"How did the phone call go last night?"

"Fine." No way was I going to share what happened. I knew better. Or at least I thought I did. "Why are you waiting for me?"

"How long have you volunteered here?"

"Since I started working in the department. So about five years. Why?"

"Just—" He looked around. Clearly to verify we were alone. Since the animal shelter was on five acres of land, there wasn't another building in sight, and the parking lot was empty save three vehicles for three people, I figured he was being a little paranoid. He pursed his lips. “I heard a rumor, and I wanted to ask you if you know anything about it.”

“You know the price of questions.”

He cocked his head.

“Take me to dinner. I know this great Mexican place. Hell, I’ll even pay. Follow me.” Without waiting for him to respond—or even to ask if he liked Mexican—I got into my truck. I waited until he was in his SUV before I headed out of the parking lot.

Is this really a good idea? You didn’t answer his questions yesterday and now he’s got more today...can you keep everything straight?

I probably could. More importantly, though—did I want to?

For that question, I didn’t have an answer.

Chapter Eleven

Ulysses

I wasn't a huge Mexican food fan. Well, more like I didn't frequent the restaurants. As I was following Finn, though, my stomach rumbled. Okay, so food would be a good idea. *But not sex. Answers first—bedtime activities later.* He still hadn't explained why he'd booted me. Retribution for me having left? A way to protect himself? Or truly a phone call he didn't trust me not to listen in on.

Spring's overheard rumor about the shelter had felt far-fetched. And with boy scout Finn as a volunteer there, the whispered suggestions felt even more ridiculous. *But sometimes truth comes from the ludicrous. Maybe Finn isn't the boy scout you think he is. Or maybe he's not involved and had no idea about the nefarious activities.*

Huh.

That notion was plausible.

He signaled a right turn into a strip mall, and I followed. Soon he pulled up before a fast-food joint with, yes, a Mexican-themed window display. We exited our vehicles at the same time and headed into the place.

"This is on me." Finn grinned. "But I know Fifties was more expensive."

I waved him off. I wasn't keeping score. Whatever it took to get information.

I opted for a bowl of beef with rice, black beans, lettuce, chopped tomatoes, diced onions and corn with a dollop of sour cream on the top. I had no idea how Mexican the meal was, but it smelled amazing.

Finn chose basically the same things but in a wrap. He grinned as he entered a tip into the machine and tapped his card.

The server wished us well, which I could barely hear over the music playing. I didn't recognize the tune, but that wasn't surprising. My tastes ran to classic rock and classical concertos. Quite a contrast. Newer music didn't tend to sway me. I wanted comfort—which I got from things from my past.

Nostalgic doesn't suit you. You're supposed to be up on the current trends. On the new. On the latest buzz.

That didn't pull me in, though. So I'd leave those things to Spring and our freelancer, Tyler. He had an unpaid internship and was eyeing journalism as a career.

"Here okay?" Finn pointed to a corner table—as far away from the employee as possible.

"Sure."

We placed our trays—holding our food and fountain drinks—on the table, and then we both removed our jackets.

As I sat, Finn chuckled. "Fall is definitely in the air."

"You had pink cheeks when you were out with the dogs." Heat rushed to my face. Not exactly subtle.

"Will that show up in the pictures, do you think? The fresh-faced firefighter with the pink cheeks?" He plopped onto the plastic chair and unwrapped his sandwich.

"Don't you wash your hands?" I eyed him.

He rolled his eyes. "Sure. Whatever." He got up and headed to the washroom.

Maybe that was out of line. He's an adult. If he wants dog guck on his food, that's his issue, not mine. Except...I didn't want to watch him and think about dog guck. I'd never had a pet growing up. That said, I didn't mind dogs. Tiffany, Healing Horses' therapy dog visited the newspaper office once or twice a month when Rainbow Dixon visited her sister Spring.

I tried to remember where in the pecking order Rainbow fell, but I couldn't. A middle child? As an only child, I couldn't fathom seven siblings—let alone seven brothers or seven sisters.

"Happy now?" Finn sat back down.

At that moment, the sun angled in such a way as to hit his head. His red hair turned a burnished auburn with gold highlights while his dark-blue eyes appeared even more vivid. Objectively, the man was gorgeous. With the body to match the good looks.

I'd never been a guy who picked his partners based on looks. Well, perhaps in the early days. As time went on, though? More and more I wanted someone with personality. Intellect or street smarts were a bonus. Someone to carry on a conversation with.

Finn was all those things.

"So...the shelter—"

He waved me off. "Food first."

I let out a sigh of frustration as he dug into his wrap. With more force than necessary, I used my wooden fork to dig into my bowl. I didn't *love* wooden cutlery or paper straws. I also didn't want to leave a legacy of plastic everywhere. Hell, even the bowl that my food was in was a strong paper-fiber product instead of plastic. Only the lid was plastic. So hey, I'd done my part for the environment today.

"When do you go back to work?" I took a forkful of food and delicately put it in my mouth.

My dinner companion, on the other hand, was eating like he was starved, and food was dropping from the wrap onto the paper. He swallowed. "Tomorrow night. Then I work for three nights."

"Then you're off, right? Must be tough—switching from days to nights and back."

"When I get the full three days off, it's not so bad. I just stay up all day after my last night shift—that pretty much resets my internal clock."

"Don't shift workers have a higher rate of cardiovascular disease? Of cancer?"

"Yeah. Same with firefighters. I still wouldn't want to be doing anything else. So, why journalism?" He took a huge bite. Unlike me, he hadn't opted for onions.

Maybe he just doesn't like them. So maybe I shouldn't have picked them either.

Right.

Except this isn't a date.

Or is it? He'd said the price of information was a meal and he considered meals as dates.

I was so confused.

He gestured for me to answer his question.

"That's both complicated and simple. I believe in truth, and I believe the expression that sunlight is the best disinfectant. The more people know the truth, the less likely others are able to get away with crimes."

"You've broken some big stories." He grinned.

"You searched me."

"Well, you knew that was going to happen eventually. So, did you do that shit they accused you of?"" Another bite. Accompanied by an arched eyebrow.

I eyed my food. I pushed it around with my fork. "I'm not certain the truth matters. Because did I do what they said I did? Yes. Do I regret the horrendous mistake? Yes. Did I trust the wrong person? Also, yes. But was I malicious or sloppy? No to either of those. But apologies and explanations after the damage is done are always too late. Retractions and mea culpas only go so far. In my case, not far enough." Bile rose in my throat.

Finn laid his hand on mine. "I'm sorry I brought it up."

"It really is in the past. I've made a new life for myself in Mission City." *Liar. Fucking liar. You think about this every damn day.* I tried to silence my inner voice. Now *so* wasn't the time for regrets and recriminations. In the dead of night, when I was all alone, was when the demons could come.

Would come.

I again tried to decide if I was hungry enough to finish my meal.

He squeezed my hand before releasing it. "Ask your question."

I met his gaze. "What do you know about the shelter?"

Finn eyed me as if trying to work out my intentions. "That I've been volunteering there for years. They're good people. They submit their books for audits regularly. They screen everyone who steps in the door. Uh—" He scratched his nose. "Like other stuff too. They work with the city and the cops when there are abuse situations. They vet all potential adoptive homes." He shrugged. "Everything's aboveboard."

"You don't *know* that."

"Yes, I do *know* that." He met my gaze with his penetrative stare. "What are you getting at?"

"Are you...have you heard anything about animals...disappearing?"

His brow knit. "I have no idea what you're talking about. All the animals are chipped and tracked. The shelter staff know exactly how many dogs and cats they have at all times. No animals *disappear*." He glared.

Maybe I was barking up the wrong tree. Maybe Spring had misunderstood. Maybe Finn was as clueless as he appeared to be. All three things could be true at the same time. "I'm just saying...if something nefarious was going on...who might be involved?"

He sighed. "No one. I would trust them all with my life. Hell, if I was in any way worried about the animals, you'd better believe I'd be the first to speak up." He shoved the rest of his wrap into his mouth.

Clearly, this conversation was over.

The biggest dilemma journalists and police detectives faced was—keep pushing or back off?

After a long moment, I chose the second, at least for now. "I'm sure you're right. Must've been mistaken."

He swallowed then arched that damn perfect eyebrow again. "Mistaken about what, precisely?"

I waved him off. Then put my fork at the five o'clock position to indicate I was finished eating.

"You coming back to my place?" Finn quirked his eyebrow.

His question caught me off guard. "Huh?"

He leaned forward. "Sex? Do you want it? I mean, it's been an entire twenty-four hours and—"

"Hell fucking yes." No way was I passing up great sex.

"But you're not staying the night." He held my gaze.

"I can leave. When you kick me out." *Is this the right answer?*

"And not before?"

I shook my head.

"Fine. You know the way?"

"I'll follow you."

"Right. Good."

We rose, disposed of our recycling and trash, then made our way to our vehicles.

I'm happy to follow wherever he leads.

Right back into his bedroom.

Dusk was upon us by the time we got behind the bedroom door, and the light streaming in from the widows, with that last gasp of sun, showed off his sculptured muscles to perfection.

As he handed me the lube, he gave me a wicked grin. "I want to ride you."

"Then you shall. But first—" I held up the bottle.

He lay on his back and gave me the most tantalizing view of his hole.

My cock, already very much interested, leaked a drop of precum. As I coated my fingers, he moved his cock and balls out of the way.

His cock curled happily toward his belly—clearly on board with tonight's adventures. When I brushed his prostate, a bead of precum formed on the tip.

I licked it off.

His hips flexed.

I tut-tutted.

He whimpered.

Within a minute, I was sheathed and lying on my back.

After straddling my thighs, he lowered himself onto me. He was all tight heat and big grins.

From there, we did what came naturally. He sank down. I thrust up. He rode me hard. I struggled to keep up. We both knew what we were doing, and when I grasped his cock, he moaned. I jerked him to the rhythm of thrusts, and we tried to stave off our orgasms.

And also to see who could make the other come first—like this was a contest of wills or something.

"Goddamnit, Ulysses. Fucking come already." Mirth danced in his eyes.

"You first, Finnegan." I rotated my wrist slightly to give more friction to his cock.

"Jesus. I—" His rhythm faltered as he came. He spurted cum everywhere even as he spasmed around me. "Holy fuck. Holy fuck. Holy..." His eyes drifted shut.

"No, look at me." I squeezed his softening dick. "I want to see you."

His eyes flew open as his mouth made a silent *o*.

"Yeah. That." I thrust up into him twice more, then held myself steady as my own release thundered through me. I resisted the urge to close my eyes as I held his gaze. *This. This is what you do to me.* I'd had sex plenty of times since coming out of the closet in my first year of university. Plenty of guys and plenty of good times.

None compared to the gloriousness of this man.

And that scared me more than anything else in the world.

Chapter Twelve

Finn

When we dragged ourselves back to the fire hall after the latest call, I could barely see straight. My eyes were gritty, my limbs ached, and my gut still roiled.

Miriam parked the truck as Giancarlo, Albert, Krish, Toby, and Dulcie sorted their gear.

I stood toe-to-toe with Marlon—engaging him in an epic glarefest.

"I didn't fuck up." Marlon stuck his chin out.

Dulcie cleared her throat. Whether calling bullshit on Marlon's assertion or warning me to tread carefully, I couldn't tell. I certainly hoped that was an *I call bullshit* rather than trying to dissuade me from my mission.

"You *did* fuck up. Giancarlo could've died—"

"He's right fucking there." Marlon flailed a hand as he gestured to Giancarlo who was, in fact, *right there*.

If only by the skin of his teeth.

I poked my finger in Marlon's chest. "You said everyone was clear. You said we were all good." We'd been retreating. I'd counted and was certain we were missing someone. Things had been so damn chaotic at the house fire. But the neighbor swore the family was inside. And their car was in the driveway, so that assertion was logical.

We'd cleared the house even as we tried to fight the fire.

No one. We hadn't found anyone.

And we'd retreated.

I'd thought we were down a person, but Marlon assured me we had everyone.

Until I realized we *didn't* have everyone. We were missing Giancarlo.

Heedless of the risk, I'd barreled back inside. I located Giancarlo in a back room. He'd been...confused. Instead of trying to sort things out, once I realized he hadn't found anyone, I'd grabbed his hand and dragged him out the back door.

We made our way around to the front to find the family standing there. They'd been out at the movies—in their other car.

No harm. No foul.

Except for Marlon saying we'd been clear when we weren't.

"You're a fuckup, Marlon. You could've gotten Giancarlo killed."

"Well, he's not dead. Everyone's fine. Hell, you even had the paramedics check him out."

"Logically. You thought I wouldn't?" I was incredulous. No question something had gone wrong back there. I wanted my friend checked out thoroughly. Hell, if I'd found Marlon confused, I'd have wanted him examined. Not just because we needed everyone to be on their game at all times—but because I actually gave a shit about people.

Unlike Marlon.

I tried to tell myself I was being unkind. But his cavalier attitude was going to get someone killed one day. I was certain of that.

Miriam rounded the truck. "You guys need to get out of your gear. We might get another call, and you won't be ready."

She was right, of course. But I couldn't back down on this. This was too fucking important. "Just give us a minute."

"No." She shook her head. "You can hash it out once everyone's gear is ready to go. I don't want things to be disorganized if another call comes in. Hell, it's a night ending in *day*. Anything can happen."

As always, she wasn't wrong. She was also one of the smartest women I knew—and my life was full of smart women.

"What's going on?" Chief McInerny's voice rang through the fire hall.

Well fuck. This isn't going to end well.

"He's giving me a hard time for something I didn't do." Marlon pointed his finger in my direction. At least he had the smarts not to fucking touch me.

"A hard time you deserve." I turned to face the chief. Marlon's dad, of course. "Marlon said the entire crew was clear of the structure. Giancarlo was inside. Your son's incompetence could've gotten Giancarlo killed." *Way to be blunt. You could've eased into it...*

"That's a hell of an accusation you're leveling. You're probably wrong." The chief glared. At me, naturally.

"We're all a little frazzled. Close call. Tough fire." Miriam placed her hand on my arm, but she addressed the chief. "We need to get sorted before the next call out."

"Of course." He glared at me. "Thin ice. Be very careful about leveling accusations without proof. Marlon might've misunderstood. He obviously thought Giancarlo was clear. He would never endanger anyone." With that, Chief strode away.

His mere presence in this fire hall is a danger to everyone—including himself. My gut twisted. Not just at the near-miss tonight—although that was bad enough. No, I was panicked about the next time. About what happened when someone was injured, or even killed, on Marlon's shift. I was absolutely certain that was going to happen. I couldn't be on every scene every shift. Marlon and I weren't always working together. And as good as I was at keeping my ear to the ground, I still chafed at not having been let near the tire fire on Friday.

Miriam had called me. She hadn't been able to articulate why things had felt off—but they had been.

Yet nothing had come from those concerns. The fire inspector determined a faulty electrical panel had started the blaze. A plumber working the day before had shut off the water to the sprinkler, and no one had noticed.

Way too convenient. Or just shitty timing. Perhaps something more nefarious. But she didn't have proof. And supposition wasn't going to get us anywhere. Plus, to what end? The tire shop had been a profitable business. By estimates, rebuilding would take months.

By the time I finished my ruminations, Marlon was long gone and Miriam was organizing her gear. Firehouse Three covered us during the blaze, but we needed to be ready for the next call. Because it would come. Rare was a night we had a single call.

My thinking was borne out as we got two overdose calls—both young men. We revived one, but the other was already dead when we arrived. Which was super shitty. Apparently there'd been another young man found in a local park earlier in the day. Dead as well. Drugs were killing off our young people, and all we could do was watch. Interventions weren't helping. Treatment programs weren't working. Government at all levels claimed to want to solve the problem—yet none of them had a winning strategy.

I struggled into my front door the morning after that shift with barely an ounce of energy. I wanted to sleep, preferably for a month, but two days would do.

Instead, I took a shower, downed a coffee, and headed to Hearts and Paws. I nearly fell asleep in the cat enclosure. A particularly tubby orange tabby curled up on my lap. Her purrs nearly lulled me into unconsciousness so, after I left, I made my way to Timmies for another extra-large coffee and a chicken wrap. Having consumed that, I drove up to the high school. When I had Wednesdays off, I helped coach a basketball rec league for interested teenagers. Mrs. Gustafson coached both the boys' and girls' teams for Mission City Collegiate. And she was freaking amazing. Had taught me a thing or two, back in the day. The co-ed games I ran were for fun—for kids who'd never make the school team.

When I arrived, though, I immediately knew something was wrong. The group was huddled in the corner of the gym—not tossing balls like they normally would be. No one was practicing shots or dribbling. No one even noticed my arrival.

As I approached, and my shoes squeaked on the floor, Tenyce turned my way. "Did you hear about David?"

I shook my head.

Tears brimmed in her eyes. "He died. They say he OD'd."

I stood still—trying to take in that news. David was on the verge of making the school team. Likely next season. He worked harder than anyone here and showed the most potential. He was shorter than most of the kids, though. I kept praying for a growth spurt to give him the height he needed to compete.

Leroy glared. "He didn't do drugs. So he couldn't have OD'd. That coroner has it all wrong."

"When did he die?" Because I needed to orient myself.

"Yesterday morning. In the park." Rue wiped her eyes. "But it doesn't make sense."

Drugs rarely did. Addiction took many forms, and not all users showed signs of abusing.

"You folks want to talk?" I gestured toward the bleachers.

To find Ulysses standing next to them.

"Wait here." I gestured to the kids to stay where they were, and then I strode over to the guy who haunted my every waking moment as well as all my erotic dreams.

So not the time.

"What are you doing here? Do you have permission to be in the school?" I had a pass that allowed me to come and go, but not every community member did. The doors weren't guarded—or even locked—but adults and students from other schools weren't allowed to just show up and enter school grounds.

He shrugged. "I was here to talk to some kids about their friend's death."

"Does Mr. Clayton know you're here?"

"The principal?"

I nodded.

"No. I didn't realize—"

"Bullshit you didn't. You know very well you can't go skulking around schools uninvited or questioning minors about traumatic events without permission."

He shrugged. "Did you know the kid?"

I arched an eyebrow. *I should just report him. Teach him a lesson about trespassing. Show him that I follow the rules and breaking them isn't a good idea.* All very good ideas.

None of which I actually did. Instead, despite my upset at David's death, I offered him a wicked smile. "You know the price. Do you like sushi? I know this great little place."

Two hours later, after letting the kids talk about their grief and encouraging them to go home and touch base with their parents or the school counselors, I met the intrepid reporter for dinner.

Chapter Thirteen

Ulysses

"You're not kicking me out?" I yawned from the comfort of Finn's embrace.

Sushi dinner—with very few answers—had led back to Finn's place where, again, we'd fucked like gay rabbits.

This time, in our post-coital bliss, I had my head on his chest and I was curled around him. Awkward was the word I'd use. I should've been comforting him. He'd admitted he knew David.

"I'm too tired to kick you out."

"Do you want me to go?"

His grip tightened on me. "Only if you want to."

Progress.

"I'm comfortable."

"Then stay." He said the words on a yawn.

Better catch him before he falls asleep. "So did you know the kid who ODed?"

"David? Yeah. He played basketball in the rec league I run. I've known him for about a year. I didn't know he was doing drugs, though. Don't bother to ask about that."

"Someone has to know something, though, don't you think? I mean, unless that was his very first time—"

"It might've been. Hell, they haven't formally said he died from an OD." He sighed. "He likely did, though. And that's just shit."

"I agree. But wouldn't it be better to know what's going on so you can prevent it from happening again?"

He snorted. "You're assuming I have any sway over these kids. News alert—I don't. They'll do whatever they want and I have little say in the matter."

"But they look up to you, right? Admire you?"

"That's possible. But David didn't trust me enough to come to me with whatever he was facing."

I winced—even though he couldn't see. "Look, I'm not here tonight to write a story about the kid. His life is a tragedy—and yes, reporting on it might stop another kid ODing. But what I really want to know about is where he got the drugs."

"Why?" Finn gripped me a little tighter.

I considered. "That's the bigger story. But also, I like investigating crime. I report it, then hand everything over to the police."

"That sounds simplistic. Shouldn't the cops be investigating?"

"I'm sure they do. But they've got dozens of crimes. I'm focusing on just one." I stroked his chiseled abs. "So tell me about David?"

He sighed. "Good kid. Good grades. Natural aptitude on the basketball court. He was planning to try out for the school team next year. He was on the short side. He was good, for certain. He'd hold back, though, with the other rec kids. He never showed off. More often, he was willing to help them. Almost acted like my assistant coach. Which is why him doing drugs makes no sense."

"Do drugs ever really make sense? I read the autobiography of this really successful business guy in Vancouver. Top of the world. His company was doing great and he was happy. He started dating a woman from Seattle who coaxed him into trying crack. Why? He was never able to articulate that. But his entire life changed on a dime. He spent the next few years down the addiction rabbit hole. He'd do whatever it took to chase that high again. It affected his work, it impacted his relationship with his children, and he blew through all the money he had."

"Jesus. He survived to write about it?"

"I can get you a copy of the book. It's a damn fascinating read." I pressed my hand to Finn's sternum. "The guy hit rock bottom. For some people, that's death. For him, he'd lost everything and had ceased to function at work. He went to a friend and confessed everything."

"Please tell me the friend was understanding."

"Yep. We should all have such good friends. He got the executive into rehab and the guy hasn't touched drugs since. But it's not usually that easy. He found reasons to put his life back together—but it had to be for himself as much as for other people. Eventually, he repaired his relationship with his daughter. And he's gone on to be successful again. But he can't get those years back." I ran my fingers lightly across Finn's abdomen. "I don't understand that kind of high. And I'd never risk finding out. Some people are more prone to addiction, and maybe he was one of them."

Finn ran his hand across my scalp. "You don't have any burning obsessions?"

I stilled. The words were on the tip of my tongue. Here, in this quiet space, I could reveal all.

And yet I didn't.

"Work is a bit of an obsession. Hence me wanting to know about David. Hence me attending the fires and trying to find answers. Or me going to the animal shelter to find out if they're involved in anything illicit."

"Ah." He sighed. "That's a lot of juggling. You can forget the shelter, though."

"I'm good at splitting my focus. And Spring's got a few things she's working on as well."

"Spring's a very bright woman."

"She seems to be on par for the Dixons." I smiled and pressed a kiss to Finn's chest. "I like strong and brilliant women."

"You're bi?" He caressed my cheek.

"Not even a little bit."

"Ah."

"You?"

"I've dated a few women. Strong preference for men, though. Especially sexy older men who ask way too damn many questions."

I laughed. "Oh really."

"Yes, *oh really*. You intrigue me, Ulysses. I want to know everything about you, and yet you hold yourself apart. You have secrets."

I swallowed. Hard. "Everyone has secrets, Finn. Everyone. Even you."

"Nope. My life is an open book."

I considered my next words carefully. "We've all done something in the past that we regret. Someone we hurt, something we did—inadvertently or advertently—that did real damage. A careless word. Even an ungracious thought. It's there for everyone, Finn. It's part of being human."

A long silence followed.

Eventually, Finn said, "I...I don't know about that. I really do try to live my beliefs. I suppose I've had uncharitable thoughts on occasion. Impure ones as well." He pulled me tighter. "Like all the things I want to do with you."

I angled my head up so I could gaze into those gorgeous dark-blue eyes. "And? Care to be precise?"

"Eating your ass? Fucking you into oblivion?"

"I didn't realize you wanted to top me."

And I'm not sure how I feel about that.

Finn laughed. "I pretty much want to top every guy I'm with—as well as bottoming on a regular basis. I just happen to love everything about sex."

"Okay. You haven't shown me that side."

"We've had sex almost every time we've gotten together."

"Because you won't answer my questions if I don't sleep with you. That sort of sounds like...extortion?"

He chuckled. "Only you would see it that way."

"How do you see it?"

"As a way of us both getting what we want. You're always free to say *no*. But for an old guy, you definitely have more stamina than I'd expected."

I pushed off him. "Old guy? Old guy?"

He grinned impishly. "Forty is close to over the hill."

"Twenty-seven isn't a young pup. How old is your mother?"

"Forty-nine. Why?"

"Is she *over the hill*?"

"Of course not. She still does long shifts as a nurse. She still contributes." He appeared to consider. "You know, you're closer in age to my mother than you are to me."

"Oh Jesus." That hit. Hard. "Am I robbing the cradle?"

He chuckled. "Oh hardly. If you are, I'm choosing to be stolen." He coaxed me closer. "Can I show you how young you actually are?"

I cocked an eyebrow. "And how, precisely, do you plan to do that?"

"Well, we'll start by eating you out, and then I see myself fucking you into—"

I launched myself toward his head. I grasped his cheeks and sealed our mouths together.

Yeah, I'm game for this.

And so I was.

He edged me as he fucked me into oblivion—after having eaten me out.

In the morning, with great regrets, I had to leave. I gave him a blow job before I headed out.

Only later did I realize how few questions he'd actually answered.

Chapter Fourteen

Finn

Miriam slapped me on the back. "Holy shit, dude, that was amazing."

We were back at the station, having just executed one of the toughest calls I'd ever been on. Extractions were brutal at the best of times. This one? Off the charts.

"Yeah, you should get a freaking medal." Giancarlo beamed.

I removed my turnout gear and tried not to grin. "Okay, enough. Team effort." These calls were always tough. Today's was truly one for my, *holy shit I really did that* book. "I need a fucking shower." I stank. I couldn't remember ever having sweated so much. So much on the line and so little time to get everything done.

"Yeah, you go shower. I'll heat up some pasta." Miriam grinned. "Lasagna."

"Oh God, my favorite." I placed my hand on her biceps. "Thanks for this." I gestured to Giancarlo with my chin. "You too, eh?"

"Yeah." His dark-brown eyes shone brightly.

We did good.

I made my way to the shower and was under the hot spray within moments of stripping. *Please let us not get another call. I need to come down.*

Someone else stepped into the shower and started humming tunelessly.

Marlon.

Krish had once—tactfully—suggested that maybe being silent in the showers would be acceptable.

Twitty Marlon had lost his temper and thrown a hissy fit.

Since none of us wanted Chief to come down on us, we opted to stay silent.

I'd watched Krish's back until the furor had died down. Seriously, one would think we'd asked Marlon to make...some great sacrifice or something.

Instead of lingering, I finished washing up and hopped out. I was sore as fuck, but that was as much about the stress and adrenaline that'd been running through me as any physical exertion. I'd done exactly what I was supposed to. Textbook perfect. I was glad rookie Toby had been along for the ride so he could see what a successful extraction looked like.

After putting on jeans and a department T-shirt, I spent about ten seconds drying my hair. I added gel and then beat a retreat since Marlon had started singing louder. His voice was so terrible that I didn't even recognize the song he was massacring.

Sigh.

I rounded the corner to the smell of lasagna and the sight of a familiar man standing next to Giancarlo.

Ulysses saw me and grinned. "I understand you're to be congratulated."

"What are you doing here? This is a private area." I tried to keep my tone neutral.

And apparently failed since Giancarlo shot me a warning glare I'd have had to be extremely dense to miss. I arched an eyebrow.

Ulysses's smile broadened. "I got permission."

I was about to ask from whom when Miriam popped her head out from the kitchen. "First come, first served, and the reporter's joining us. To get a sense of our work, right?" She gave him a bright smile.

Sheesh. Everyone's fucking smiling tonight. And I should've been as well. Except I'd been trying to keep a clear delineation between Ulysses and work. He was asking too damn many questions. Questions for which I either had an answer I didn't want to share or, worse, didn't.

"Lovely." I pasted on my best smile as we made our way into the kitchen.

The tomato sauce scent assailed me, and I inhaled deeply.

"Hero gets first piece." Miriam handed me a plate with a massive slice.

I was hungry enough to eat it—and probably a second serving. Lunch was a long-distant memory.

"And guests after that." She handed Ulysses a plate. "Sit close to Finn." She cast me a *what the fuck is wrong with you* look I was well-familiar with.

"Yes. It'll be lovely. I'll be stuffing my face." I put the plate on the table and made my way to the counter. "Water for everyone?"

I got a bunch of *yes, pleases*. Polite bunch tonight.

After setting out water for everyone, I took my seat. Across from Ulysses. So I could look into those mesmerizing eyes and remember how sore he was able to make my ass when he drilled me hard—just the way I liked it.

He put a forkful of pasta in his mouth as he held my gaze.

Surely there must be some kind of rule...like conflict of interest?

Except we weren't paying for his meal. Weren't bribing him. Weren't attempting to sway him so we could get better coverage.

"I got some great shots of the accident. Not of personal trauma, of course." Ulysses swept his gaze along the table.

"Were you supposed to be that close?" I tried to picture the scene in my mind. The crushed cars, the highway littered with debris—

"I happened to be just a few cars behind. I didn't see the accident, but I called emergency services."

"Apparently several people did." Miriam cut a piece of her lasagna. "We responded as quickly as we could."

"I was trying to comfort the older lady. The paramedics said she was having a heart attack?" Ulysses separated a bit of cheese from the pasta.

Giancarlo nodded. "Yeah. They got there before us, which is unusual. But that worked out because they helped her while we extracted the family."

"Using the jaws of life, right? That was so impressive." Ulysses held my gaze.

"Actually, we call it the cutter. Or the spreader or the combo. Depending on which tool we use. The general public say jaws of life."

"Ah. Maybe I should get a lesson in terminology. I'd love for readers to have that insight."

"Finn would be happy to give it to you. We have a media-liaison person, but Finn's about the best we've got." Miriam gave me a pointed stare.

"He really is. I'm so lucky to be learning from the best." Rookie Toby's grin was so wide his face damn near split.

I rolled my eyes.

Giancarlo poked me in the ribs.

"Well, I look forward to getting the lowdown on the department from Finn." Ulysses eyed me. "So what happened tonight?"

"We got the call. We were the closest firehouse, so we pushed hard to get there. Two-vehicle crash at high speed. The hypothesis is the elderly driver of the pickup truck had a heart attack and, it appears, crossed the center lane. But that's up to the accident reconstruction people, so please don't put that in print. Get the final verdict from the experts."

"That's fair." He continued to hold my gaze.

"The paramedics arrived first, and they took control of the first casualty while my team worked on extracting the occupants of the second vehicle. A mother and three children. Fortunately, all were wearing restraints. Unfortunately, their car sustained severe damage."

"Pickup truck against a sedan rarely ends well for the car." Giancarlo winced.

"But Finn had that car open in no time, and we were able to get the lady and her kids out." Toby beamed.

I could've pointed out we'd all contributed. Just because I'd held the machine, didn't mean I deserved any more of the credit.

"Just in the nick of time." Ulysses held my gaze.

"Yeah." Toby nearly bounced out of his seat. "The baby went into respiratory distress and Miriam stepped in and...uh..." He squinted.

"Latest reports from the paramedics are that the baby's been stabilized and has been transported to Children and Women's Hospital in Vancouver." Miriam poked at her food. "I didn't do much. The second set of paramedics arriving in the rig made all the difference."

Perhaps. But she'd kept the baby from going into shock and, more importantly, had kept the baby's airway open.

"I saw the second ambulance. And, obviously, the helicopter."

"Yeah." I let out a breath. "We thought we might be transporting the elderly patient to the hospital that way, but she was holding her own and the baby was going downhill fast."

"Tex was piloting, right?" Giancarlo offered a small smile. "Best we've got."

"Tex?" Ulysses gazed over at my friend.

"Yeah. Long story. He grew up in Mission City, then joined the army, then got injured and left. He sort of flitted around from here to there until he got his accreditation to fly life flights. At that point, he settled in Mission City with his husband and now he runs flights in Cedar Valley." Giancarlo offered a smile. "Now there's someone worth interviewing—he's got quite a story. And an adorable husband to boot, who is some fancy scientist guy. Something to do with physics, right?"

"Yep." I returned the smile. "Good memory. Davey teaches at the University of British Columbia and is some kind of genius. Talk to him, though, and he's just sort of adorable." I considered. "He might make a good human-interest story as well."

"So many residents, so little time." Ulysses offered me an enigmatic expression I couldn't identify.

"You planning on going somewhere?" My stomach lurched. I'd sort of assumed he was making his home in Mission City for the foreseeable future. *Have I read that wrong? Is he really itching to leave?* Small-town life wasn't for everyone. I loved it. So did many of my friends. Other people definitely didn't.

Marlon entered the room. He helped himself to a huge serving of lasagna and then, inexplicably, took off. Or maybe explicably.

"How about him? Was he involved today? You all sort of look the same in your turnout gear." Ulysses was adjusting his proverbial reporter's cap.

"He was there, yeah." Miriam's jaw set.

Well, fuck.

"Oh, what was his role?" Ulysses just not wanting to quit.

Giancarlo caught my gaze. He cleared his throat. "He was helping coordinate with the police."

Ulysses wrinkled his nose as if he caught the undertones. "Is that normal? You all looked pretty busy—"

"Things vary." *Shovel the bullshit as best you can*. "All good." *Nothing to see here. Move along.*

"Well, I'd really like to talk to him."

"Talk to who?" Chief McInerny sauntered into the room. "Good job, everyone."

"I'd love to talk to the fireman who was coordinating with the RCMP officers." Ulysses grinned. "I'm trying to get a sense of how the team operates and—"

"Who the hell are you?" Chief glared.

"Ulysses MacDonald. I'm a reporter for the Mission City Gazette."

"You shouldn't be in here. Who let you in?" He turned his attention to me. "This your doing, O'Sullivan?"

"I, uh—"

"My doing." Miriam shrugged. "He wants to do a piece on the department. I figure it would be good for us. And we can slip in some important things like fire safety, wearing seatbelts, not drinking and driving. Right?"

"That's for the city liaison officer to deal with. Your job is to fight fires." He stared at Ulysses. "You can just move along, son."

Ulysses offered a broad smile. "I had permission to be here, and I don't want to get anyone in trouble. I'm not doing a fluff piece—I saw the teamwork involved today. I think that should be highlighted. You've been busy fighting an awful lot of fires recently. Most people in

Mission City probably don't even know about the other heroic things your people do. They are your people, right?" Sweet...but not syrupy.

"This is Chief McInerny." I had to try to get this back on the rails. "Why don't I give you the official tour when we're done eating? Any official information can come from the media person."

Ulysses cocked his head.

Work with me here. Please don't make things worse than they already are. I'd thought this was a terrible idea for an entirely different reason—my bad for not thinking about *all* the ramifications.

"That's a good idea, O'Sullivan. Quick tour and then we can send our...visitor...on his way." The chief eyed Ulysses. "Stay away from my people." He took off, leaving in his wake clear confusion as well as distress.

Ulysses was confused.

I was distressed.

"So that was the chief?"

I nodded.

"And the other guy was...his son? Nephew?"

"Son." Miriam sighed.

"Ah. I see." He dug into his lasagna. "This really is great pasta."

With a small smile, Miriam nodded. "Thanks."

"My pleasure."

Oh shit—this is not going to end well.

Chapter Fifteen

Ulysses

I tapped my pen on my desk. As much as I was all about the technology, I often wrote things out by hand. Especially when I was trying to piece something out in my mind. Finally, I grabbed my phone and hit Finn's number.

"Yes?" Said on a yawn.

"Crap." I winced. "I thought you were off."

"I am." Another yawn. "And I shouldn't be napping, so it's a good thing you called."

I wanted to call bullshit on that, but it wasn't for me to say one way or the other. "How are you?"

"Tired. We've had a couple of major calls and a bunch of small ones in the last few days. I'm also not sleeping well. But that happens from time to time."

"Do you want to talk about it?"

"Nothing to talk about. How come you called?"

"Well, uh...can I ask you out to dinner?"

"Is this a real date or a business date?"

"Business."

"Oh…okay."

Does he sound disappointed…or is that my imagination?

"Well, good. Just so you know, I don't put out on the first date. So if we ever have one of them, don't expect it to end up in the bedroom."

And apparently Finn was as good as his word. We had a *business date* at, of all places, Subway. Then we wound up in his bed.

Again.

In a tangle of sweaty bodies, and harsh breaths, he scratched my scalp. "You're really talented at that."

I chuckled. "I've had some practice."

"Not celibate all these years?"

"Uh…no. Perhaps less sex recently, though."

"Less than the two of us fucking like rabbits?"

I chuckled. "That wasn't what I meant." *Jesus, how do I say this?* "I meant less since moving to Mission City."

He stilled—his fingers resting on my scalp. "Like how much *less*?"

Fuck it. "Like I haven't had sex with anyone except you since *that* night."

"*That* night?" He sounded confused. "Oh, you mean after the fire?"

"Nope."

"Oh. Oh." He elongated the word. "Seriously? You went more than three months without sex?"

This time, I laughed. "You make it sound like it's the end of the world."

"Might just be." He resumed his scratching. "I, uh, wasn't celibate during that time. Well, not like…"

I chuckled—unsure of what he meant by *not like*. "I didn't expect you to be. You didn't even know who I was. You certainly didn't know I'd be back or we'd wind up together again."

"Ah. You're forgetting what a small town Mission City is. I knew you were the new editor almost from the moment you left my bed. Spring Dixon has a big mouth—in case you're wondering from whom I heard it." He stilled again. "Or maybe Sarabeth at Fifties told me. Well, possibly both."

"So word got around about the new gay guy in town."

"Yep." He sighed. "And I was sort of hurt and sort of mad and then we met in the bar and—" He chuckled. "Why I didn't drag you home that night, I'll never know."

"Bad timing."

"On whose part?"

"Mine? The universe's? We just maybe weren't ready." I rubbed my forehead.

"Really?" Said with no small amount of sarcasm. "But you're ready now."

"Uh—"

"That's what I thought. Okay, we've had our *business* date. Ask your questions."

I didn't particularly like his tone—but that was my fault and not his. "You saw the article I wrote about the firehouse?"

"Yes. Very flattering. Too much about making me the hero." He tightened his grip on me as I continued to lay my head on his chest.

I traced my fingers along his ab muscles. "I thought I accurately portrayed everyone as playing their part. Except that guy. The chief's son? What was with him?"

"I don't know what you mean." Said with wariness. And even a bit of weariness.

"That guy was a jackass."

"Who? Marlon or Chief?"

"How about both?" Based on two minutes of exposure, I'd bet the answer was both. I gave him time to respond.

Another one of his sighs replete with so much meaning. Yet which actually told me nothing at all. "Marlon's not all bad—"

"He didn't help you on that accident scene."

"I had it handled."

"I meant the royal *you*."

"Ha." His belly rippled as he chuckled. "I don't think that's a thing."

"Well, if it isn't then I'm making it a thing."

"I'm not sure that's possible either." He continued to massage my scalp. "I don't know what to say."

"The truth is a good place to start."

"Truth is in the eye of the beholder."

I angled my neck so I could meet his gaze. "What's going on, Finn? What aren't you telling me?"

"Nothing. Marlon...well..."

"Nepotism?"

He chuckled. "That's the word."

Somehow, I was certain he knew that word all on his own.

He cupped my cheek. "Marlon's a twit. If he's directing traffic, that's not a bad thing."

"Yeah, but would you trust him to have your back?"

"I trust you when I'm on my back." He licked his lips. "Come and kiss me. I'm not sure we did it right the last time."

Of course we'd done it right the last time. And we did it right again.

The next morning, after reluctantly leaving Finn's warm bed, I dragged myself to the office.

"You look like shit." Spring placed a coffee on my desk.

"Late night."

"I saw the story you posted about the car accident. How's everyone doing?"

"Elderly driver is going to recover. Her husband confirmed she had a heart attack and feels incredibly guilty."

"Ouch."

"Yeah. She'd been feeling unwell, but figured she just had indigestion and didn't want to miss dinner with friends. There's going to be a lot of guilt around that decision."

Spring plopped onto her chair and put her feet on her desk. "Women have different symptoms for a heart attack."

I nodded. "Maybe time to do another reminder?"

"Sure. I'm certain I can find an expert. There's that new cardiothoracic surgeon in Abbotsford, right? What's the guy's name?"

"Dr. Leopold Rodgers. I suppose you could do a profile on him as well, right?"

She sipped her coffee. "Yes, to a story. How was the family who were in the accident?"

"All expected to make a full recovery—including the infant. She was taken to Vancouver."

"That must've been scary." Spring nudged open her bakery bag and pulled out an actual donut.

"Scary? Yes. Fried dough?" She tended to only eat actual donuts on tough days.

"The best." She grinned. "What are you planning?"

Apparently not a tough day. "I'm going to do an in-depth piece about the fire department. I want to understand the ins and outs of a small-town FD and what goes into running the department on a functional and community level."

She rolled her eyes. "That's hardly a news story."

"It's been more than twenty-five years since anything substantial's been done on firefighting in town. Firefighting is a whole new ballgame since then, and readers will be interested. Very few people left over from back then."

Spring squinted. "Hell, I was barely around back then."

"In diapers?"

"If I'd been born at all. Seriously nothing since then?"

"Nothing I could find. An occasional piece on a particular firefighter. And when the first woman joined and—"

"Man, that was such a commotion. Seriously. One would think women were incapable of everything."

"Right? I remember when Vancouver got their first female firefighter. Now, there are plenty."

"I've heard there's a lot of nepotism in Vancouver."

"There might also be a lot in Mission City as well." I wasn't going to throw Vancouver's fire department under the bus—even if they did deserve it a little bit. Misogyny existed everywhere.

"We're getting better—at least with gender parity. Nepotism is a whole other can of worms."

"Oh?" I cocked my head.

She narrowed her eyes. "You've met Chief McInerny, right?"

"I have."

"And Marlon?"

"I have."

"Well, I suspect you can put two and two together to make a kid riding on coat tails rather than being worth his pay."

"That bad?"

She arched an eyebrow.

"Finn didn't elaborate."

"Finn? Finnegan O'Sullivan?"

I nodded.

She straightened so fast that she nearly spilled her coffee. "Holy shit."

"What?" I widened my eyes in alarm.

"You're *still* shagging Finn O'Sullivan?" Her voice took on a note of incredulity.

"I didn't say that. Did I say that? No, I did not."

"Well, with an answer like that, it's pretty damn obvious. Shit. I thought that was a one-off."

"Yeah—" I scratched my chin. "You know..."

"Right." She sipped her coffee. "Still, there's some logic."

"What? That he's gay and I'm gay?"

She rolled her eyes. "Plenty of gay men in Mission City. And enbies. And lesbians. Even have one of those in my family."

Before I had a chance to query if she meant a sister or some other relative, she barreled on. "So like, man, Finn. I sort of had a crush on him when we were younger. He's older than me—obviously. But he went to school with Sunshine? I got glimpses of him and thought *yeah, he's yummy*. And such a good guy to boot. Hometown hero and all that. So you're shagging him."

"I'd prefer we not talk about my sex life—or at least use a word other than *shag*. You sound British."

She laughed. "Well, I'm not that. You're so prudish."

"Not so much. Just, well, we haven't—to the best of my knowledge—told anyone."

"Do you have anyone other than me to tell?"

"Touché."

"That was mean of me. I shall rephrase." She took a deep breath. "Other than me, do you have someone you can share your feelings with?"

"What feelings? I'm shagging him."

"Oh God, and here I didn't think you had a sense of humor."

This time, I arched an eyebrow.

"Isn't it breaking some kind of journalistic code? You don't sleep with your subjects?"

"In a town this size? That would make things tough."

"Oh please. Three hundred people? Sure. Mission City's got thousands. I'm quite certain you could find someone."

Her words hit me. I had known I was taking a risk—and yet I kept going back to his bed. "I'm...well..."

"Uh-huh?"

"I can focus on the entire department, rather than just him."

"Have fun with Marlon." She rolled her eyes. Then she sobered. "That family's had some tragedies, so I shouldn't be so harsh. Just...well..."

Better look up that tragedy. Or tragedies. She had used plural.

I told her, "You can proof the story to ensure there's no bias. But Finn's coworkers were damn impressed with his skill the other day."

"Oh, skill, is it?" She waggled her eyebrows.

I laughed "And what are you working on today?"

We settled down to work, but that feeling of disquiet followed me around for the day as I tried to figure out how close to the journalistic-ethics line I could come without crossing it.

Chapter Sixteen

Finn

I ached in muscles I didn't know I had, and my joints felt like the Tin Man's after a heavy rain. Hell, even my head pounded.

Yet, when my phone rang with that special ringtone—that one dedicated just for the guy who was regularly fucking me into the mattress—I answered.

"Yeaaah?" *God, could I sound any more pathetic?* In truth, I wasn't certain I could. In fact, that my eyes were open at all was a goddamn miracle.

"Rough day?"

"You saw the fire." *Shit.*

Ulysses chuckled. "You saw me, eh? I wasn't sure if you had. Miriam waved. You didn't."

"Did I hurt your feelings?"

"Not in the least. You were working—I'd never interfere."

"Well, that's good. What's up?"

"I need a date. A business date. And, well, this has nothing to do with questions."

"What do you mean?" My mind was so befuddled that I couldn't figure out what he was trying to say.

"I need to check something out. And going to a target location on a date would make me look less like I'm poking my nose around in stuff."

I laughed. "You hardly need me as a cover. Why not take Spring?"

"Right. Two reporters. That's not conspicuous at all." No missing the sarcasm.

"Where are we going?"

"You know Tully's?"

"On the highway? Sure, I've been there." Wasn't my favorite place, but if he'd wanted to go to Fifties, then we would've been going to Fifties. I was just as glad my favorite diner wasn't the *target location*. I yawned.

Ulysses immediately said, "I'll swing by to pick you up."

I barked out a laugh. "Ulysses, I'm fifteen minutes in the wrong direction."

"Just stay put and I'll get you. I want to pick your brain." He hung up.

I stretched. If I put my head down, I was liable to go to sleep. I sniffed myself. *Yep. Another shower's in order.* I still had an odeur de smoke—even though I'd already scrubbed down at the hall. Or maybe the lingering scent was just my imagination.

Still, I hopped in, washed quickly, and was dressed and towel-drying my hair when Ulysses arrived. I opened my door to him. *Scrumptious. I could totally eat him up.* Those blue jeans and his black leather jacket with the aviator sunglasses. Damn.

He arched an eyebrow. "Keep looking at me like that and we'll never make it to dinner."

"I've got some leftover pasta. Or I can whip up a batch of Kraft Dinner after we've dirtied my sheets."

He stepped forward and yanked me in for a hard kiss. "As much as I love KD—and I truly do and will one day take you up on that offer—my questions aren't going to get answered if we stay in."

I pouted.

With a grin, he yanked me out through my front door. He stepped back inside, grabbed my jacket, keys, and sunglasses. He handed me the jacket and glasses, then he locked the door.

"I could've done that myself." Since the sun was only now beginning to hit the horizon, I donned my shades. By the time we headed home, I wouldn't need them.

Ulysses slapped my ass. "I know you can. Now, get in."

I did. And by the time he was on my street, I was fast asleep.

With a start, I awoke when his tires hit gravel. "Oh shit."

He laughed. "I wasn't going to wake you, Sleeping Beauty. Except for the snoring, you were adorable." He pulled into a spot, put the SUV in Park, but didn't turn off the engine. "I almost turned around—I really didn't realize how tired you are. That's on me. We can go back—"

"No way." I stretched. "Turn the engine off and let's go in. That twenty-minute power nap will carry me through until I get home. Just don't let me fall asleep on the way home—that'll really fuck with my internal clock."

"You're sure?"

I reached over and hit the ignition to shut the engine off. "I'm sure."

"Yeah, okay." He unplugged his phone from the charger. Then we both got out and headed inside the restaurant.

Tully's was sort of a cross between a bar and a restaurant. The pool room in the back was the sort-of-a-bar part, while the restaurant was...well, pretty much as advertised. The grub was decent, but the place was on the opposite side of town from me. I had to put in some effort to make it out here. Generally, I didn't find it worth the effort. But with Ulysses? Always willing.

We removed our sunglasses. I tucked mine into the neck of my jean shirt.

Ulysses put his in his jacket pocket.

"Don't forget they're in there. You might break them."

"Cheap pair. Because yes, I've done that before." He gestured to the sign. "That true?"

"We seat ourselves? Yep."

He put his hand to the small of my back. "This table looks perfect."

"Uh, sure." Right in the middle of everything. I would've picked one of the back booths—more privacy. More intimacy. More chances to feel each other up. Because tonight only four other tables were occupied.

Ulysses pulled a chair out for me.

"Thank you, kind sir." I grinned. "I don't think anyone's ever held a chair for me before."

"Then you haven't been dating the right sort of guys." He sat next to me. "What's good?"

I glanced around. "Their burgers aren't bad. Not as good as Fifties'. Their onion rings are pretty good. Not as good as A&W's, though. The pasta's decent, although not—"

"Point made." He laughed. "I'm here for a specific reason."

"Uh, okay." I opened the menu. "I'm probably going to have an order of chicken wings and an order of nachos. Want to share either or both?"

"Only if we get extra guacamole."

"You can have mine." I scrunched my nose. "And I'll have extra sour cream."

"Hey, Finn." A smooth female voice had me looking up.

"Debra." I grinned. "I didn't know you worked here."

She shrugged. "My degree in biology isn't as useful as I'd thought it would be. I make decent tips here, so that's something."

"I promise to leave a large tip." Ulysses cut me a glance before focusing on Debra. "I'll have a cola."

"I'll take a root beer." Some caffeine—but not too much.

"Sure. Y'all decided about food?"

"Double order of the bourbon barbecue chicken wings and a double order of the nachos—extra sour cream and extra guac."

"You got it." She snagged our menus and sauntered off.

Ulysses pulled his phone out of his jacket pocket. "How long have you known Debra? She looks older than you."

"Younger by three years and careful when you start commenting about women's looks." I glared. "She's had a rough go of it."

"Ah." He gave me a sort of sheepish gaze, but his eyes danced with delight, probably at getting an unguarded comment out of me.

Then he looked at his phone again and started typing.

"Seriously? You bring me here for a date and you're texting?" I rolled my eyes.

"You didn't actually say how long you've known Debra."

I scrunched my nose. "I think I've just sort of always known her. The way kids do in small towns."

"You just reminded me that Mission City is bigger—"

"Than you think." I chuckled. "Yeah, I get that. I—" I rubbed my forehead. "I can't think like this."

He placed his hand over mine. Well, the one not trying to coax a memory from the recesses of my mind. He squeezed my hand. "It's okay. I just...want to get a sense of you."

I squinted. "What does that have to do with how long I've known Debra? Oh, she was selling Girl Guide cookies at the front door of the grocery store and Mom handed me cash. I remember thinking this girl was kind of scrawny, but she stuck her hand out and introduced herself. Brash as could be. Then, when I spotted her around school, she'd always wave and call my name. Like we were friends or something."

"Or something." Ulysses released my hand and started typing again. "So she's a friendly sort?"

"Yes. Which will stand her in good stead in a restaurant, right? Hopefully get more tips? A shame about her biology degree."

"Not many jobs around these days in any field."

Slowly, I nodded. "Like, there'll always be fires. I'm never going to be declared redundant."

He stopped typing long enough to scratch his stubbled jaw. "And as good as AI is, they're not yet able to watch a city hall meeting and write an article. Or interview people. Although—" Another scratch.

I so wanted to be the one doing the scratching. All that prickly stubble under my fingers... "Although?"

"Well, I suppose I could feed the interview into the AI and ask it to summarize and write an article."

"Would you ever do that?"

"Hell fucking no."

"Right. So there are still things AI won't be—" I cut myself off. "Seriously?" I gestured to where he continued to type. "Worst date ever."

"I have to go to the bathroom. When I come back, I'll tell you about the worst date ever." He rose, leaned over to peck my cheek, then sauntered off to the bathroom—phone in hand.

I watched him go. As if he knew, he jiggled his butt.

"One root beer and one cola." Debra offered me a warm smile and her brown eyes shone. "Your date seems interesting. He new in town? I don't think I've seen him before."

I was on the verge of telling her that he was the new editor of the Gazette. *But he said two reporters here would be conspicuous. Which means...*

In fact, I had no idea what that meant. Still, I offered her a smile. "Yes, new in town."

"And he's...like you..." Here, her smile diminished just a little.

"Queer? Yeah." Might as well just lay it on the line.

"I meant a firefighter. He seems a little old." She bit her lip.

Nope, that wasn't what she meant. I'd never thought her homophobic. I couldn't tell, even now, if she was or not. "Don't let him hear you say that." I winked.

"Right." Her full smile returned. "Food up soon."

"Great. Thanks." After she headed back to the kitchen, I took a sip of my drink. *Had I made an assumption? Was she trying to tell me something?* Tully's never seemed unpleasantly redneck—but then I'd never come here on a date.

Ulysses sauntered back. He grinned as he dropped into his chair. "I'm thirsty."

"Okay." I took another sip of my drink. Something was up...I just couldn't put my finger on it.

"This is actually a fairly big property." Ulysses glanced around.

"You mean the restaurant? I suppose."

He shook his head. "No, I meant the actual lot. About an acre. That seems like a lot for a restaurant and a parking lot. Are there any outbuildings?"

I scratched my elbow. "I have no idea. I've only been here a handful of times—and usually after a day shift. When it's dark. Like it is now." The sun had set, and the bright lights of the parking lot illuminated the gravel.

"Ah, got it."

What does he got? I was so confused.

"Chicken wings. Hot in both taste and temperature." Debra grinned. "Nachos will be up in a few minutes."

"No rush." Another devastating Ulysses's grin. "We've got all night."

As soon as Debra was gone, I muttered, "Speak for yourself. I'm liable to fall asleep in the plate of nachos."

He winced. "Sorry. I should've waited."

I waved him off. "I'm assuming you had your reasons for wanting to come here tonight."

"Uh, yeah. I just—" He cut himself off as he stared at the front door and the new arrival.

Fuck. My. Life.

Marlon.

He caught my gaze, let that gaze travel to Ulysses, and then settled his attention back on me. He nodded before heading for a booth at the back. Near the kitchen.

"He come here often?" Ulysses gingerly handled a chicken wing.

I shrugged.

He bit into the wing and sucked in air.

I rolled my eyes. "She warned you those things were hot."

"No shit." He swallowed, then blew on the other half. "I was hungry."

"So am I...but I'll wait until it's not going to burn me." I sipped my drink.

"You're adorable." He sucked the rest of the chicken off the bone and tossed said bone on the spare plate. Then he picked up the next one.

"Hey, leave some for me." I snagged one. "And what do you mean by *adorable*? I can't tell if that's a compliment, an insult, or something in between."

"Compliment." He devoured another wing.

I blew on mine. Despite fighting fires, I wasn't a fan of heat. Well, too hot, anyway. "I'm never quite sure where I stand with you." I bit into the wing.

"I'm not certain what you mean." He shrugged. "I try to play it straight—"

"You're anything but straight—and I'm not talking about your sexuality." I chuckled.

"Nachos with extra guac and extra sour cream." Debra put the heaping, steaming plate on the table. "Can I get you anything else?"

"No. This is fantastic. These wings sure are hot." I put the bones on the spare plate.

"Cook does a good job."

"How late are you open today?" Ulysses held her gaze.

"Until ten. Eleven on Fridays and Saturdays."

"So not super late?"

She shook her head. "Fifties is open all the time. The two bars in town close later. We're mostly here for the lunch and dinner crowd." She glanced around. "Well, crowd is relative. Most nights you can just walk in and grab a seat."

"Tough economy to run a business in."

A moment passed—whether because she had to think about her answer or whether because she thought he was asking strange questions—I couldn't be certain. "We offer good grub at a good price. We're not as fancy as some places."

I was going to assume she meant Stavros's Greek or the fine dining Italian place whose name I could never remember.

"Excellent grub at an excellent price. I can't wait to try the nachos." Ulysses gestured toward the heavenly smelling platter of food.

"Well, I'll leave you to it. Just flag me if you need something." With that, Debra was off again.

"I have to go to the washroom. Don't wait for me." Then he was up and gone again.

Well, hell fucking no, I'm not waiting. I'm starving. Heedless of the temperature of the nachos, I dug in.

And wound up gulping a lot of root beer.

Still, I'd finished my half of the wings and made a dent in the nachos by the time my *date* returned. I arched an eyebrow.

He started texting.

"Swear to God—"

"Texting myself." He shrugged.

"Oh." Which had me even more confused. What was so important that he had to make note of it?

He put his phone on the table—screen down. "Look, I'm a terrible date. Can you make your way home? I need to do a stakeout here."

I blinked. "So much to unpack in what, three sentences? Sure, I can make my own way home."

"Great." He yanked out his wallet and handed me a hundred-dollar bill.

I was too tired to argue. I wouldn't need that much, but I could give him the change the next time I saw him.

He nodded as I put the money in my wallet. "Call me tomorrow?"

For what? I still don't know why we got together today... "Uh, sure. I'll take the rest of my nachos to go—"

"Oh, I didn't mean for you to leave this instant—"

I flagged Debra and indicated a takeaway box. "I'll fall asleep in the cab if I don't go now." I pulled up the app for the local cab company and ordered a car. "All good."

Debra arrived with the box. "Everything okay?"

"I'm just super tired. My friend here's picking up the tab."

"No dessert to go? I've got a fresh lemon meringue pie."

"Well, I won't turn that down." I glanced at my *date*.

He gestured for me to go ahead.

Fifteen minutes later, I was in a cab and on my way home.

Artie chatted the entire way.

I gave the cabbie an extra big tip and was in bed seven minutes after hitting the door. Even the puzzle of what the hell Ulysses was up to couldn't keep me from sleeping straight through until the next afternoon.

Chapter Seventeen

Ulysses

I didn't see you at the fire today. Are you okay? —

Finn's reply pinged back immediately. —*Sick.* —

—*I'll bring chicken soup.* —

—*Contagious. Stay away.* —

I put my phone back on my dining room table as I stared at my laptop. Colds and flus weren't unheard of this time of year—but October felt early in the season. Still—

I texted again. —*Are you okay?* —

—*Yeah. Not really. I'm out on sick leave for the next week.* —

Fuck it. —*I'm coming over.* —

I didn't wait for a response. I tucked my laptop back into my messenger bag and headed out the door. Ten minutes later, I was sitting in the lobby of the country-style restaurant while they dished up two bowls of soup and heated some garlic bread. Oh, and I decided an entire lemon meringue pie would be a *forgive me* gift.

Thirty minutes later, I let myself into Finn's cabin. He hadn't locked the door, but that wasn't a huge surprise. He maintained no one would bother to rob him.

I tried to point out he didn't *know* that. And that, in fact, robbers might not know he only had a big screen television to steal. If he had anything else, I hadn't seen it.

"Said not to come." A feeble voice from under a pile of blankets on the couch.

"Do you have chills? Are you hot?" I moved to the kitchen. "I brought soup, garlic bread, and pie."

"Lemon meringue?" A little less feebly.

"Yes. Soup first." I found a spoon, opened the lid of the container of soup, and headed to the living room. The cabin was really just one large open space with the loft above and the two bedrooms with the bathroom in the back. "Sit up."

He pushed himself up. His cheeks were flushed, and his eyes were bright. His hair was a disaster.

I'd never thought him more adorable. I handed him the soup and spoon. "What does your mother the nurse say?"

"Keep her out of this." He pouted.

"You haven't told her."

"It's a cold. Or the flu. Or COVID. Or something."

I arched an eyebrow. "Do you not know the difference between a rhinovirus, coronavirus, and influenza?"

He rolled his eyes. "I just feel like shit. Thank you for the soup." He took his first sip. "This is awesome."

"Fifties didn't have the soup or the pie."

He eyed the container. "Oh, these folks are great too."

"I hoped so."

"Are you having some?'

"That's the plan."

He pointed to the chair. "Stay well away from me."

I rolled my eyes. "I think I can keep my hands off you. You look like shit."

"Well, I feel worse." He sipped. "This really is appreciated."

"My pleasure." I headed back toward the kitchen. "How did you catch this...whatever this is?"

"No clue. Miriam says no one else is sick. I thought maybe I got it from you."

I laughed. "Nice try."

"Well, we were at Tully's together two days ago." He sneezed. "How's your *investigation* going?"

No missing the invisible air quotes.

"I have a couple of leads. Waiting to see if things come together the way I suspect they might."

"You going to share?"

"Absolutely not. Do you have a sore throat?" I put the pie in the fridge, put two pieces of garlic toast on a plate, and grabbed my soup.

"Nope."

"Oh good." First, I offered him the toast.

He smiled and snagged it. Then he took a bite. "Almost as good as my mom's."

"Far be it for me to argue." I sank into the recliner and raised my feet.

"Tough day?" He grinned. "A lot of shoe-leather detective work today?"

"Nope. Just going through property records."

"Sounds boring as shit."

"You wouldn't be wrong." I sipped the soup. "Yeah, this really is good." I eyed his television. "You want to watch something? Or just hang?"

He gazed up toward the loft.

I followed his track, but couldn't figure out what was so interesting.

Finn cleared his throat. "I was hoping you'd come with me to the high school."

"Tonight? Are you sure you don't have a fever?"

He shook his head, swinging his gaze back to me. "Tomorrow night. It's really important that I'm there."

"Risking your health and risking making other people sick?"

"I'll wear a mask."

I winced.

"Fine, I'll drive myself—"

"No, you won't. If it's that important, I'll take you." But I was going to make sure he had a lot of fluids and an early night first.

Twenty-four hours later, when I landed on his front doorstep, he did look better.

He shrugged. "I think it was a twenty-four-hour thing."

"If you say so."

He donned his mask.

I wanted to tell him not to bother. Then I remembered how miserable he'd been yesterday. Since I didn't want to be that way, I kept my mouth shut.

Twenty minutes later, we entered the gym at the high school.

Two basketball teams were warming up at opposite ends of the room. I recognized Mission City Collegiate's light blue and gold. I squinted to read *Abbotsford* on the opposing red-and-white team jerseys.

"Old rivalry?"

Finn gestured to a corner of the bleachers away from everyone else. Once we were settled, he spoke. “Yeah.”

“And the black armbands on the Mission City team?”

“For David.”

“Yeah, okay.” Now his wanting to be here—no matter what—made sense.

A couple of the boys moved toward us and waved.

Finn gave them the thumbs-up.

They returned to their warm-up.

I scanned the crowd carefully. “Is that woman related to David?” I pointed to a woman wearing all black and dabbing her eyes with a handkerchief.

“Yeah. Marcia. His mom. She’s got three kids and a police-officer husband. He works for the Abbotsford Police Department.”

“Not Mission City RCMP?”

Finn shrugged. “Not everyone wants to be associated with the baggage of Canada’s national police force.”

“Good point.” The Royal Canadian Mounted Police had both a storied history and, thanks to some truly bad apples, a notorious reputation. Especially in racialized communities.

A group of girls clustered in a corner caught my notice as well. “Who are they?”

“David’s younger sister Patrice and three of her friends.”

“Aren’t two of those girls from your rec league?” I was pretty sure I recognized them.

“Yes, Rue and Tenyce. Good memory.”

I shrugged. “I try.”

He chuckled.

Then the game began, and he grasped my hand. Part of me was surprised—not that he was willing to show affection, but that he needed some kind of support.

Several times he clearly wanted to yell encouragement, but his chest rattling kept him relatively peaceful.

"I hope you don't get pneumonia," I whispered into his ear.

"Worth it. Had to be here."

Although I understood the sentiment, I couldn't say I had anyone in my life that I'd risk further illness for. Not even my intrepid Spring. Well, if she was in trouble, then of course. And if Finn needed me. But just two people after forty years on the planet. That felt...pathetic. Still, two more than I'd had when I'd ridden into town— "Is that...?" I knew who he was, of course, but I wanted Finn's reaction.

He nodded. "Marlon. I, uh, don't remember ever seeing him here for a game before."

"Might he be here because of David? Of his death? Did he respond to the call?"

"I'd have to ask. I just don't remember." He eyed me. "I'm getting to know that look. You're about to go to the bathroom again, aren't you?"

I shrugged. Then headed to the bathroom. By the time I returned, Mission City was leading by ten points and halftime neared.

In the end, they won the game.

Finn gave plenty of thumbs-up, but stayed back.

Some of the kids looked disappointed, but Mr. Clayton, from a distance, expressed gratitude. "Glad you could make it, Finnegan. Sorry to hear you're sick. Also grateful you're keeping your distance. My wife would strangle me if I came home with a virus of some kind. Our kids are already germ factories."

I chuckled.

The principal turned his attention to me. "I appreciate all the great articles your paper writes about our school—as well as the rest of town."

I nodded. "I've been welcomed here."

"I hope so. Small-town living can be an adjustment. My wife had rarely left Vancouver before she came out here. The quiet disconcerted her. You're from the city, right?"

"Born and bred, as the expression goes. Do you have a moment to speak?"

He eyed Finn. "Are you okay?"

I pivoted my attention and found Finn's brow sweat-slicked. I turned back to Mr. Clayton. "You're right. I'm his ride, so I'll get him home."

"Come by my office tomorrow, and we can chat about whatever's on your mind." He glanced over toward the students gathered around David's mom. Then he gazed back at me.

I nodded.

"Only so much I can say—but I can certainly discuss drugs and how they affect our community. That's your thinking, right? Or something else?" He waved it off. "Whatever comes up. Tomorrow?"

"That would be great." I grasped Finn by the elbow.

He didn't even put up a token protest—which told me just how sick he was.

Within an hour I'd sponged the sweat off him and had him in bed.

"I'm just going to sit at the dining room table to get some work done," I told him.

"Okay." Mumbled.

"And I might crash in your spare room."

"I'm fine." Slurred. He was headed into sleep.

I brushed his damp hair back from his forehead. “Indulge me. Otherwise I’ll worry.”

“Thought I was getting better.” He coughed.

I winced. I should’ve donned a mask when he’d taken his off. “Well, going out tonight probably wasn’t a good idea. But I understood.” Better to head off that argument before it started. “Take care, okay. Just call if you need me.”

“Yep.” He rolled onto his side, curled into a ball, and was asleep within moments.

I worked at the table for a while. I watched television for a while. Eventually I crawled into his spare bed for a fitful night.

In the morning, his fever appeared to have broken.

So, reluctantly, I headed to work.

Chapter Eighteen

Finn

I miss you. —

I hit send before I could reconsider my choice. Then I didn't give Ulysses a chance to respond before I sent the next text.

—*When did you say you'd be back?*—

Probably too needy, but I was still recovering from a bad bout of the flu. Dr. Raymond said that as soon as I was healthy, I needed to get my flu shot. That, because of the different strains, I might not have immunity for all the crap I might be exposed to.

Getting a flu shot, along with everything else, had been on the list for the next time I was off. Damn virus had caught me first. I'd happily roll up my sleeve for a shot if it meant not going through that again.

And now Ulysses was out of town. *Tracking down leads.*

—*I miss you too, Sunshine. Home soon.* —

I didn't even mind him calling me *Sunshine*. We were kind of like that romance trope—grumpy/sunshine. A few couples I knew were like that. Correction—had been like that.

Maddox the recluse until he met Ravi—the sunshine pediatric nurse.

Recluse Adam until he met sunshine Aussie forester Dean.

Leo the surgeon before he met and married the perpetually happy nurse Quinton.

Except...had Ulysses been grumpy when we'd first met? Aside from nearly being taken out by Rodney Saunders joyriding in his mom's minivan—and running that red light—Ulysses had seemed chill. Relaxed. Horny.

Kind of like I was now. Being alone was not conducive to getting laid.

Problem was, I didn't want just anyone. I certainly wasn't going to do a run into Vancouver or take a look at my app to see if anyone new had suddenly appeared. To the best of my knowledge, Ulysses didn't have a profile there. When he'd first disappeared—and I hadn't known who he was—I'd kept my eye out for any new additions.

Then I discovered who he was—and I'd kept my distance. Because I was dumbass hurt when he'd left my bed.

Now? Now I wanted him down to the marrow of my bones—which made no sense. How he'd become so important to me wasn't clear to me. *He brought you soup. He took you to the game—even though you might've made him sick. He's taken you out on dates—even though they weren't real dates. He's drilled you into the mattress repeatedly—even though he could be out looking for someone else.*

My phone rang. My heart leapt until I checked the screen.

Mom.

"Hey, Mom. How's it going?"

"Busy. More than usual. Early flu season and it's hit hard. Most people haven't even gotten their shots. You're getting yours, right?"

"Yeah...but I already got the flu. Was a bastard. Or is that a bitch?"

"You'd have to ask a language that assigns gender to all nouns." She laughed. "I don't speak French or German."

"Neither do I. Well, I did okay in my high school French classes."

"You're okay now?"

I sighed. "Yeah. Dr. Raymond said to get the shot anyway. Something about variants—"

"Your doctor is very smart. Make certain you listen to him."

A chuckle escaped me. "Yes, Mom."

She snorted. "When do you ever listen to your mother?"

"Hey! All the goddamn time."

"Like when I admonish you for swearing?"

I laughed again. "I remember—usually after I've said the curse word."

"Are you coming for dinner this weekend?"

"Why don't you come here?"

"Really? You won't be busy this week?"

"I can cook up something on Sunday before you come over. I, uh, might have a friend for you to meet."

"Oh." She paused. "A *friend* friend or just a friend?"

"Yes?"

"Is that a question or a statement?"

"Yes?"

She chuckled. "You always were a dark horse, Finnegan. It's why I love you so much. Sure, I'll come to dinner. What can I bring?"

"Caesar salad and lemon meringue pie?" I licked my lips.

"Sounds great. About five?"

"Yes, that would be amazing. Thanks."

"Finnegan?"

"Yes, Mom?" She was one of the very few people who full named me—even when she wasn't mad.

"I'm so damn proud of you. Whomever this young man is, I can't wait to meet him."

"Yeah, about that..." My mind flashed to the odd silver whisker in Ulysses's scruff. Hopefully he'd shave before meeting Mom.

"Yes, my dear?"

"He's...maybe not my *young* man."

She chuckled. "Is he as old as I am?"

"No."

"Well, then he's your *young* man. See you Sunday. Love you."

"Love you too."

She cut the call.

I sank farther into the cushions of the couch. Well, that was something. Perhaps a big something.

I texted Ulysses. —*Will you come to dinner Sunday? Shit, will you be back by Sunday?*—

I waited. Rather impatiently.

—*Yes. To both.*—

—*Great.*—

I hesitated. Then added, —*I'll cook. We'll have company.*—

—*Oh? Anyone I know?*—

—*My mother.*—

My phone rang.

I answered. "Hey. Was this a bad time?"

"For you? It's never a bad time. So, is this a casual, here's my friend, Ulysses? Or is this a *meet the parents* moment?"

"Yes?"

He chuckled. "Okay, that's fair. Anything I need to know?"

"I might've warned her that you're not my *young* man."

He snorted. "Didn't we figure I was closer in age to your mother than to you?"

"Had we?" I considered. "Well, not quite up there."

"But close." More amusement.

"Well, maybe." He wasn't wrong. No regrets...but he wasn't wrong.

"I'll contact you as soon as I'm home."

"Okay." My heart did a little pitter-patter. To my memory, he hadn't referred to Mission City as *home* before. Or maybe he meant me—which would be even sweeter. *I'm falling for this guy.*

"Hey, Finn?"

"Yeah?"

"How are you feeling?"

"Better, why?"

"Oh, good. I'm just thinking about all the things I'm going to do to you when I'm back."

"Yeah?" I adjusted myself. "How about you tell me?"

And he proceeded to.

A day later, he was on my doorstep.

I opened the door with a huge grin on my face, glad he hadn't waited until Mom-day to come over. "Do you want dinner now, or—"

"I'll take the second option." He held up a bag from Fifties. "We can heat this up later. Right now, I want you naked in bed."

"You don't have to ask me twice." I hotfooted to the bedroom and was stripping as he sauntered in.

"So eager."

"Hey, it's been—" I squinted.

"Seven days."

"Longest we've gone. Well, since, you know..."

"Yeah, since we started this...whatever this is..." He yanked his henley over his head, revealing an expanse of dark skin.

I licked my lips.

"Yeah?" He grinned as he unbuttoned his jeans, pulled down his fly, and then yanked off both jeans and boxer briefs.

His gorgeous erection sprang free. He arched an eyebrow. "You got here first and you're still dressed?"

Well, my shirt was unbuttoned and my fly was down. But yeah, I'd gotten distracted. So off came the rest of my clothes, and I dove for the bed.

He laughed as he followed me down. Levering himself, he lay flat against me.

My skin tingled every place his touched mine.

Our cocks brushed and a shot of electricity arced through me.

I held his gaze. "My doctor ran the tests. I'm negative."

"Oh really." He grinned. "I went to a clinic, and they ran all the tests for me. I'm negative as well."

"And we're not seeing anyone else? Well, I mean I'm not. But you might not—"

"Just you, Finn. I can't imagine that changing but, for now, just you."

I didn't know how to interpret his words. They sounded like a commitment of some kind. Like if we stopped using condoms then we were all in with this relationship thing. "I've never gone bareback."

He held my gaze. "I haven't either. Never met someone who made me want to. Not until I met you."

"Okay." I brushed our cocks together.

He groaned. "Yes. That. Can I prep you?"

"I'd love that." Because somehow, when he did this, his care and attention deepened the bond between us.

He rolled off me and snagged the lube from my nightstand.

I opened my thighs to welcome him.

From there he did what he always did—but with the new anticipation there wouldn't be a barrier between the two of us. I wasn't nervous. Deep in my soul, I trusted him. Even as he carried secrets. I didn't. I was an open book.

He crooked his finger to brush my prostate.

A drop of precum leaked from my cock.

He licked it with a Cheshire cat grin. "You ready for me?"

"Always." I didn't try to keep the need from my voice. Because he'd become an important part of my life. Hell, I'd invited him to meet my mother.

He slicked his cock, and lined himself up.

Our gazes met and held.

I nodded.

Slowly he pushed inside me.

The feeling was both the same and different. Knowing I was laying myself open to him. Giving him the opportunity to deeply hurt me—if he chose to.

It goes both ways—you could easily break his trust as well. But I wouldn't. I knew enough of myself to know I'd never do that.

"God, Finn. I'll never get enough of you." His jaw clenched as he bottomed out.

"Then don't. I'm right here." I wrapped my legs around his waist and dug my heels into his ass.

He chuckled. "Trust me—I know." He withdrew and thrust in, pulled back then pushed forward. He teased and tormented and pushed me higher and higher.

All at once it was not enough and too much, an electric sizzle in every nerve that had me ready to explode. Too much, pushing me to the brink of the highest cliff.

"Come for me. Just do it." He held my gaze.

I came. Hard. Spectacularly. In a way that robbed me of both breath and words. That totally overwhelmed my senses as I flew high above us.

Ulysses thrust twice more before holding himself still. He came inside me.

This is going to change me. Change us.

Hopefully for the better.

But I just didn't know.

Chapter Nineteen

Ulysses

"So, what are your intentions toward our Finnegan?" Giancarlo eyed me across the firehouse kitchen table. With a sparkle in his eyes.

"I intend—" *How the fuck am I supposed to answer this?* "He deserves to be treated well, and I plan to do exactly that."

The fireman gave me the once-over. "I think you might be good for him. God knows, he deserves someone special. Too long playing the field, if you know what I mean."

"I do." Probably because I was guilty of much the same thing. Before Finn, I'd never met someone who made me consider removing myself from the, uh, game. "I appreciate you letting me in."

"Chief's not here, and you said you had a few questions about our gear?"

"Yeah. If you can take me through what happens after a call comes in, that would be amazing."

"Sure. Finn should be here soon." He eyed me.

"I don't want to be seen as having favorites. Now, apparently there have been more calls than usual."

That derailed him sufficiently that, along with the questions I peppered him with, I was able to keep him occupied for a full forty minutes before Finn showed up.

When my ginger fireman arrived, he didn't appear pleased to see me—given the furrow in his brow. "Can I talk to you?"

Giancarlo's gaze shot between the two of us. He held up his hands. "I'm innocent." With that, he headed toward the kitchen.

Finn gestured for me to follow him out of the station house.

Once we were outside, he rounded on me. "Stop poking around my station. I'm getting to know how you operate. You think there's something hinky going on. I'm telling you—there's nothing wrong with my team. Keep your nose out."

I held his gaze. "If there's nothing wrong with your team, then there shouldn't be an issue with me asking innocent questions."

He snorted. "Nothing is innocent with you. You're a disaster waiting to happen. I just can't figure you out."

"There's nothing to figure out, Finn. I am exactly as I seem. Now, can you point me to the bathroom?"

He rolled his eyes. "Now I *know* you're up to something. Care to share?"

"Nope. I've just got to take a leak. Literally that simple."

"Nothing is *that simple*. Nothing is literal with you either. You've always got an ulterior motive. The problem is I just can't figure out what it is." He scrunched his nose. "And you're not as you seem. You're keeping secrets from me."

I leaned closer. "Finn, there's nothing between us. Literally or figuratively."

A blush stole across his cheeks.

Oh my God, that's so adorable. Then I replayed the words in my mind. "I didn't mean *nothing* between us. I mean—"

He pressed a finger to my lips. "I know what you meant. And I suppose I can show you the bathroom. I'm not certain I trust you, though."

"I'm an honest guy."

"Yeah, I've heard that before."

Before I had a chance to interrogate him on that one, he headed back into the fire hall, and I followed.

Since I really did have to piss, that took a few moments as I gathered my thoughts. What did I know versus what was actually conjecture? I just wasn't certain.

Finn was there to escort me out. As I got into my SUV, he held my door open for a moment. "What are you doing, Ulysses? What do you know that I don't?"

I offered a cocky grin. "Sorry, if you want me to answer your questions, you need to buy me dinner first."

He rolled his eyes. "I'm off shift in twelve hours. How about breakfast at Fifties?"

"Sounds delicious." I gently brushed my hand against his—both to move it out of the way and because I really needed the skin-on-skin contact.

He didn't smile as I closed the door...but he didn't scowl either. So I took that as a win.

Since dinnertime was near, I swung by Wendy's drive-through for a burger and poutine. At home, I set up my laptop on the dining room table. Then I pulled out my notebook and started writing on index cards—one for every notable incident. One for every person who I'd spoken to. Finally, one for every location I'd investigated.

A shit ton of cards and not a single cohesive thought.

I dug my fork into the fries—smothered in gravy and melted cheese curds—and tried to piece things together in my mind. Either I was looking at several separate incidents or they were somehow collectively linked. Neither explanation made sense. Mission City didn't—at least by all appearances—seem to be a hotbed of criminal minds. So, did that rule out everything being unrelated? That one person, or persons, was responsible for everything? Or did that mean there happened to be multiple people involved in multiple crimes.

And what were the crimes?

Finished with the poutine, I moved on to the cheeseburger.

If a pattern existed, I simply wasn't seeing it. Nothing was coming into sharper focus and, the longer I looked at this, the less sense it made.

I picked up the phone and hit speed dial. I needed fresh eyes on this stuff, and no eyes were fresher than Spring's.

"Hello Boss. How's it going?"

"Hey, Dixon. You have a moment?"

"Sure. Just a sec."

Muffled voices.

I winced.

Spring came back on. "Okay, what's up?"

"It can keep until tomorrow. You've got other stuff—"

"I have a sister who had a bad day at work. She'll survive."

I frowned. "The psychologist, vet, dog trainer, ranch manager, or bookstore clerk?"

She burst out laughing. "Oh my God. You remember?"

"I do try. Your sisters are...infamous."

"They're something." She chuckled. "Zephyra. She had a cat die today who shouldn't have, and she's super upset about it."

"This can wait—"

"You called, so obviously it's important. What do you have?"

"Fires, hinky restaurant goings-on, and an animal shelter."

"Ah." Rustling. "You think they're connected."

"Don't you?"

"I'd say this is farfetched." She sighed. "Take me through it."

"Okay. So you heard something was going on at the animal shelter."

"Unusual adoptions, yeah."

"And we've figured out there's likely a dog-fighting ring being run out of the back of Tully's." I rubbed my forehead. "So those are probably connected."

"Yep. Which leaves the unusual number of fires."

"Hmm." She was silent for a moment. "Again, you think they're all connected."

"Possibly. But you know this town better than I do. You'd know if something was up—right?"

"Boss. Darling. I do not have an *in* with Mission's criminal elements. Hell, I get more from the police department than sources. Possibly because my ex-brother-in-law likes to give me a hard time."

"The RCMP officer? Sunshine's ex-husband?"

"Yep."

"I would think that would mean you'd get less information."

"You'd think." She snorted. "Constable Seth Jacobs—Colton's good friend—feels sorry for me because Colton's *so mean*."

I heard the air quotes.

"So he feels sorry for you?"

"Whatever works. Seth's a good guy. Colton's an asshole. Does it really matter who my source is? Anyway, Seth didn't give me either the restaurant or the animal shelter."

"Who did?"

"Ah…can't share that. And you're forgetting the tainted drugs."

"David. Fuck. Yeah, I forgot about that." I put the phone on the table and wrote the young man's name on an index card. "How does he fit into this? How does any of this connect?"

"You ever consider they might not?"

I sighed. "That many criminals in one small town?"

"Sheesh. Small towns are crawling with all kinds of people up to no good. A hotbed of sinners."

"Good God."

"I think that's the point. Look, what are you thinking? Because I have a few ideas, but they're so outlandish that I haven't said them aloud to anyone."

"Well, you have my full attention. Will Zephyra be okay if you come over?"

"She took off. I'll text Torah and ask her to follow up. My dog-trainer sister's all about forward action and getting on with the work that has to be done. Zephyra has a full roster of pets who will need her tomorrow. She can afford tonight to grieve, but tomorrow she's got to go back and do the best job she can. I'll leave it up to Torah to drill that into her."

"Sounds like tough love."

"If I wanted woo-woo, I'd send Sun. If I wanted coddling, I'd call Rainbow. If I wanted tough love, I'd sic Kennedy on her. The psychologist is the toughest one amongst us. Hence Zeph coming here rather than heading to the ranch."

I rubbed my eyes. "That's way too confusing."

"Are you at your condo?"

"Yeah."

"Give me ten."

"Appreciate this."

"You owe me."

"Yeah, I do."

She cut the line.

What have we got?

I wish to God I knew.

Chapter Twenty

Finn

Ulysses canceled breakfast. Something about running down a lead.

I wouldn't have made great company either—what with the continuous yawning. But I was off for the next three days, so staying up all day was imperative to reset my internal clock.

In the end, I went to Fifties by myself and sat at the counter as I devoured my omelet, tomato, and sourdough toast. Three cups of coffee later, and after a visit to the washroom, I was off to Hearts and Paws.

Yanna the shelter manager greeted me. "Oh, Finn, so glad you're here. I need to go out for a few hours to run errands and Selah called in sick. Could you keep an eye on the front area? When I'm back, if you want to stay, you could visit the animals then? I just gave them all their walks, so they're good."

Disappointment panged within me, but I couldn't very well say *no*. "Would you like me to run the errands?"

She shook her head. "I need the break, and it'll be easier for me since I have all the accounts. If you could just hold down the fort?"

"Of course." I waved her off. I'd been trained in and done this several times, so I would be fine. "Oh, can I bring Poppin out to keep me company?"

"Sure."

"And how's Thelma doing?" The pittie mix still had my heart because she'd been surrendered.

"She's been adopted. Her new owner is picking her up on Tuesday."

"Oh, that's great." Relieving as well. "Any takers for Walter or Poppin?" It was always so hard to place the oldest seniors like Walter, and it'd take a special home to handle Poppin's health issues, but I kept hoping.

Yanna shook her head. "None yet."

"Did Ulysses ever come back to do those spotlights?"

She shrugged. "Not while I've been here. Maybe he came when Selah or Meyer was working?"

I frowned. "I'll get on him about that." I hoped Ulysses was just busy, not using these precious pets as pawns in his investigation.

Yanna blinked. "You can tell the new editor of the community paper what to do?"

I batted my eyelashes. "I can be very persuasive."

She chuckled. "Man doesn't stand a chance. Whatever you can do to help, Finn. It's always appreciated. Gotta run." She grabbed the keys off the rack and headed out to the van.

After nabbing the keys to the dog runs, I locked up and went to retrieve Poppin.

Damn dog was thrilled to see me and insisted on sitting on my lap while I flipped through the paperwork.

"This is so boring." I yawned. "I planned on walking all you folks so I wouldn't fall asleep."

She licked my cheek.

"Yes, I love you too. I so wish I could bring you home with me." *You knew working here would be tough. That you'd want to bring every dog and cat home with you.* I eyed the list of cats available for adoption. Maybe if I brought two home together? Might they keep each other company while I put in such long hours? Would that even be fair to the cats? If I was working all the time? And if not working, then out gallivanting about? I'd spent more time at home in the past three weeks since Ulysses came back into my life than I had the previous six months. I was always out. Now I wanted to be home on the chance of getting laid.

It's not just about getting laid—you actually really like the guy.

Yeah. I did. Which was going to inevitably lead to pain. He wasn't the staying type. He wasn't going to stick around. He'd want to go back out into the world again. Not just some small hick town. What he did before would blow over. Or he'd find a much-larger town where he could restart without baggage. Where people would give him a chance.

People in Mission City have given him a chance.

Yeah, he hadn't been run out of town by pitchfork-wielding folks. But how many had actually dug into his background and discovered what he'd been accused of? Hard to say. And how accurate were the reports? Didn't everything have elements of exaggeration?

I thumbed through the recent adoption applications. Locating Thelma's was easy enough. The adoption was scheduled for ten days from now.

Maybe I know the person rescuing her? Maybe I can arrange to see her from time to time? She really does have the sweetest disposition.

I squinted at the application. I couldn't make it make sense. So I yanked out my phone and, while holding Poppin securely in my lap, I pulled up a map app. Then I entered the address of the new owner.

Uh. I was right. This address doesn't exist. Well, what the fuck does that mean? Maybe they'd transposed the digits. Except the number wasn't even close to any others on that street. Giancarlo lived on that street—so I knew the sequence of numbers.

On a hunch, I pulled the last fifteen adoption records. The first eight checked out fine. *See? This is Ulysses's doing. He's got you all paranoid for no reason.*

Except—

The crunch of tires on gravel had me quickly tidying the papers and putting them back in the filing cabinet. I was back at the desk when Yanna stepped in.

"I don't suppose you can help—" She gestured toward the van.

I grinned. "Happy to. Then I need to stretch my legs and give the dogs some time in the fresh air."

Again, Poppin licked my cheek.

Yanna smiled and we traded off—she sat at the desk while I unloaded all the purchases from the van.

Within twenty minutes, I was out back with Thelma.

"I only ever wanted you to go to a nice home." I blinked. "Now I don't know where you're going, and that scares me." Because who the hell used a fake address on an application for a dog adoption? And, just as importantly, who didn't flag that when approving it? I ran through the papers in my mind and realized they'd all been signed by the same shelter worker.

Son of a bitch.

Two hours later, I was hitting the buzzer at Ulysses's condo—desperately hoping he was home.

"Hello?" His voice was tinny through the speaker.

"It's Finn."

"It's 412."

The door buzzed.

I yanked it open, stepped inside, removed my sunglasses, and headed toward the elevator.

The ride up took mere moments, and I stepped out to find Ulysses waving from a unit down the hall. I strode his way and brushed past him, sweeping into his condo.

And coming up short.

"Oh, wow."

He chuckled. "Yeah. That." He shut the door. "Can I take your jacket? Are you staying?"

I removed my jacket and handed it to him. Then I headed to the floor-to-ceiling windows. "You can see Baker."

"Yep. Want to step onto the balcony? View's even better from there."

"Will I need my coat?"

"Nah. I installed the glass last week when the nip in the air appeared permanent for the winter. I can still open the windows, but it's not cold unless I do."

"Ah, so the balcony becomes a solarium?"

"Yes, exactly."

"Okay, let's go. I mean, I could've gone out without my jacket on regardless." Because I didn't want Ulysses to think I was a wimp.

"Of course you could've." He patted me on the back. Humoring me.

We stepped onto the balcony and headed right to the edge. "Yeah, what a beautiful day." Nothing like this view at my little cabin.

"We've had a run of those." His voice softened. "I'm not looking forward to the rain—but it's a small price to pay."

"What do you mean?" I turned to him.

"Just that we live in Canada, and most of the rest of the country deals with snow for the winter. We only have a handful of snow days."

"And maybe this year we won't get any." I grinned.

"Highly unlikely." He brushed his hand against mine. "But I don't think you came here to talk about the weather—or to see my spectacular view of Mount Baker."

"Given I didn't know if you'd be home, and I certainly didn't know about the view, you'd be right."

He cocked his head. "What's up?"

"You got something to drink? I've just come from the animal shelter, and my throat is dry."

I needed to tell him what I'd learned. But I also still didn't completely trust him.

"Water? Soda? Coffee?"

I blinked. "Uh, cola would be good."

"Great." He headed toward the fridge. "How about some grilled cheese? You hungry?"

"Sure."

"And tomato soup?"

"Sounds great. I, uh, need to wash my hands. And maybe take a leak?"

He pointed. "Guest bathroom. Whatever you need."

"You have two bathrooms?" I grinned. "That's a freaking luxury."

"What I don't have is a magical cabin in the woods with bears." He pulled a tin of soup out of the pantry cupboard.

I slid off the stool and headed to the bathroom. The walls and tile were a sterile white, but the pale-yellow towels softened the space.

After I'd done everything I needed to do, and was still struggling to wrangle my thoughts, I headed back to the kitchen. As I passed the dining room table, a display caught my notice. "You planning a feast?"

"Huh?" He gazed over at me.

"All these recipe cards."

"Yeah, no. Come slice some cheese."

As I made my way to the bar stool again, he hustled over to the table and gathered up all the cards lightning fast.

"Were they in some kind of order?" I used the knife to open the plastic wrap covering the cheese.

"Nothing I can't recreate." He headed back to stir the soup.

"Are you hiding something from me?" I cut the first slice.

He eyed me. "Maybe. Just...some incomplete research."

"Sounds serious."

"Mostly speculation."

I cocked my head. "I have something I want to talk about."

He echoed me. "Sounds serious."

"Because—" I toyed with the knife. "The thing is...I don't know if I've found something or not. You've got me all paranoid. Looking for conspiracies where there aren't any."

"How do you know there aren't?" He continued stirring the soup. "Mission City has secrets, Finn. Even if you claim you don't—"

"Hey, I don't."

He glanced over his shoulder. "And that might be true. For you. But that doesn't mean it's the same for everyone. Otherwise, why would you need police?"

I winced. "Yes, sure, we have criminals, but this is...weird."

"Okay...so we're in agreement that there's likely something going on. What have you found?"

"There's something hinky about the adoption papers for almost a dozen dogs."

"Oh?" Ulysses flipped the bread.

More sizzling.

My mouth watered. Then I let out another breath. "Yeah."

He pulled two plates down from the cupboard. "You want to stay where you are or sit at the table? Oh, or we can sit on the couch."

"Table's fine."

We pulled up chairs at the table and settled into eating our meals. My stomach churned, but Ulysses ripped the crust off a piece of his sandwich and dunked it in the soup. "So...you ready to talk?"

"Talk? Oh, right." *Now or never. I just have to trust him.*

And so I did.

By the time we were finished our dinner, I'd told him everything I knew—which, admittedly, wasn't much. Just that Selah and Meyer had handled all the questionable adoptions, and different fake addresses had been used for each. All the pets involved were bigger dogs. Each had been a surrender who'd been at the shelter a few days. "I just don't know what it all means."

Slowly, he nodded. "I think I might, but it's too early to speculate."

I gestured to the pile of index cards. "Part of that?" I frowned. "I want to know what the fuck is going on. Why do I have the feeling Thelma's in trouble, not heading to a forever home?"

Ulysses rubbed his face. "Okay. I'll tell you what I can. But I have to protect my source—"

"That's bullshit. You know I won't say anything."

He stared at me. "I trust you, Finn. But you can't go off half-cocked. If you get involved, things might go further underground. We might never be able to expose them."

"Expose who?" Exasperation rose within me. "What are you not saying?"

"Okay." He tapped the table. "A friend of Spring's approached her. They'd heard about a dog-fighting ring behind Tully's—operating long after the restaurant closes."

"Oh my God." My gut churned. I'd thought this might be bad—but I hadn't envisioned this. Yeah, I understood there were depraved people in the world...but dog fighting? "And you think they're using shelter dogs?"

"I don't know. You've given me another piece to the puzzle. But I don't know what I have yet. I've met with the source—"

"Who?"

"Finn."

Even I couldn't miss the warning tone.

"What?" I might've snapped that. Then realized that approach wasn't going to get me anywhere. "Can you tell me anything else?"

Ulysses shook his head. "Let me keep researching and investigating. You said Thelma has ten days?"

I nodded.

"Then I have a deadline." He held up his hand when I opened my mouth. "Sooner if I can, okay? But I have to make certain I don't miss any of the pieces. If I go public too soon—or get exposed—then things can all go to shit. This isn't just about dog fighting. I think it goes deeper, and human lives may be at stake."

"Does this have something to do with Vancouver? Because we haven't discussed—"

"Not tonight." He rubbed his face. "I can't face that tonight. I should...but I just can't."

I wanted to argue. He was keeping so much from me. *Yes, but what right do you have to demand more? You haven't even defined your relationship.* I hated when my inner voice was right. Goddamn it.

Ulysses gave me a small smile. "Look—I'll add what you've told me and see where I end up. Now, you up for a hockey game or something? Or do you need to be heading to bed?" He rose.

Slowly, I followed. Obviously, we were done for tonight.

He reached for my hand.

I gave it easily.

He pulled me into a hug.

I sank into the embrace. I had no idea what was going on—but this comfort and strength meant everything.

Chapter Twenty-One

Ulysses

"Why are *you* not nervous?" I smoothed my shirt.

Finn chuckled. "Because she's *my* mother. I'm never nervous when I see my mother. Relax, okay? She's going to love you."

I had my doubts. Still, as I perched on the edge of Finn's sofa, I waited as patiently as possible.

Last night, after the hug—which had been a little epic—I'd followed Finn home. To make certain he got here safely. He'd been wrecked.

Only he'd invited me in.

And we'd made love. No fucking into the mattress. Just...slow lovemaking. And he'd fallen into a deep sleep. I hadn't been able to find it in myself to leave. So, I hadn't. Today, while he'd been cooking, I'd chased down two damn leads that led nowhere and I was no closer to solving the mystery. I'd run home to grab a fresh shirt. He ribbed me for being *so gussied up*. In truth, I couldn't remember ever dressing up for him. *I need to do better.* I needed to show him how much he was coming to mean to me. A thought I wasn't willing to examine too closely as his mother was due any moment.

Headlights cut across the front window.

"Good timing on Mom's part, but I have to pull the lasagna out of the oven."

"Oh, let me do that. I'm sure your mother would prefer to be greeted—"

"Go let her in, Ulysses. Don't make Mom wait." He opened the oven.

I hustled over to the front door and opened it.

The woman before me wasn't quite who I expected. Sure, Finn had photos of the two of them—but I'd never studied them carefully. I certainly had never noticed how short she was. Especially in comparison to her rather tall son.

"Hello Mrs. O'Sullivan. Lovely to meet you." I offered my biggest grin.

"It's Ms. O'Sullivan. I never married Finnegan's scoundrel sperm donor." She eyed me. "You may call me Valerie."

"Okay." I sounded the word quietly.

She grinned. "And you're Ulysses."

"Yes, ma'am...Valerie." I cringed.

"You'll do." She handed me a pie plate. "Blueberry—Finn's second favorite. I was going to bring lemon meringue, but the berry crop this year was a good one. I hope you like it as well." She also had a salad container.

"I love blueberries."

"These were fresh from the summer's bumper crop. Now, let's go see what my son's been up to while we've been out here introducing ourselves." The curvy redhead, who was barely five feet tall, swept past me and into the house.

Obediently, I followed.

She'd shucked her shoes and was already in the kitchen hugging her son by the time I closed the front door.

"Lasagna?" She sniffed.

"Yep." Finn beamed.

"From scratch?"

"Yep. With extra cottage cheese for you."

"Oh, lovely. And I brought blueberry pie." She gestured for me to move into the kitchen—which I did. "As well as the salad I promised."

Finn took the pie and put it on the counter. "You ready to eat? We can have the Caesar salad while the lasagna cools a little."

"Sounds lovely." Valerie turned to me. "I'm wanting to hear all about how you two met."

Heat rushed to my cheeks. I was grateful my dark skin hid what would've been, I was certain, an epic blush.

"Mom." Finn used his best chastising voice.

"What?" She batted her eyelashes. "I want to hear about the man who's stolen my son's heart."

I sputtered.

Finn rolled his eyes. "You promised. You're exaggerating. Now, please sit. Water okay?"

"Of course." Valerie sat at the head of the table.

Finn and I would be sitting to either side of her—facing each other.

I grabbed three glasses of water and delivered them while Finn brought the salad. He and I sat and watched as Valerie served herself.

She passed the salad to me. "My son has never introduced me to someone in his life. He can try to tell me that you're *just a friend*, but a mother knows." She cast her blue-eyed gaze upon her son.

He blushed. Then he ran his hand through his copper hair—so like his mother's. Finally, after a long moment, he served himself some salad. "It's not like that." He handed me the salad.

"Finnegan." I gave him my sternest voice.

His gaze shot to mine.

I took the salad bowl and held his gaze. "Don't lie to your mother. It's exactly *like that.*"

Valerie snorted.

Finn cussed.

I grinned and dished up salad.

We ate in silence, then, when Finn rose to get the pasta, Valerie again turned her attention to me. "I like your writing style. And I like how you've freshened the paper. So in need of an update."

"I'm trying my best."

"So how long are you sticking around?"

"Mom." Finn placed the glass container holding the lasagna on a trivet. "No interrogations."

"Asking casual and insightful questions is not the same as interrogating. Police interrogate. I seek answers to burning questions. Ulysses understands, don't you? The need for answers?"

"Yes, Valerie, I do."

Finn gestured for his mother to hold her plate up so he could put a piece of lasagna on it.

I did the same. Then waited until he had his pasta as well before picking up my knife and fork.

My first bite was barely onboard when Valerie continued. "Did he meet you on Davie Street? Or through an app? I've heard those things are wild—"

"Mom." Total Finn exasperation.

Something I was familiar with.

Glad I'm not the only one who pushes his buttons.

"What?" Valerie cut a piece of pasta. "I'm trying to be a hip mom. Someone who's accepting, but also cautious."

"I am capable of taking care of myself."

"Like when you got the flu?" She eyed me. "You brought him chicken noodle soup?"

"Yes. Seemed the least I could do."

"Well, you seem to be a good man. You'll do." She took a bite of pasta.

Finn caught my gaze.

I smiled.

He smiled back.

Dinner meandered in easy conversation after that. I directed any probing questions into my work history or my personal life into ferreting out anecdotes about Finn and his childhood. Apparently he'd always had a daredevil streak in him.

Valerie's refusal to let him play football still rankled.

"You did just fine in soccer." She pointed her fork at him. "And now you help by coaching basketball. See? No expensive gear needed." She turned to me. "And you?"

"None of the above. I tried hockey. Once. Complete disaster. I was not designed for skates."

"I could teach you. I'm pretty proficient." Finn grinned.

"Uh, no. But thanks." Memories of my bruised ass after my one attempt was enough to keep me off blades forever. I gestured to Valerie's empty plate.

She handed it over. "I think I need a break before I tackle dessert."

I snagged Finn's cleared plate, created a pile, and headed to the kitchen. "That sounds like a good idea."

"Ulysses owns a motorcycle. Likes to drive it fast."

I put the plates on the counter and turned to face Finn as he stood.

Valerie pivoted her attention to me. "Seriously? Do you know what nurses call motorcycle riders?"

"No. And I probably don't want to." I glared at Finn.

Who just gave me a shit-eating grin.

"Organ donors." Valerie picked up her glass of water and headed to the couch. "I've seen it happen. A shame. Those things are so damn dangerous."

Finn snickered.

"You think I don't know about you riding Bobby Jansen's motorcycle in grade eleven?" She wagged her finger at him.

He blanched.

I chuckled.

He glared.

"Mothers know these things. You never could keep secrets from me." She sat on the couch. "Which is why I'm surprised you kept Ulysses a secret for so long."

"We've only been dating a few weeks." Finn held my gaze.

"But you hooked up in the summer." Valerie sipped her water.

"Who told you that? Spring?" Finn rubbed his forehead. Then he pointed an accusatory finger at me.

I pressed a hand to my chest. "I swear I didn't tell anyone anything."

Valerie laughed. "You two are a hoot. Now come and sit with me."

Obediently, we moved to the living room. I sat in the recliner while Finn joined his mom on the couch.

I told Finn, "I think it's nice to have someone who cares that much about you. Even if they are a little...intrusive." I met Valerie's gaze.

She snickered. "You'd think Finnegan would've learned by now. Nothing's a secret."

"Slowly it's dawning on me." I sipped my water.

"Anonymity in the big city?" She eyed me.

"Something like that."

"You've never married?"

"Mom." Part exasperation. Part warning.

"Never met anyone who made me want to tie the knot. Hell, it wasn't even legal when I was in high school. Then Canada legalized same-sex marriage and I graduated high school and...it never happened."

"You studied journalism?"

"Yes. At UBC."

"Good school."

"Yes." *And very expensive*. Even back then, I'd had to borrow a pile of money to make it all work. The day I'd paid off that loan had been one of the happiest of my life. I liked living debt-free.

"Why journalism? That's an unusual career path."

"Pie?" Finn stood. "Technically anything is an unusual career choice since every job is different, right?" He made his way over to the kitchen. "Are we heating the pie and adding ice cream?"

His mother persisted, "I'm just saying—"

"What?" Finn reappeared from behind the corner. "Careful." He directed that to Valerie.

I cocked my head.

"I'm not a racist, Finnegan. You bloody well know me better than that. Your grandmother would have something to say about this relationship, but that's on her, not me."

"Mom." More admonishment than frustration.

Clearly I was missing something. "Is this because you don't see as many reporters of color? Because that's certainly changing." Even in the eighteen years since I'd earned my degree, several of the lead anchors of news shows in Vancouver now were *minorities*. The top echelon was still whiter than perhaps necessary—but things were changing. They were improving.

Valerie met my gaze. "I just didn't picture you behind a desk."

"Because I'm more of a shoe-leather reporter. I have no interest in being in front of the camera—I never have."

"You're attractive enough for it."

"Mom." Now complete exasperation.

"I thank you for the compliment. I prefer the written word."

"You used to do some hard-hitting reporting in Vancouver. Nothing like the fluff you've been relegated to doing in Mission City."

"Oh my God." Finn handed his mother a plate with a slice of pie and a scoop of vanilla ice cream.

"It's okay." I smiled. "You can't always believe what you read in the newspapers."

"Well, that's a damning statement." Valerie pointed her fork at me. The look in her eyes told me, yes, she'd seen not just my longtime byline but the whole mess at the end.

I shrugged, acting like I didn't care what Finn's mother had read about me. "I'll admit to making a bad mistake and coming to Mission City for a fresh start."

"How's that working out for you?" She ate a forkful of pie.

"Looking brighter by the day." I met Finn's gaze as he handed me a plate.

He rolled his eyes.

I sank my fork into the ice cream. "I'll endeavor to do right by Finn, if that's what you're asking."

She nodded as she swallowed. "I suppose that's all I can ask for. I just want Finnegan to be happy. I want him to be with someone who will treat him properly."

And my misjudgments of the past meant I might be a bad bet. I understood her skepticism. I wouldn't be able to sweet talk my way out of this mess. "I'll do my best."

"See that you do."

"Mom." Complete exasperation. Finn sat on the couch next to his mother with his plate of pie. "Don't make me regret inviting you."

I chuckled and it didn't sound too fake. "All good—we're just getting to know each other."

Valerie nodded her evident approval.

I'd passed muster.

At least for the time being.

Chapter Twenty-Two

Finn

"How could you be so stupid?" I glared at Michael, one of my rec teenagers.

He glared right back. "It's not what you think."

I jutted my chin. "That very much looked like you were buying drugs from that guy. Who was he? Why was he on school property? And, like I said, how could you be so stupid? David died of a drug overdose. You want to wind up like him? Dead?" I was full of steam and ready to go all night at this.

"He wasn't selling me drugs." Even as Michael made the denial, though, he couldn't meet my gaze.

"Is he hassling you? Do you want me to tell Mr. Clayton? He can make sure the guy isn't at the school again." Except the principal couldn't be everywhere at once. And nothing was stopping Michael from crossing the street and buying drugs from some random person sitting in a car on the side of the road. If he wanted drugs, they wouldn't be hard to find.

Between Giancarlo just not showing up for his shift today—without even calling in sick—and now interrupting Michael buying drugs, my whole day was going sideways. Badly. "Look—" I took a deep breath. "Are you addicted?"

"Is this an intervention?" Said with all the sarcasm a teenager could manage.

"Does it need to be? You know I can call in a guidance—"

"I'm not an addict."

"So you were just buying drugs for the hell of it? Have you heard about the tainted drug supply? You can never be sure what's in the drugs or in what quantity. Dying is really easy. Drug dealers don't care about whether you OD or not—they'll always find another buyer." Which, to me, was a fault in the logic. Except it proved true over and over again. People died. And yet drug dealers never went out of business.

"Can we just play ball?" The teenager tipped his chin up at me. In defiance, most likely.

I hadn't witnessed enough to go to the cops. At most I had suspicions with a very generic description of a very generic guy. Nothing I could swear to. Nothing that would help them put an end to the drug trade in Mission City, that was for certain.

Rue and Leroy stood off to the side—watching us intently.

Finally, something broke in me. Not acceptance—more like resignation. "Yeah, let's play. And promise me you won't do anything so monumentally stupid as buying drugs—okay?"

"Yeah. Okay."

I didn't really believe him—but I'd done everything I could.

That night, as I ate leftover pie, I was surprised to get a text from Ulysses, asking if he could come over. The answer, of course, was *hell, yes.*

Half an hour after that, he sat in the recliner enjoying a slice of pie as well.

"You survived my mother's inquisition." He'd left last night—not long after she had. I'd asked him to stay, but he'd said he had something to do early in the morning and hadn't wanted to wake me. I was pretty certain I could sleep through just about anything...but I'd also wondered if he'd needed space after the intense interrogation from my mother.

Now, twenty-four hours later, he was back. But he kept gazing at me—as if trying to take my measure.

"I have some news." I poked my pie.

"I do as well, but why don't you go first?"

"Sure. I, uh, think I stopped Michael from buying drugs today. I mean, he says he wasn't..."

"You don't believe him."

"I don't believe him. And I can't imagine I've dissuaded him from doing it again in the future."

"Ah. What did you see?"

I shrugged. "An older white guy looking like he didn't belong. Some kind of furtive movements—I just charged over there. Scared the guy off, that's for sure. If he had a legitimate reason for being there, he would've said something, right?"

"Yes, very likely." He put his plate on the side table. He'd devoured the pie. "And Michael?"

"Claimed I'd misunderstood."

"Teenagers are tricky."

"What do you mean?"

"Might there have been another reason for them meeting?"

I scrunched my nose. "Christ, I hope not. The guy was older than me. Bad enough if he's coming around with drugs."

"Did you tell the cops?"

I shook my head. "I didn't tell Mr. Clayton either. Hell, I couldn't even give a good description of the guy. Brown hair. Nondescript face. Average height and weight. Nothing remarkable about him."

"Those guys do make the best dealers."

"Right? I know a guy who's got a scar on his face. He'd make a terrible criminal because he'd be easy to describe. And Michael didn't confirm he was buying drugs. At best, it would've been my word against his."

"You're the adult."

"Who's upset after David's death and seeing bad stuff everywhere."

Ulysses cocked his head.

"This is totally irrelevant—but Giancarlo didn't turn up at work. And didn't call in sick. I can't remember him ever doing that. I wanted to go over to his place, but we were slammed. Miriam has a key from the last time he was away and she watered his plants. She was planning to check on him. I should've gone, but I had basketball practice."

"What did she find?"

"Nothing. She texted me that he wasn't there and nothing looked amiss. She called the hospital and—"

"I know where he is."

I shook my head, as if trying to clear my thoughts. "I'm sorry, did you just say you know where Giancarlo is?"

"Yes."

"And you didn't think to tell me that straightaway? Like when you walked in the door?"

"In hindsight, that might've been wise. But you offered pie and—"

"Jesus Christ, Ulysses." I wanted to throw a pillow at him. I wanted to throttle him.

I did neither.

He held up his hand. “He’s at the detachment.”

I blinked. “He’s at the police station?”

“Yeah.”

“Okay.” I frowned. “Why didn’t he just call and tell me that? What’s with the secrecy and, for that matter, how do you know about it?”

“Well...I have a source I can’t reveal.”

I started to launch myself off the couch.

He held up his hands—clearly in self-defense. “I can’t, Finn. But I thought you’d want to know. I needed to know what you knew before I said anything. Hell, you might’ve been aware and didn’t care—”

“Ulysses.” I ground out his name with a clenched jaw.

“Right. He was arrested last night.”

“What?”

“He was pulled over for erratic driving. The cop figured Giancarlo was high.”

“What cop? How did he know? Or she? Was it a she?”

“Constable Seth Jacobs. Giancarlo was all over the road and Seth needed to pull him over. They ran a drug test at the detachment and the result was positive. Giancarlo's facing a driving-while-impaired charge.”

My world bottomed out, and my stomach plummeted. “Giancarlo’s not an addict. Hell, he isn’t even a user. That’s...just wrong. All wrong. You must be mistaken.”

Ulysses shook his head. “Confirmed. Charges are going to be laid tomorrow. I, uh—” He rubbed the back of his neck. “I was waiting to see if you were going to say something. Whether you knew or not. Because I probably shouldn’t be telling you—”

“Will I be able to work backward to figure out who told you?”

He nodded.

"Right." I blew out a long breath. "I won't say anything. I promise. I appreciate you coming here to tell me. I just...how is he using and I didn't know?"

"Because he didn't want you to see? Or maybe this was the first time?"

"You don't believe that." I eyed him.

"Not for a second. The odds of being caught DUI your very first time using are pretty slim. Cops can't be everywhere all at once."

I slid back into my comfortable seat. "I don't understand."

"About addiction or your friend in particular?"

"All of it. Fucking drugs. He's going to lose his job."

"Yeah, which sucks—but do you really want someone using drugs while on the job?"

"He probably never used while working."

Ulysses arched his eyebrow.

"Well, I certainly didn't see any sign of it."

"People are good at hiding things, Finn. You, of all people, know that."

I did. That didn't make things easier to swallow, though. "So, arraignment?"

"Yep. Probably he'll get bail. Stupid driving high—but he didn't crash. Like you said, there'll be professional ramifications. I think he's going to need your friendship—if you're comfortable offering it."

I frowned. "Why wouldn't I? I'm supposed to be empathetic to drug users. Not their fault..." Even as I said the words, though, I remembered all the times I'd had uncharitable thoughts about addicts and how they just needed to get their act together and stop using. All while understanding that wasn't always possible. Often, addiction didn't respond to pulling up one's bootstraps. "I feel like I don't know him—like everything that's ever happened between us was a lie."

"Now, that's harsh. Maybe listen to his side of the story?" He looked down at his hands. "Okay, so there's more."

"What do you mean *there's more*? Why aren't you just spitting it out?"

"Easing into it?" He winced. "Look, I know Giancarlo's a friend. I just—"

"Spit it out. I can take it." I put way more certainty into that statement than I should have—but what the fuck ever. I couldn't figure out why Ulysses wasn't just laying things out. Consistently, I preferred to have all the facts before me so I could take everything in all at once and deal with the consequences—whatever they might be.

"Okay." Again, he gazed at his hands. "This wasn't the first time he got pulled over."

"What the fuck?"

"Right? I don't know who the officer was the last time. But Giancarlo wasn't arrested—even though he'd clearly been using. So either Seth got fed up with letting him off or—"

"No way. If Seth pulled him over, and there was any sign of impairment, Giancarlo's goose was cooked. Like last night. Seth doesn't fuck around with that. I might not know much—but I know that. You don't know, though?"

Ulysses shook his head. "My source is already sticking their neck out even just to tell me Giancarlo had been pulled over. But—" He stopped.

"But? No point stopping now."

"The last time? He wasn't in the car alone."

I blinked. "He was driving while under the influence with someone else in the car? Again, what the actual fuck?" I rubbed my face. "I almost don't want to ask."

"But you want to know."

I cracked an eye. “Yeah, I suppose I do.” I exhaled. “Who was it?”

“Marlon.”

“What?” Again, I blinked. Like, trying to align the pieces of a puzzle that just wouldn’t fit together. “But they’re not even friends.”

“No. But my source thinks they have the same dealer.”

Chapter Twenty-Three

Ulysses

"Hey." I offered my best smile as I found Finn leaning against my door the next afternoon. He looked as tired as I felt, after an evening when we'd had no answers and no recourse except to distract each other in bed. "You waiting long?"

He shook his head. "Cody let me in. Even offered to let me hang at his place until you came home. I didn't want to intrude."

I unlocked my door. "If Cody offered, then I doubt he saw it as an imposition. I've never seen him with anyone. Well, except his Aunt Genessa. That woman's a hoot."

"Can't say I've ever met her." Finn stepped into my condo.

I flipped on the light, closed the door, then locked it. "You okay? You look tired. I don't think you slept much last night."

He shrugged. "I was restless. Sorry if I woke you."

"You didn't. And you had to be at work early this morning. Long day?"

"I confronted Marlon."

"Oh." I put my messenger bag on the island and removed my coat. "Can I take your jacket?"

"Uh, sure." He removed it. Finally, he met my gaze. "Marlon said some things about you."

"Oh." I hung our coats in the front hall closet. "Do I want to know?"

"A bunch of shit—about what happened in Vancouver." He scratched his chin. "I don't know if he was pulling shit out of his ass or if there's more going on than what you've told me."

"Oh." I moved toward the fridge. "Would you like a drink? You look exhausted, and I don't want to give you caffeine if that'll knock your schedule off."

"Diet cola's fine. That amount of caffeine will be okay. I don't want to nod off."

"If you're tired, feel free to crash. What do you want for dinner?" *Because I'm just going to act like nothing's wrong. Fucking Marlon.* In truth, I didn't know what Finn was trying to say—but pushing felt like the wrong move. Better to let him come to me.

"I'm easy. Whatever's quickest."

"Usually pizza. Although I can run to the taco place. That takes, like, five minutes."

"I don't want to go out."

"Right. I'll go—"

"I don't want you going out."

"Okay. So, pizza?"

He nodded. Then rubbed his face.

I yanked out my phone and, since I knew what we both wanted, ordered two large pies. Leftovers were a good thing—he could take them for lunch tomorrow. "Thirty minutes."

"Huh? Oh, thanks."

"Are you okay?"

He held my gaze—those stunning blue eyes assessing me. "I need you to tell me exactly what happened in Vancouver."

I opened the fridge, grabbed two diet colas, and closed the door. I handed him one, then gestured toward the living room.

He toed off his boots, then headed to the couch.

I removed my shoes and followed him.

Night had fallen, and all the city lights twinkled in the distance.

A train whistle sounded—likely the commuter train bringing weary workers home from Vancouver after a long workday.

I cracked my can open and then sat on the couch. Near Finn—but not touching. Not because I didn't want to—because I certainly did. No, that wasn't it. He was holding himself apart, and I had to respect that. Obviously, Marlon had said something and Finn was trying to work things out in his mind. A man conflicted.

That, I understood.

I sighed. Then sipped. Finally, I considered. "It's both a long and short story."

Finn cocked his head.

"Well, I graduated from the University of British Columbia with a journalism degree almost twenty years ago."

"Okay." Said with some obvious trepidation.

"I have a point."

"Yeah, okay."

"I got a job reporting for a local radio station. And I enjoyed it enough—but I wanted more of a challenge. So I took the plunge and went back to school to do a Master's degree."

"Well, that's cool." Although he was still eyeing me.

"I thought having the letters after my name would open more doors. That didn't exactly happen."

"Oh."

"Yeah. But I was determined and I kept pursuing all avenues. Newspaper and magazines—along with television, obviously—were still the main ways of reporting. Internet journalism's much bigger now. But I thought the way to legitimacy was through legacy media."

"Right." He rubbed his forehead.

"Eventually I landed a job at the Sun."

"Okay. That's good, right?"

"Yes. But I worried it might not've been for the right reasons."

"Ah. Because of your skin color rather than your writing abilities?"

"Precisely." I rose and walked over to the window. "Stupid, right? I was a damn good journalist. Impeccable credentials. Several writing awards. Little stuff, but it all added up, you know?

"I do. Guys like Marlon, who get in because of nepotism? They should be working twice as hard to prove they earned their spot and it's not just because of who they know."

"Exactly. I was put on the metro desk. I started out doing little human-interest stories. Slowly, I made a name for myself. I got a couple of big scoops and broke a scandal involving a city counselor." I swallowed. "Accolades came. I got recognition for the work I was doing. And I still did stories about my old neighborhood—"

"Which neighborhood?"

I didn't turn to face him. "Downtown Eastside."

"Ah." He didn't have to say more. The poorest urban neighborhood in Canada. Extreme poverty butting up against extreme wealth. Crossing Cambie Street heading westward was like entering a new universe. Plenty of poverty existed in Canada—which was a travesty in and of itself. Indigenous communities suffered the greatest inequality—both on and off reserve. Another horrendous truth the country had truly to grapple with.

And if one wanted to find the most destitute in Vancouver, one went to the Downtown Eastside.

"I tried to separate myself from my past, you know? Even as I wrote stories about my old neighborhood. I wanted to prove I was—" I flailed my hand about.

"I get it."

Since I didn't want to say out loud the tumult in my mind, I just kept going. "One day I was approached by a guy from my old neighborhood. Someone I'd known. Someone I'd known to steer clear of."

"Okay."

I rubbed my face. "He had a really good scoop. A politician on the take. Lots of proof, too. He was willing to show me all of it."

"Just like that?"

"My exact reaction. Everyone wants something. But I couldn't figure out his angle. I didn't have money to give him. He didn't want his name in the papers, so fame wasn't his aim either. He claimed he was doing it for the greater good. To better society."

"Ulysses?"

I turned to face Finn. "Yeah?"

"Too good to be true?"

"Yeah." Memories flashed through my mind. *How much dare I share? Do I really want him to lose all respect for me?* "I took all the evidence and wrote a three-part hit piece. I tore that politician to shreds. I had the documents, after all. Proof of all the wrongdoing she'd been up to. Ironclad. Hell, I figured the prosecutors could use the roadmap I'd drawn to convict her of corruption and bribery."

"But it wasn't true."

"Nope." My gut clenched. "None of it. Not a single word. Everything I'd been presented had been fabricated—by some damn smart people." I rubbed my forehead again. "I thought I was so smart. That I'd never be taken in. I followed all the rules—and still got hoodwinked."

"That's...shitty. You had to write a retraction, right?"

I cleared my throat. "The very first thing I had to do was explain myself to my editor. Worst conversation ever. She eviscerated me. And rightly so. Then yes, she sent me to my desk to write the biggest mea culpa ever. No excuses. Unequivocal *I fucked up and every word I wrote was a lie*. I wasn't given even an inch of print to give my side of the story. No one was going to give a shit about me. Nor should they have. This was about almost ruining someone's life."

"You weren't malicious. Hell, it sounds like you weren't even sloppy."

"Intentions don't mean shit when you fuck up as badly as I did. I was looking for recognition. For someone to pat me on the back and acknowledge I was the best."

"Obviously that didn't happen."

"Nope. Lawyers descended to sort out the mess. Cops even got involved because it looked like I'd intentionally attempted to cause damage."

"Which you had."

"From the outside? Yeah, that's what it looked like. The paper wanted to cover their asses."

Finn tilted his head. "They didn't think to do that *before* shit went down?"

"My editor was the biggest check—and she took everything I showed her at face value—like I had. But she was responsible for a bunch of reporters. She trusted us to do our jobs. And I honestly thought I had." I moved back to the couch and dropped. "I was blind."

"Why?" His voice was quiet. "You seem like one of the most level-headed people I know. Cynical too—which is why I'd have thought you'd be more...questioning."

"She really looked guilty. I mean, our lawyers struggled to find fault in the documents I'd been given. Someone went to a lot of trouble to make it all look legit."

"To what end?"

"That was what was so confusing. She was just one member of council. She wasn't known for being a troublemaker, and she certainly hadn't done anything controversial."

"And yet....? I'm sensing a but."

"You'd be right. She was about to block a major development project in her neighborhood. Big money was involved. Look, all levels of government are pushing for an increase in housing supply and rules are being bent—if not broken. She was about to speak out."

Finn scratched his nose. "Sounds extreme. To go to those lengths—"

"His secondary motive was to take me down."

"Okay, that you've got to explain."

"I told you that I knew the guy."

"From your old neighborhood."

"Yeah."

"Okay." He held my gaze. "Just spit it out."

"Apparently I rejected his advances." I rubbed my scalp with my fingernails. "The thing is...I'm pretty sure I would remember if I'd done that. Because I was struggling with my sexuality with all the other crap going on in my life. I mean—" I grunted. "I have no memory of anything between this guy and me. Like none. Which makes me wonder if I was either truly that clueless or if this thing—whatever it was—only happened in his head."

"Or he's lying."

I squeezed my eyes shut. "I don't understand."

"This is incredibly complicated. He wanted to take down the council member so a building project got approved."

"Yes."

"And he used you because...you turned him down when you were younger? Does that make sense to you?"

For the umpteenth time, I rubbed my forehead. "No, it doesn't make sense. It never did. Which is why I didn't see it coming. Anyway, he's in the wind, the development wound up getting approved, and the council member—" My breath hitched.

Finn sat straighter. "What happened to her? I only saw the retraction and your apology. I never did see anything more."

"The Sun didn't want anything to do with the whole mess. They were very happy to cut me loose." I gazed up at the ceiling. "Things...didn't go well for her."

"But she was innocent. She didn't do anything wrong."

"Sure. But the stress of being accused...that was a lot."

The moment held. *Please don't ask me. I don't want to go back to that place. I don't want to admit the depth of my culpability or my breathtaking stupidity.*

Finally, Finn broke the silence. "Can you talk about it?"

"She was pregnant. Miscarriage—" I waved my hand. "It's not publicly known and obviously, you can't say anything."

"I would never."

"I know. And I don't know if the stress caused the miscarriage or if she would've lost the baby anyway. That's just something I have to live with. If I'd been less reckless—" I swallowed. "If I'd asked better questions. If I'd taken the time to question motives. If I'd looked at things objectively. If only—"

"You know that's not productive, right? That overthinking thing?"

"But—"

"Ulysses."

"Yeah." Finally, I met his gaze.

"You didn't set out to cause harm. You didn't deliberately target her. You did what you thought was best at the time. In retrospect, you can see all the choices you made and how they impacted her. But you didn't have that knowledge with you at the time and you didn't calculatingly aim to harm anyone."

I nodded.

"Have you told her how you feel?"

I shook my head. "The lawyers wouldn't let me within a mile of her."

"Would they even know?"

"You mean you think I should write to her now? Share how I'm feeling? How sorry I am for what I put her through?"

Finn nodded.

"That's just going to make her relive it. There's no absolution for me. I fucked up. I lost my job—which was only right. I became a pariah in Vancouver. So I left. And in some ways, I don't think Mission City was far enough."

"But the publisher offered you a job."

I shrugged. "Pretty much. But no matter what your mother thinks...I'm not just hanging out here until things blow over back in the city. That's never going to happen. I'm not getting my old job back. I'm not getting a new and better gig. In the end, I'm just grateful I landed on my feet and relatively unscathed."

"*Relatively.*"

"Yeah. That."

My phone buzzed. I pressed the keypad. "Pizza's here."

"We're not done with this conversation."

I rose. "Finn, there's nothing else to say. You knew most of this. Well, some of it. Maybe not how stupid I was. Or how I ruined a woman's life." I rose and made my way to the front door.

Inga stood on the other side with two boxes in her arms. She offered me a wide smile. "Doubly hungry tonight?"

"Company." I took the boxes from her.

"Oh?" She subtly tried to look over my shoulder. Well, given how short she was, it was more like her trying to gaze around me.

"Friend."

"Okay." She attempted to look disinterested.

I wasn't fooled for even a moment. "Thanks for coming."

"Thanks for the big tip. Have a nice night." She headed back toward the elevator.

I re-entered the condo.

Finn was in the kitchen, retrieving plates. He offered a grin. "Curious delivery driver?"

"You heard that?"

He nodded.

"Yep. Inga. Do you know her?"

"No one delivers pizza to my place. Well, there's one place...but I don't like their pizza."

"Ah. So you either have to cook your own or head into town?"

He put the plates on the counter. "It's called planning ahead. When you live as far out as I do, you make lists and check them twice. You figure out what you can get done before and after shift. I mean, I suppose I could run into town more often than I do. But I hate polluting the environment and wasting time. I love Domino's, though. So good choice."

"Ah. I don't need to ask if this is the place that delivers but you don't like them."

"They don't deliver my way, and I love them. When I'm treating the folks at the firehouse, this is what I pick. Others are okay...but these are the best."

"You want carrots or celery or—"

"I just want pizza. But, thanks." He waited for me to put the boxes on the counter.

Where I expected him to dive in, though, he didn't. Instead, he held his arms open wide for me.

After a long moment, I stepped into the embrace.

"You're not a bad person." He whispered the words in my ear. "Maybe, eventually, you might be able to forgive yourself? Just something to consider."

I clung to him. How many times had I tried to tell myself those exact words? That although I'd been stupid and naïve, I hadn't been malicious. I hadn't intended to hurt someone. Well, someone innocent. "I don't know if I can. Forgive myself."

"Which is why I think you need to reach out to her. But that's between you and her." He squeezed extra-tight. "Now...I'm fucking starving."

Chapter Twenty-Four

Finn

My mind wouldn't settle.

Over and over.

Round and round.

My words to Ulysses about overthinking things were now coming back to bite me in the ass. Because this time I was the one doing the overthinking.

While my—

I squinted up at the ceiling in his bedroom. A sliver of light came through the drapes and slid across the space.

Light pollution.

My place in the country was pretty dark, but I needed blackout blinds because of the shift-work. Right now, I should've been at home in my own bed. Instead of here in—

What the fuck, dude? How hard can it be to say?

Really hard, apparently.

Boyfriend.

Right?

Except...were we that? Yes, he'd met my mother. So that moved the relationship from beyond the realm of fuck buddies.

Right?

On the other hand, he hadn't introduced me to his pizza-delivery person.

Right?

But was that a sign of wanting to keep me hidden, respecting my privacy, or just not wanting to get into a long-winded explanation of who I was?

Boyfriend? Partner? Fuck buddy?

I just didn't have an answer.

Instead, I squinted at the clock radio.

2:50 a.m.

Too late to go home to try to get some rest.

Too early to go to the fire hall.

Aside from Fifties, there weren't a whole lot of places open at this hour. *I could go and try to sleep in the pickup.* Except if my mind was working overtime here, nothing said it would calm inside my vehicle. Between the animal shelter, my kids with drugs, and Giancarlo, I couldn't settle.

I slid from Ulysses's grasp and got out of the bed.

He resettled quickly.

Instead of trying to sort my clothes, I headed for the door. Fortunately, it didn't creak when it opened. I made my way into the main room.

We hadn't closed the blinds here, so artificial light flooded the room.

Rain lashed the windows. I hadn't noticed the wind picking up earlier, but it blew with force.

Glad I'm not out in that tonight.

I headed to the guest bathroom, where I pissed, washed my hands, then threw cold water on my face.

Still no answers were forthcoming.

My fight with Marlon was on repeat.

Me—demanding to know if he was the reason Giancarlo was using drugs.

Him—acting all affronted that I would even consider asking him such a question. Because he was innocent, of course.

Right.

Me—demanding to know why he was involved with drugs at all.

Who said something? Your reporter boyfriend? He's lying. Trying to frame me. That's what he does. You should go and look up his name.

I'd already done that, though. And I thought I'd known the whole story.

I'd come here.

And Ulysses had laid himself bare to me.

I'd basically made him relive all that—to alleviate my sense of unease.

Because fucktard Marlon had one thing right—I didn't know everything about Ulysses. Even now, I didn't feel like I knew everything.

And who says you need to? Who's keeping score? Even if he is your...boyfriend...who says your relationship isn't solid enough as is?

I caught sight of the open door to the second bedroom.

Curiosity might've killed the cat—but it had never stopped me from venturing where I maybe shouldn't have been going. Asking forgiveness instead of permission and all that bullshit.

Instead of questioning the wisdom of my actions, I made my way into the room.

The blinds were open here as well, and that artificial light flooded in. The desk, pressed right up against the window, was the first thing that caught my attention. It dominated the space.

I advanced toward it and did some calculations in my mind. During the day, sitting at this desk, there would be a direct line of sight to Mount Baker. Unobstructed and phenomenal view.

My desk in my loft—with the view of the forest beyond—had nothing on this.

A shiver ran through me.

Well duh. You're naked. It's nearly the end of October. What were you expecting?

Ulysses didn't have his heat on yet. Wasn't cold enough for that—but it would come soon enough.

Another lash of rain against the window.

I glanced down the desk.

And squinted.

Okay, there's a difference between asking forgiveness because you inadvertently went somewhere you weren't supposed to and actually snooping deliberately.

And yet—

I found the switch for the lamp and flicked it on.

The neat pile of papers must've been five or six inches.

In Each Their Time.

A novel by H.R. Webb

My jaw dropped. I knew just enough about publishing to recognize a manuscript. And, having read every single H.R. Webb novel, I could also recognize this was a new book. *Why would Ulysses have—*

"Can't sleep?" Ulysses's deep voice resonated through the room.

Involuntarily, I put a hand over my heart. As if I could somehow calm the racing. I turned to face him. While I was naked, he wore a black silk robe. In some ways, the garment was incongruous with the man I knew—soap and water, motorcycle-leather wearing dude. Yet he looked fucking sexy in it.

Again, I shivered.

"You want a blanket?" He moved toward the closet, opened it, and pulled a blanket from the top shelf. "I have more blankets than one man might possibly need. But I always worry about being cold. I suppose because of—" He handed me the scratchy gray wool blanket.

"Because of…?"

He turned to close the closet door. "Doesn't matter."

"What if it matters to me?" I could guess—but I wanted to hear it from him.

Our gazes clashed.

He took a deep breath. "Our heat got cut off a few times when I was a kid. That's all."

"That's a lot. My mom and I might've had a few lean times, but we always had electricity and wood for the fireplace."

"You don't have many fireplaces in four-story walk-ups."

"In the Downtown Eastside."

"Yeah."

I wrapped the blanket around myself. Warmth would be slow in coming because I'd let myself get chilled. Another shiver ran through me.

"Why don't you come back to bed? I can warm you up. Or we could have a shower. Plenty of things I could do—"

"Why do you have an H.R. Webb novel? A manuscript, right? Do you, I don't know, write reviews for them or something? Beta reader? ARC reader?" Advance reader copy. Because there had to be some kind of an explanation why he had an unpublished manuscript by one of the biggest thriller writers in Canada. Right?

He sighed. "It's sort of a long story." Something flickered in his eyes.

The penny dropped. Or was it the shoe? Both dumb expressions. "You're H.R. Webb."

For the first time in our acquaintance, he bit his lower lip. "It's complicated."

"No, it's really not. You're either a prolific thriller writer who sets their gritty crime dramas in Vancouver or you somehow have gotten a hold of their manuscript—possibly through unethical means."

"You would believe that of me?"

"I don't know what to think—you haven't told me anything. You haven't given me any kind of an explanation as to why you have this. My feet are getting cold. Hell, they are cold."

"Come back to bed." He extended his arm.

I shook my head. "Not until you explain."

"Ah. Stubborn."

"Yep. Goes with the red hair—or so my mother tells me."

"Right. Okay. I am H.R. I've been writing these books for almost fifteen years."

"But, why? I mean, I get why you write—but why do you write *and* have a day job?"

He shrugged. "Being an author has always felt ephemeral. Like it might all end at any moment and I'll be left with nothing. So it's easier to just keep fiction writing as a side gig. I put all the royalties aside. I guess, a nest egg, should the worse ever come to pass and I lose my *day job*." He emphasized the words.

"Man, I don't understand. If I could write all day, instead of fighting fires, I totally would."

"Would you? Or might you grow bored? Feel the need to be part of a community. Writing is a fairly solitary act. I have writer friends with whom I communicate—but all over the internet. I don't have real-life friends who know my truth. My editor, my agent, and a couple of people at the publishing house know—but that's it."

"There's been speculation that H.R. is a woman."

Slowly, he smiled. "I've heard those rumors. Obviously not true. The assumption is also that H.R. is Caucasian."

"You know, I've never thought about it."

"Because those authors still dominate the market. Another reason I didn't identify myself—I don't want to be labeled as a certain kind of writer because of my skin color, you know?"

"Yeah. I really do." I closed my eyes. "You haven't told me about this. You're a writer? You didn't bother to tell me? You think I didn't need to know?"

He eyed me. "Why do you need to know? It's just something I do in my spare time. It's not who I am. Look, even after I published my first book, I went back to UBC to get a Master's in Journalism. Writing fiction is...my stress outlet."

"And when you left town?"

"I took a vacation."

"You said you were working."

"I was." He held my gaze. "I was meeting my agent and editor in Toronto." He pointed to the manuscript. "Sometimes it's easier to have the meetings in person. Plus, checking in can prove to be a good thing. My editor wanted a different approach with this book. I argued if this formula worked, why mess with it?"

"Don't you get bored of writing the same thing over and over?"

He shifted from foot to foot. "Maybe? Sometimes? But my fans want the same thing over and over." He scratched his scalp with his fingernails. "I know what poor looks like. I don't ever want to go back to that."

"You've hit the bestseller lists. That means sales. That means money. You don't seem to have some extravagant lifestyle."

"That's true. But I might lose my job tomorrow. I might have things fall apart and I have to dip into my nest egg. And the next book might be a flop. Lots of horrible things can happen. So I just balance everything precariously and wait for things to fall apart."

I didn't want to be swayed by his words, but I understood what he was trying to say. "Because of your childhood."

"Probably."

"Right." I took a deep breath. "I've had you all wrong, all along, haven't I? I thought you were beginning to care for me." I gestured toward the papers. "But you didn't even trust me with the truth. With your truth. You planned to keep that side of you hidden from me. For what, forever?"

"I didn't know." He met my gaze. "I didn't know we were going to turn into something. And I like what we are. I don't want to fuck that up with bringing something that doesn't matter into the relationship."

"Doesn't matter? Writing is a huge part of who you are. Hell, I write poetry. So I understand about having the need for a creative outlet. And before you go razzing me for not telling you, let me say I've had six poems published in the last five years. Not exactly something worth writing home about. Especially since only half of those actually paid me money. You're H.R. Freaking Webb, for Christ's sake. So not even on the same plane of existence."

"Six published poems is impressive, Finn. You could've shared that with me. Poetry journals are notoriously hard to get published in. I've never tried writing poetry because I know it's harder than it looks." He extended his arm again. "Come back to bed."

I shook my head. "Is this why you haven't made progress on the shelter? Because you're busy writing fiction?" I gestured to the manuscript. "I'm going home now. I need some space."

"Finn—"

"No. Not this time. Just...let me go." I brushed past him—heading to the bedroom to get dressed.

He didn't follow me.

Chapter Twenty-Five

Ulysses

As I sat at the basketball game, I kept my eye on everyone.

Most especially Finn.

He wouldn't look at me. I sat in the bleachers, across where he was coaching—and he wouldn't make eye contact.

Three days. He'd worked two of them, had a day off, and was now here. And yet he'd made no move to contact me. And my three texts had gone unanswered. Just one a day. *See? I can be reasonable. I'm not obsessive. I'm not obsessed.*

Or so I keep telling myself.

Over and over, I replayed that night in my mind. Should I have said something different? Would it've given me a different outcome? Or had the die been cast when I chose not to tell him about my writing? I didn't have a ready answer for that. If Finn wasn't a writer himself—a poet no less—would the omission have cut so deep? Again, I couldn't say. I'd kept my mouth shut—as I had for the last almost fifteen years—and had never considered sharing. H.R. wasn't part of my day-to-day life. I fit writing and publishing around my day job as a reporter and now, as editor of a small-town paper. If I'd thought the pace of life would slow once I moved to the boondocks, I was sorely mistaken on that count. Mission City kept me hopping.

Michael scored a three-pointer, and the crowd erupted in cheers. No one louder than Finn. He embraced everything in life with enthusiasm. *Did he ever reach out to Giancarlo?*

I'd tried. And been rebuffed. I'd explained the story was coming out in just a day and I was offering him an opportunity to set the record straight. He'd slammed the door in my face and ignored my repeated emails. Not that I'd believed he had a record to set straight. Probably his lawyer warned him about speaking to the media—or anyone else—about his situation. He was unlikely to make the situation better—but he could make it a whole lot worse if he wasn't careful.

So I'd backed off, and the story had run as front-page news today. The paper would be distributed throughout the day and, as of yet, I hadn't had anyone approach me about my plea for more information, complete with a promise of anonymity. I doubted the people at the game had yet seen the paper—but with the way word traveled around here, someone was bound to hear something.

Plus, time was ticking on Thelma's adoption. I might have to break that part of the story before I had all the pieces. I absolutely didn't want to do that.

"Mr. MacDonald." A deep voice caught my attention.

"Mr. Clayton." I rose and extended my hand to the principal.

He shook it. "Please, it's Gage."

"Then I insist on Ulysses."

The little crow's feet around his eyes crinkled when he smiled. "That's fair. Do you have a moment?"

"Certainly." Mission City had the game well in hand.

Finn didn't appear the least bit interested.

My mind kept wandering anyway.

So I followed the tall, imposing man into the hallway.

"How are you finding things in Mission City?" He gestured toward the long hallway.

"I'm adapting."

He chuckled. "I've been here twenty years, and I still say that."

"You're not from here?"

"No. I grew up closer to Vancouver. I graduated from teacher's college and got a job in Mission City. My girlfriend became my wife, and we started a life here. Life proved interesting as I eventually became principal at this school and she was a guidance counselor. But we made it work."

I cocked my head. "I thought your wife was a lawyer."

"Ah. Rielle's my second wife. Cara, my first wife, died suddenly a number of years ago. I'd sort of given up on love—and then fate threw Rielle in my path, and I had no chance to swerve and avoid the collision."

"Sounds painful."

Gage chuckled. "Best kind of collision. Meeting of the mind, body, and spirit. I used to think love was a once-in-a-lifetime thing. I'd only ever loved Cara. Now, I see that simply isn't true. That a really lucky person, if they lose one love of their life, might find happiness with a second person. I don't know how to describe it."

"I think you just did." I smiled. "And now you have two young children."

"Yes. Fatherhood at over forty caught me off guard. No regrets—but it's a demanding thing."

"I can imagine." The man had gray threaded through his dark hair. "I don't know how you do it. I look at parents and see the awesome responsibility."

He gestured up and down the hallway. "I have a lot of responsibility—here and at home. I'm lucky I have a strong partner."

"Sounds like it." I eyed him. "Why are we having this conversation? Not that I mind talking—"

He chuckled. "I figured you'd want me to get straight to the point." He sighed. "I read the article about the firefighter and drugs. You know we just lost a student to drugs."

I nodded.

"I'm wondering if there's a connection."

I stilled. "Isn't that a question for the police? The RCMP are in a much better position to comment."

"And yet they won't."

"Ah." Things crystalized. "I can't tie the two events together. But I'm seeing a pattern. I can't go public until I have confirmation."

"Can you share with me?" His dark eyes held hope.

I shook my head. "Too premature. I will say if I had a direct link to the school then I'd be telling you."

"Finn mentioned he thought he saw a man trying to sell drugs to Michael. Michael denied it, of course."

"Yeah. It's not like he's going to admit to buying drugs—especially to someone he respects as much as Finn."

"I'd hoped—" He ran his hands through his hair. "Finn's so good with the kids. I hoped he could help keep them out of trouble."

"Can anyone do that?"

He chuckled. Ruefully. "Uh, no. They're teenagers. They're chaos incarnate. Good point."

"Yet you love them."

"I do. I really do. When I lost my wife, I had this place as a reason to keep going. Successes like Finn help a lot in soothing the ache when things don't go well."

"Like David."

"Like David." He extended his hand.

I shook it. "I promise I'll let you know."

"That's all I can ask. You going back to see the rest of the game?"

I shook my head. "It's all good. I'll get the final score to print in the paper. You've got a good team."

"Yes. With a good coach. And Finn helping the kids not strong enough to make that team. We work hard."

I liked how he included himself in that statement. Like he understood that leadership from the top was as important as lower ranks. That Finn was as important as the other adults in these kids' lives.

Gage held my gaze. "You ever think about having kids?"

I blinked. *Wow. Okay. Holy personal question.* "Not in the cards for me. For some guys? Yeah, I can totally see it. I'll happily watch from the sidelines."

"Fair enough. Might you consider mentoring some of our kids? Even a single kid? We need good role models..."

His original question now made more sense. My immediate thought was mentoring kids in creative writing—teaching them about the world of publishing.

Gage didn't mean that, though.

"I'll see if we can organize something. Spring's a local graduate, right? She might have some ideas of how to get a student more involved."

The laughter from Gage was unexpected. The grin was also a contrast to the serious nature of our previous topic. "Spring Dixon. Oh God." He rubbed his forehead. "Kennedy was before my time, but I've taught or been principal to every other Dixon sister. I doubt it'll come as a surprise when I say Spring was—" He made a rolling gesture with his hand.

I arched an eyebrow.

"Challenging. In a good way. She had to question everything. And I mean *everything*. She was the editor for the school newspaper, and I never knew what to expect. The teacher responsible for supervision wasn't great at, uh, supervising. I survived that year—barely. Autumn was such a treat by comparison."

Spring's younger sister. "And her twin, Summer?"

Another chuckle. "Not as...defiant...as Spring. But still a handful. And I can't say more."

"At least I'm now able to identify all of them. I've never met seven sisters who so resemble each other." Most of them had long black hair and pale-blue eyes, like carbon copies of Spring at various ages. Only Kennedy had chestnut-brown hair.

"Yes. I can say the same—except I don't even think I've met seven other sisters at all."

I laughed. "True that. Okay, I should be going."

The doors to the gym opened, and people started pouring out.

Finn was near the front of the pack and, when he spotted me, he made a beeline my way. "Hey, Mr. Clayton. Ulysses." He gave me *that* look. Clearly, he was still annoyed.

"I need to go speak to the players. Nice to see you, Finnegan." With that, Gage headed toward the gym.

"Can I talk to you?" Finn gazed around at the milling students.

"Sure."

He gestured toward the door to the outside.

I followed him.

When we arrived in the parking lot, he stopped. "Why are you here?"

"The basketball game?"

He arched an eyebrow. The streetlamps cast shadows across his face.

"Seriously, Finn."

"Did you go to the bathroom?"

"What?" I stared at him. Then I laughed. "Uh, no. I didn't go to the bathroom."

"This time." He didn't appear the least bit appeased.

"Finn—"

"Did you talk to Mr. Clayton? About what's going on?"

I nodded. "And I'll tell you what I told him—I don't have a complete grasp of what's going on. When I do, I'll let him know." *I'll probably go to print first...but I will tell him.*

"What about Thelma? She's being *rescued* in a couple of days. Look, I'm going to go down to the shelter myself." He ran his hands through his hair. "Unless you promise me you're working on it. That you're going to save her."

Be careful. "It's coming together, Finn, I promise."

He didn't look convinced. "I have to go."

A pang of disappointment resonated in my chest. We hadn't talked about what happened the other night. I still didn't have a read on his feelings. Well, upset with me for keeping a secret—he'd made that abundantly clear. The rest? I didn't have a clue. "I'll see you around though, right?"

"Yeah. Sure." And then he was gone.

Chapter Twenty-Six

Finn

Mission City Man Grows Prize-Winning Petunias.

Nine-Year-Old Violin Prodigy Taking Classical Music World by Storm.

Meet the Nurse Who Cared for Preemie Babies for Fifty Years.

I scrolled and scrolled and scrolled.

All of the stories Ulysses had written since coming to Mission City in July. And I found tons of them. Standard ones about crime and politics. Stuff one would expect from a small town.

But also, a huge number of human-interest stories. About people who might've otherwise be forgotten in the hustle and bustle of everyday life.

"Watcha doing?" Miriam plopped onto the couch next to me.

I closed the browser on my phone. "Nothing important."

"If you say so." She eyed me. "Have you spoken to Giancarlo?"

I shook my head. "His arraignment was yesterday while we were at that accident on the mountain road."

"Crazy driver."

"Yeah. Seth said the woman must've been going almost a hundred klicks when she crashed."

"I can't believe she's alive."

"Me either." Although her injuries were pretty devastating and she faced months in rehab to recover from all those broken bones. The human body just wasn't designed to withstand those kinds of forces. "I mean, I was on shift and so couldn't have gone anyway. And we're down a body because we lost Giancarlo—"

"Yeah." Miriam sighed. "It's just...a mess. He got bail, right?"

I nodded. "So he should be around his place. I'll go by after work."

"Tell him I think he's an asshole *and* I hope he gets his shit together sooner rather than later."

I laughed. "I can try. He's more likely to listen to you than me."

She cocked her head.

"He's scared of you. I don't intimidate him."

"You're a pussycat."

"I think that's my point. When did I become such a soft touch?" I groused.

"Oh, Finn, really? You were always the guy who was going to rescue kittens and escort little old ladies across the street. It's why you're such a great firefighter—you do it for the right reasons." She examined her fingernails. "How's it going with the reporter?"

My gaze shot to hers.

She both snickered and rolled her eyes. "Jesus, Finn. You're so damn obvious. You're trying to keep a decorous distance and act like nothing's going on while it's so clear you're going at it like—"

"I wouldn't finish that sentence if I were you." I gave her *that* look. Pretend-threatening.

She laughed. In my face.

More proof I was just a softie at heart. I pressed my hand to her arm. "It's complicated."

"It always is. Do you want to talk—"

The alarm sounded.

We leapt off the couch and headed toward the rig.

Iris was at the wheel today, and we were soon racing toward a warehouse fire in the business district.

I tried to push aside the question of how many more fires we were going to see as we pulled up to the massive blaze.

"Goddamnit." Miriam cursed as we unloaded.

"Let's get the hoses—"

Seth ran over, waving his arms. As frantic as I'd ever seen him. "There's a woman unaccounted for. She works in the back office."

My heart rate kicked up. "Any chance she got out and wandered away?" Stuff like that happened.

"No. Her car's still in the lot and no one has seen her. The back's not on fire yet. I can't get the door open."

That he was even trying spoke to his both dedication and stupidity.

"We've got the hoses." Iris joined Miriam, Toby, and several others.

"Marlon, you're with me." I gestured.

He didn't complain—but he didn't hustle either.

I grabbed the axe, and we headed around to the back. As Seth said, the back half wasn't engulfed yet—but that was coming.

On instinct, I tried the door.

Nope. Locked.

Grateful the door was wood, I took a few really good swings and was able to pop the lock. So many things could've gone sideways by this point—and so many still could. But I had faith we were going to be okay.

Thick, black smoke billowed out as the air provided fuel to the fire. Still, I had to try. I felt my way around until I came to the first closed door. I pushed it open.

Empty office.

I moved to the next door, labeled washroom.

More smoke and the noise from the fire was growing louder and louder.

This door didn't open as easily, and quickly it became apparent why—someone was lying against the door.

I dropped to my hands and knees and then tried to push the door with my shoulder.

The body shifted. Whoever they might be—they'd be damn sore tomorrow. If they weren't already dead.

After a couple of really good shoves, I managed to dislodge her enough to maneuver her out. Her dress caught in the door, and I clumsily ripped at the fabric.

Smoke continued to surround me.

Have to get her out. Have to get out. Have to survive.

Marlon gestured that he'd take her.

Between the two of us, we secured her over his shoulder.

He was halfway to the door—with me just a step behind—when a loud explosion sounded.

The whoosh of air knocked me down.

Marlon staggered, but he kept going

A beam crashed within inches of my face. *That should've killed me.*

Except now, my route of escape was cut off.

Marlon turned, waved, and then pushed his way out of the building.

Was that a wave that he'll be back or a wave goodbye?

Panic engulfed me as my breathing intensified.

I'm not going to die today. I have Mom and Ulysses. I haven't told the stubborn fool how I feel about him. There's so much I just haven't done.

I tried to dislodge the beam.

It wouldn't budge.

Another crack.

Something hit my head.

Everything went black.

Chapter Twenty-Seven

Ulysses

"I don't care who you say you are, you're not getting in to see my patient." The Asian nurse with the piercing dark-brown eyes stared at me with his hands on his hips.

Quinton. The nurse's name's Quinton. We'd met at Fifties weeks ago.

"He's my boyfriend. You saw me with him." Because desperation was in order. Yes, Finn and I hadn't defined our relationship in terms of words—but he had, somehow, become my everything.

Quinton's eyebrow arched.

"Fiancé." I jutted my chin. "New engagement."

"Still not a spouse or a family member."

"But—"

"Quinton?" A soft, female voice came from behind us.

We both turned to find Miriam. She had bags under her red-rimmed eyes. "Quinton, this is Ulysses. He's really special to Finn. Please let him in. As a favor to me?"

"Oh dear." Quinton moved to the firefighter. "You look like shit."

"We almost lost him."

"He's going to be okay."

I hoped the nurse had some insider knowledge I lacked because *injured in a fire* sounded really fucking bad to me.

"Yeah?" Miriam gazed at Quinton hopefully.

Or at least what I read as hope. I just didn't know her well enough.

"Yeah. The doctor says once we get his oxygen levels higher, that we can move him out of the ICU. He's a bit of a mess, but he's going to recover. Okay?" He patted her arm.

"So can Ulysses see him?"

I had no idea what that request might be costing her. Surely she'd want to see Finn as well.

Quinton eyed me. "His mom's away on a cruise. Finn's insisting we not call her."

Despite myself, I chuckled. "Ms. O'Sullivan is *not* going to like that."

"Nope." The nurse grinned. "Fierce Mama Bear alert. She's almost as bad as my mom. Nurses, eh?"

I remembered having heard Quinton's mother used to be a nurse. She'd retired about the time Quinton married the surgeon Leo with his two kids. "I wouldn't know about nurses. Fortunately, I haven't spent much time around medical professionals."

"Oh, you're a lucky one. Yeah, nurses are fierce protectors of their patients." He eyed me. "Even if we're not mamas."

"No, but you're a—" I floundered for the word.

"Technically a stepfather." He cocked his head. "But I only use the *step* part because the kids have two dads. As far as I'm concerned, there's no daylight."

"They're lucky to have you." *And I wish we could stop this fucking chitchat so I can see Finn.*

"All right, let's get you in to see Finn. I need to check his vitals first, though. Give me a minute?"

"Take as long as you need."

He arched an eyebrow.

"Within reason? It's killing me—being out here when he's in there." I gestured toward the room.

"All good." Quinton turned and headed into the room.

"How are you holding up?" I wanted to pat Miriam's arm. Something. Anything. Some kind of grounding—to assure me she was okay. To affirm Finn was going to survive.

"I'm okay. We did what we had to do. A few minutes more, and—" She shuddered.

"Okay, you can go in." Quinton made his way over to us. I wanted to demand of Miriam what she meant—but getting to Finn was more important.

"Thank you."

"Fifteen minutes. Don't wear him out."

"Yeah. Okay." I hustled in—hoping Quinton could take care of Miriam.

The room was dimly lit with the blinds shut tight. Night would fall soon. Darkness to shroud the world.

Finn's vivid red hair stood out against the stark white of the sheet. As well as his sallow pallor.

I expected an oxygen mask, but he only had a canula to deliver that crucial pure life-sustaining gas.

His eyes fluttered open—the vivid blue almost completely eclipsed by the black pupils. He reached out.

Within a step, I was by his side. I grasped that hand—clinging to it as if it were a lifeline. "I was so worried."

He swallowed. "I need water."

"Are you allowed?" Even as I asked, I spotted a jug of water and a cup on the nightstand. Reluctantly, I released his hand so I could pour some water. "There's a straw."

"Thanks." His voice rasped.

I held the straw for him, and he sucked greedily. "Maybe not too much?" I had no idea.

Finally, he pulled back.

I put the glass on the nightstand. Then I pulled a chair over so I could sit. Finally, I did what I really wanted to do—I grasped his hand tightly in mine. "You're alive."

"I'm okay. Truly."

I feathered his hair back. "You look like shit. Although I think Quinton said much the same thing to Miriam, so hopefully some of it's due to your shift."

"She's here?"

"Outside. She told Quinton to let me in."

"He checked with me." He swallowed. "I'm grateful he did."

"You realize your mother's going to be so pissed when she hears you didn't call her."

"She's near Alaska. She's been wanting to take this cruise forever. I'm not going to ruin it."

"You're her child."

"She'll get over it."

"I don't know if I would. I'd want to know."

"Miriam called you?"

"Actually, Toby did. Although I'm certain Miriam told him to. Actually, I have no idea. I just raced here. To get to you. Now, can you talk about what happened?"

Finn gazed toward the closed blinds.

"Do you want me to open them?"

"Nah. My head hurts like a sonofabitch. Light'll be brutal. Not that it'll stop Quinton from shining that damn light in my eyes."

"Because he has to."

"Because he has to." Finn confirmed that. "I get it. Really, I do."

"So relax and talk to me." I wanted him to get on with it—but that wasn't my place. I still had no clue what was going on.

His troubled eyes met mine. "Bad fire."

"Yep."

"Someone inside."

"And you went in." Seemed pretty obvious, but I needed a clear picture.

He nodded. "Broke wood door, went in. Found her. Marlon hauled her onto his back—"

"Really?"

Another nod.

"Oh, okay. I wouldn't have predicted that, but whatever. Uh, good for him."

Finn winced.

"Ah. So not good?"

He flicked his hand. "He got her out."

"But...?"

"A beam fell in my path. I—" He swallowed. "He saw. He waved, and then he left."

My stomach bottomed out. "Left you there to die?"

"I don't—" He closed his eyes. "Maybe he was waving that he'd send someone in, right?"

I didn't—for even a scintilla of a second—believe that. Still, I couldn't know what had been in Marlon's mind. In his heart. "But you got out."

"More debris fell on my head and I think I passed out."

"Jesus."

"Yeah. But Miriam and Toby got me out. Or at least that's what the paramedic said. Leda. Yappy woman. Insisted on talking the entire time."

"Because she needed you to stay conscious?"

He wrinkled his nose. "I suppose."

"And you did?"

"Yeah."

"Did they scan your head?"

"Yeah."

I waited for more—but nothing was forthcoming.

"Have you seen the doctor?"

"Concussion."

"Yikes. I've never had one."

"This is my second."

"Oh?"

"Yeah...second in nine months."

That had me sitting up straighter.

Slowly, he nodded. "I don't know if I was blessed before or am cursed now."

"I'm always hesitant to use the word *cursed.* Maybe...unlucky?" I continued to grip his hand. "But there's more to this story, isn't there?"

"Yeah. That last concussion? We shouldn't have been in that mess in the first place. It's complicated—" He sighed. "Firefighting's dangerous. I get that...but that shouldn't have happened, and today shouldn't have happened either."

"Marlon?"

"Today? Yeah? Maybe? Giancarlo screwed up in February. But not intentional, right? And a kid died and maybe that's why he turned to drugs? Maybe?"

"I don't know. Have you told anyone about this?"

His eyes grew wide. "If I tell Chief, Marlon's just going to deny it. Say I misunderstood...or made it up or some shit."

"Yeah, I figured."

"But if I don't say something? And it happens again? What if someone gets killed? And I could've done something to prevent it?"

I squeezed his hand. "I've got you, okay? You're off work for a few weeks, right?"

"A few days, at least."

"Well, then don't worry about it."

"What do you mean?"

"Just that I've got your back. That everything's going to work out."

"I don't understand."

"And I can't say any more at this point." *Because I'm not sure what I've figured out and I still want you to be vigilant. In fact, maybe I'll just wrap you in bubble wrap and keep you with me forever.* "Look, just rest, okay Finn? You scared the shit out of me."

"I think I scared the shit out of myself." He offered a rueful smile. "But I don't understand."

"You don't have to. You just have to focus on getting better. On healing up. Then you can think about going back to work."

"Fuck, Ulysses, I'm not a child. I don't need to be petted on the head and told not to worry." He winced. "What if something bad happens when I'm not there?"

"That can't be your concern. You just need to worry about yourself right now."

"But I always worry about everyone else."

Which is something I love about you. I squeezed his hand yet again. “Just don’t go and do something stupid, okay?”

“Does that mean you care?”

I cocked my head. “Of course I care. I always care.”

“No.” He squinted. “I don’t mean like you care because you’re human and I’m human. I mean—” He rubbed his forehead with the hand not gripping mine. “You know what I mean.”

“Yeah, I do. I know what you mean *and* I care a damn lot about you. I don’t want to...but I do.”

He closed his eyes—almost like he was basking in my words. Finally, he opened his eyes. “I care about you, if that helps you. Fuck...I think I love you.” He did a slow blink, then his eyes shut.

I didn’t answer.

When Quinton shooed me out, I went willingly.

And spent a lot of time trying to figure out what to do next.

Chapter Twenty-Eight

Finn

The Fire Chief, the Corruption, the Drugs, and the Illegal Dog Fighting.

I balanced my laptop on my lap on my own nice, private couch. I wasn't supposed to be looking at the screen, but fuck it. This was too important. The top story for the Mission City Gazette.

Ulysses's byline.

I scanned the article, noting Marlon, Giancarlo, Selah, Meyer, and Debra's names.

Jesus.

Then I forced myself to read the story from beginning to end.

Marlon was at the center of all this. What had started out as harmless gambling had grown into an addiction beyond his control. He'd started a dog-fighting ring as a way to get other gamblers to pony up their money. The brutality of the fighting made my stomach churn. I'd *known* some of those dogs, walked them, cheered when they went off to "homes." I wanted to puke.

Then he'd turned to drug dealing as a way to bring in more money. At that point he'd gotten Giancarlo addicted. And yes, he'd sold the bad drugs to David—so the boy's death could be laid at his feet as well.

Then the total shit needed a place to launder the drug money—so he used the restaurant. And the dog fighting took place behind Tully's after hours with Debra's help. And yes, Meyer and Selah were involved in faking paperwork and disappearing the dogs.

Jesus.

Finally, Ulysses analyzed the fires.

Turned out, all the buildings were insured by the same company. That company was raking in money—and suddenly all Chief Gerard's money woes, including delinquent mortgage payments, were all neatly paid off. Marlon ran up the debt, and his daddy found a way to pay it all off.

Half a dozen photographs. The fighting ring behind the restaurant. A drug dealer selling to kids. Kids I fucking knew.

My head ached and I rubbed my eyes. This was all just too damn much to absorb. Improbable. Impossible. And yet clearly laid out in meticulous detail. Including an interview with the top RCMP officer in Mission City. Sergeant Gregory Wilder said they'd been close to making arrests, but now most of the arrests were in progress and the perpetrators were in jail.

Yeah, but if he'd gone public before the perpetrators get arrested, wouldn't they run?

That thought churned in my gut. That Marlon, Gerard, Selah, Meyer, Debra, and everyone else involved might actually get away with all this. But Gregory said arrests had been made. Was it too soon for Ulysses to list them?

Wrong. Wrong. Wrong.

And where did that leave me? I'd told investigators what I remembered about the fire. But I hadn't told them about Marlon's wave. *Did I imagine it? Or did he really leave me to die?* I'd never had a sense of the time between him walking out of the building with the victim, and Miriam coming to rescue me.

The neurologist who examined me said I might never get those memories back. That basically I'd been knocked in the head and she was surprised I remembered as much as I did.

I hadn't mentioned the wave—just that I had a clear memory of the beam falling and Marlon leaving with the woman. He'd been hailed a hero. If what Ulysses had just revealed was true—and I had no reason to doubt it—that hero's cap was coming off damn fast.

My phone rang.

Mom.

"Hi, Mom. How—"

"Finnegan O'Sullivan, my hard-headed child, what the actual fuck?"

I sighed. "I can explain. Uh, where are you?"

"I just got off the cruise ship in Vancouver Harbor. And I saw an article in the Vancouver Sun, written by your boyfriend, about all these shenanigans in Mission City, and when I check that out, I see you were injured by falling debris in a fire—and were in the hospital for several days—and I didn't know anything about it. Did you break your fucking fingers as well?"

"Huh?" I rubbed my temple. Valerie O'Sullivan did *not* use the f-word.

Ever.

"I assume you broke all your fingers and that's why you were unable to call me. Is that correct?"

"No?"

"Finnegan."

"Yes, Mom?"

"Was that a question or a statement?"

"Uh...both?"

"Finnegan." Laced with disappointment.

"You were on the cruise of a lifetime. Your bucket list. There's nothing you could've done for me. Miriam drove me home. Iris has checked in. Toby brought soup."

"And Ulysses? Your boyfriend?"

"See article published in the paper." I rubbed my temple. "When do you get home? Do you need me to pick you up? Did I say I would?"

"Oh, Finnegan, my love. I can hear your pain. Head?"

"Yeah, Mom." Part of me just wanted to get a *mom cuddle* and sink into the comfort.

"I'm good, my dear son. A couple from Hope were on the cruise, and they offered to drive me to Mission City."

"Mission City's not entirely on the way."

"They don't like driving the big highway, so they would've been driving through Mission City anyway. Truthfully, they would've driven me regardless. Charming couple. I've made new friends, I think."

"Well, I'd love to meet them." I liked the idea Mom had made new friends. She attracted people—but making enduring friendships could be tough. Especially with her hours at the hospital.

"You know, I might arrange that. Actually, they have a friend they want to introduce me to."

"Oh?"

"A widower."

"In Hope?" *You want your mom to be happy. Hope is just an hour away. And who's to say your mother is going to fall in love with some random stranger?*

"Abbotsford. They were all professors together at the university. The couple were a few years older and have retired."

"So this guy's a prof?"

"Yes." Mom chuckled. "A mismatch if I've ever seen one."

"Hey." I said that sharply. "You're brilliant, vivacious, and any man would be lucky to meet you."

"Oh my dear boy." The smile was evident in her voice. "It's just dinner."

"Well, I want to meet him, okay? Promise?"

"How about I meet him first? Oh, they're waving at me. I'll be home in an hour. Should I have them drop me off at your house?"

The laptop display indicated it almost six. "Go home, Mom. Put your feet up. We can touch base tomorrow—if you're not working."

"I'm not. I planned for a day to resettle. I'll worry, though."

"I'm truly fine. Tomorrow, then?" Another day for me to get closer to healing—whatever that looked like.

"You're tired?"

"Yeah, I really am. I might have an early night." Totally hadn't been the plan—but she didn't need to know that.

"I love you."

"I love you too. I'm glad you had a good time."

She huffed. Then cut the line.

I smiled to myself. *I did the right thing in not calling. She'll get over her pique eventually. She always does.* Not that I went out of my way to piss her off. But I was a stubborn O'Sullivan—so it was bound to happen now and again.

My phone buzzed with an incoming text.

Ulysses.

—Up for company? Understandable if you're not. —

I hesitated. I wasn't truly up for a guest. Still, I didn't want him to worry. *Sure, shovel some shit while you're at it—of course you want to see him.* At least here, I could be honest with myself.

—Sure. I'm...not great company. —

A long pause.

—What can I bring? —

—Yourself. —

Another pause.

—And a burger? Soup? Chili? —

—Sure. —

—Which? —

—Any. —

—Or all. Be there soon. —

—You don't need to bring all. —

I waited.

No response *and* the message went un-replied to. *Stubborn cuss.*

Yeah. Except I'd do the same damn thing. Had when Giancarlo had been laid up with that bad ankle.

Giancarlo.

For the umpteenth time, I hit speed dial. For the umpteenth-and-first time, the call went straight to voice mail. *Fucking asshole. I would stand by you. Or I think I would. I'm not such a boy scout myself. I know shit happens.* Would I forgive him for driving high? Probably not for a while. But I'd encourage him to get help. Stand by him if he went for rehab. Just...I needed to fucking talk to him.

I closed my laptop and put it on the end table. Then I chose to be nearly horizontal in the recliner—less pressure in my head. Less pressure equaled less pain. Or so I told myself. I really should've gone to lie down, but Ulysses was on his way over.

My boyfriend? Fuck buddy? Partner? What is the label for what we have? I just didn't have an answer for that.

Chapter Twenty-Nine

Ulysses

He looks so damn peaceful. I don't want to wake him.

That said, my stomach rumbled at the smell emanating from the fragrant bags of food. I'd barely eaten anything in the last two days.

The live interview in CNC's studio in downtown Vancouver had capped off the insane ride. I hadn't wanted to do something so publicly—on camera, no less—but Spring talked to me about it. Said I'd bring attention to Mission City, the newspaper, and the hardworking but under-resourced RCMP force.

Sure. Yeah. All that.

And the interview had been likely to drag up my past.

I'd lucked out.

Jake McGrath, a recent Mission City arrival himself, had taken the interview. He was covering for the regular host of a show that ran across Canada. Personally, I wasn't sure this little town deserved that much of a spotlight.

Judging by the way my phone blew up after the interview, I'd been wrong.

Despite my worries, Jake had been fair, open, and hadn't brought up the Vancouver debacle. He'd even teased me about small-town living being far more interesting than most city folk thought.

I'd laughed.

That laughter hadn't even been forced.

"Are you feeding me or just going to stand there staring at me?" Finn cracked an eye.

Then winced.

"How's the head? Are you due for more painkillers?"

"Not taking them. Pain's manageable. I'm going to live." He eyed me. "You can take off your jacket, you know."

"I know." I held up the bags. "Soup, chili, or burger?"

"What are you having?"

"Well, I brought two servings of everything so you don't have to be a polite host and take my preferences into consideration."

He grinned. "That's planning."

"And we have enough food to last several days."

"So you don't have to go anywhere?"

"So I don't have to go anywhere." I shifted my messenger bag on my shoulder. "Even brought my laptop. Spring's holding down the fort. I will warn you that I might have to do some interviews with other media outlets. I can do them from your mom's room."

"With the frilly flowers?"

I laughed. "I don't give a shit about that. I just—" I swallowed hard. "I don't want to leave you. I should've been here."

"Hey." He extended his hand.

I hotfooted to the kitchen. After dropping the food onto the counter and putting my messenger bag on the dining room table,

I made my way back to Finn. With gratitude, I grasped his hand. I knelt by the side of the recliner so our faces were mere inches apart. "I wanted to tell you. But the police asked me not to speak to anyone. And yeah, you're not just *anyone*, and I trust you with my life—"

"But you couldn't take the risk. I don't blame you. I'll never fault you for that." He stroked his fingers down my cheek. "Now, what did I miss?"

"You read the article?"

"Several times, yeah."

"Has anyone called you?"

He shook his head. "Well, Mom. I figured the fire hall is probably up in arms about the entire thing."

"I'm sure. I did a live interview with Jake McGrath at CNC."

"Marnie's husband?" His smile was a little dreamy.

I cocked my head. "Yes, they're married."

He grinned. "Don't tell Loriana—Marnie's my favorite librarian. Loriana's—"

"Intrusive?"

"Yeah. That."

"You warned me."

"Did I?" He frowned.

"Pretty sure you were the one. The matchmaking librarian."

"Who's terrible at it. Yep, that's her. Marnie's shyer. Quieter. But just as kind. Very different women." He tried to sit up. "I've only met Jake in passing. Good-looking guy."

I chuckled. "Yes, he's made for television. He's covering the national show tonight." I gently laid my hand on Finn's chest.

"Oh?" He frowned. "I can sit up."

"Chili, burger, or soup?"

"Burger."

“Great. Stay put.” I pressed a kiss to his lips, rose, and then headed to the kitchen. “Root beer?”

“Yes, please. God, I’m so tired.”

“You’re barely out of the hospital.” I washed my hands. “And you almost died.”

“I didn’t *almost die*.”

I removed the lettuce and tomato from our burgers before nuking them. “Uh...yeah. If Miriam hadn’t found you then you would have died. So that’s *almost died*. Nice try, though.” The microwave beeped. I yanked out the burgers and put in the plate full of fries and onion rings. “You want fries, onion rings, or a mix?”

“A man after my heart. God, I love you. Combination would be amazing. I’m completely salivating at the smell.”

He sighed—so loudly I heard it over the buzzing of the microwave.

God, I love you.

That was just a figure of speech. An expression. Nothing more than a throwaway line.

I cleared my throat. “Uh, you’re welcome.”

The microwave beeped. I removed the plate and set about organizing two meals. Once I finished, I grabbed a root beer and headed to the living room where he sat—still reclined, but straighter.

He offered a broad smile. “You’re the best.”

“Right. I bought a burger.”

“Sure.” He accepted the plate. “But you remembered I love onion rings and that I like root beer with my onion rings. Those are very important things.”

To that, I chuckled. “You’re an easy man to please, Finnegan O’Sullivan.”

“Don’t you forget it.”

I held his gaze. "I won't. I promise—I won't." I headed back to the kitchen.

"Hey, do you think you can find that interview with Jake McGrath?"

"Sure. Their producer sent me a private link."

"May I watch it?"

"I don't see why not."

"Cool. I'm not certain I taped the news. It didn't occur to me. That Vancouver would pick it up—let alone the show that runs across Canada."

"Mission City's profile just went up." After putting the containers of chili and soup in the fridge, I grabbed my plate and can of diet cola and headed back to the living room.

"Hopefully in a good way. That our profile went up. I mean, the bad guys were caught, right?" Finn pointed to his plate. "This is amazing."

"Make certain you tell your mother that I'm feeding you."

"Oh, she's back from her cruise. She met a nice couple from Hope, and they're driving her home. She says they want to introduce her to a professor who teaches over in Abbotsford."

"*Introduce her?*" I put my plate on the dining room table and dug my laptop out of my messenger bag. "Like, romantically?"

"That's what she implied. Hey, what are you doing? You need to eat."

"Yes, Finnegan." I opened the laptop and connected to his WiFi.

"I'm serious. Whatever you're doing—" He cut off.

I turned to face him. "What?"

"Is that your phone buzzing?"

"Yeah."

"Ulysses, it's pretty much buzzing nonstop."

"Yeah." I turned back to the laptop, located the email from the producer, and pulled it up.

Finn cleared his throat. "Shouldn't you be, I don't know, checking to see who's messaging you?"

"I will." I carried the laptop over to him and put it on the coffee table. He'd have to squint, but he didn't really need to see my mug up close—and he knew what Jake looked like. I pressed play, and then I headed back to the dining room table to grab my rapidly cooling burger, fries, and onion rings.

With only half an ear, I listened to the interview. As I devoured my burger, I scrolled through the hundreds of texts, DMs, and comments to my post on social media.

Spring's newest message popped up.

—You better be driving or getting laid or something important. Shit's blowing up.—

I blinked. Probably the clearest indication of why I had so damn many texts. Three more came in even as I took another bite of burger.

Surreal.

For years, I'd wanted this level of attention. To be noticed. Writing for the Vancouver Sun had been a feather in my cap—but I'd wanted more recognition. To be seen by a wider audience. Judging by the interest I was garnering now, my interview with Jake was even bigger than I'd realized it was going to be.

"Ulysses?"

"Hmm?" I turned my attention to Finn.

He pointed to the dark computer screen.

"Oh, did it turn off? I can—"

"I watched the entire interview. And ate my entire meal. Your food must be cold by now. And your phone is still buzzing."

Offering a sheepish grin, I nudged a French fry. "I should nuke these again."

My phone screen flashed.

—The rot in Mission City goes deeper than you know. Meet me on Friesen Road. Two miles past the dump. Come alone. —

I stared at the phone.

This made no sense. Not that I was hubristic enough to believe I'd figured everything out. But I'd put all the pieces together—and they'd fit. Not a single loose thread.

What if you're wrong? What if Gerard and Marlon aren't at the top of the food chain? What if they're acting on someone else's behalf? What if—

I tried to shut down that line of thinking. Everything. I'd turned over every single thing I could to the cops. Well, everything that wouldn't reveal sources and methods. The cop who'd sat with me yesterday, Corporal Colton Pritchard, hadn't been all that impressed. But he'd also reluctantly admitted they didn't have what I had. I'd given him eighteen hours to arrest whoever he wanted—but that I was going public at noon today. And, as promised, I had.

I shot a text off to Spring.

—You know who's been arrested yet? —

—Colton won't say. Seth and Dorrie aren't answering my calls either. —

Seth was a constable and so maybe not read in? Corporal Dorrie Duhamel was Colton's partner. So maybe she was *too* read in?

—Doesn't help that Colton's your ex-brother-in-law. —

—You think? —

I was trying to think of something clever when her next message arrived.

—RCMP Mission just announced a press conference at ten am. —

I urgently needed to be sure they'd done their part. —*We'll both be there.* —

—*Bet your ass. I'm going home.* —

I checked the time. After eight.

—*Shit. Sorry. Yes—go.* —

—*Later. Good job.* —

I rubbed my forehead.

"Ulysses?"

"What? Shit. Sorry. I was texting Spring."

"You look exhausted."

The rot in Mission City goes deeper than you know. I sighed. "I am. Look, I have to run back to the city for a few things. I'll only be gone an hour or two." *Damn. I need to text Spring to let her know what I'm doing. Because I can't tell Finn.*

"You don't have to come back." Finn's voice was soft.

"Do you not want me to come back?" Mine was a little sharper than I intended.

"Of course I want you to come back. But if you're too tired to make the drive, I'll understand."

I waved him off. "All good. I promise I'll be back." I rose and headed his way. I took his empty plate and my still mostly full one to the kitchen. "I'll eat this when I get back."

"And this can't wait until tomorrow?"

"Uh, no. I've got a press conference first thing in the morning. This needs to be settled before that."

"Okay." He sighed.

Do you really have to leave him? Isn't there another way?

I pondered that.

What? Ask the sender of the text to drop by here for a beer? Nope. I have to go.

I wrapped the food in cling wrap and put it in the fridge. Then I headed back to the living room. "You going to be okay? You need something?"

Finn shook his head. "All good. I might be in bed when you come back. Just come to bed, okay?"

"I don't like the idea of leaving you here with the door unlocked."

"So take the spare key. In the junk drawer."

Cute how I already knew which drawer was the one he used for...junk. I grabbed the key and made my way back over to him. "I'm glad you're alive."

"I am too." He offered me an endearing smile. Then handed me my phone.

I frowned.

"You handed it to me when you took my plate. Are you sure you should be driving? You're really distracted. Something you need to talk about?"

I shook my head. "All good. I promise." I pressed a kiss to his lips.

Words of endearment were on the tip of my tongue—but they wouldn't come. Or, rather, I couldn't force them.

"Go to bed. Call your mom. Just...take care."

"You're sure you're okay?"

"Yeah. Fine." I plastered a bright smile on my face and turned to leave. I forced myself to leave without turning around.

Because I had a sinking feeling things were about to go to shit.

Chapter Thirty

Finn

I gave Ulysses a five-minute head start.

Damn fool man. Thought he was going somewhere without me.

After downing a couple of ibuprofens and pissing, I was out the door, in my SUV, and following him to Friesen Road. Two miles past the dump. If my calculations were correct, that was the McFadden property. They used to run a grow-op up there back in the day when marijuana was illegal. When the government changed their tune and made the stuff legal, McFadden tried to go legit. Last I heard, he'd given up. Too damn many regulations. Old fool had never been a rule follower, and his two kids hadn't fallen far from the rotten tree. I'd thought they were all still in jail for the latest fraud.

Clearly I'd been mistaken.

This goes deeper than you know.

Silly man. Ulysses. Handing me his phone with the screen unlocked and the text open for me to see.

Maybe he intended you to see it.

Nah. If he'd wanted me to see it, he would've shown it to me. If he'd wanted my help, all he'd needed to do was ask.

Maybe he was worried about your health.

Well, shit, that might just be true.

Maybe you *should be worried about your health.*

I pushed that thought right out of my mind. If Ulysses was headed up to the McFadden property, then he damn well needed backup.

You realize a quick call to Colton, Dorrie, or Seth will get you that backup.

I needed to shut my inner voice right the fuck off so I could focus. What Ulysses didn't need was me becoming a liability. I was just...watching out for him. I'd hang back. I'd—

Shit.

I nearly drove right past his parked SUV. I hit the brakes, then carefully pulled over and reversed. I eased my pickup so I was positioned just before him. Then I cut the engine.

Damn man's smarter than you—you would've just driven right up to the old place.

Right. So I wouldn't make a good reporter. Or a cop, for that matter. Yet another reason why I'd chosen firefighting as a way to give back to my community—fires scared me less than bullets.

The moon shone—for the moment, but I spotted a few wispy clouds. The weather was supposed to turn tonight. Rain or even snow.

Christ knew, it was cold enough for it.

I ducked close to the ditch with the overgrown grass. One more small hill and I'd be at the property.

Smoke.

Fuck.

More familiar to me than any other scent in the world, the smoke curled around me. I pulled the lapel of my jacket over my nose as I slowed my pace.

When I crested the rise, the McFadden property came into view.

So far, the fire appeared to only be on the second floor of the old homestead. I whipped out my phone and dialed 9-1-1.

My eyes watered as I searched for signs of life in the windows.

Is Ulysses in there? Will I be able to get to him in time? Why didn't I just confront him at my house and demand he bring me with him? Oh, better yet—why didn't I just call Colton?

Questions I would hopefully live to seek answers for.

A shot rang out.

I hit the ground and my phone went skittering away. *Fuck.* I'd lost track of it in the dark.

"I said *get your fucking ass out here*!" A clearly exasperated voice I recognized well. My chief, Gerald McInerny.

Goddamnit.

"I'm not coming out until you tell me who else is involved." Another voice I recognized well. One belonging to a certain stubborn reporter whose hard head I was going to knock—once we got away from the gun. Because I would've laid the deed to my property on the fact Chief had the gun.

I crawled on my belly toward the blaze. The grass mostly covered my approach—and certainly no one was going to hear me over the roar of the rapidly growing fire.

A pile of pallets lay between me and the house—with several outbuildings to my left. I had to figure out whether to try to duck toward them.

Where the fuck is Ulysses?

Come to it...where the fuck is Chief?

"I'm not going to kill you. I just want to know what you know." Gerard—attempting to sound reasonable. Hell, he couldn't even pull that off. The desperation was clear in his tone.

"And I've told you that I turned just about everything over to the police. There's nothing—"

"About everything ain't everything. So just pony on over and—"

Another shot rang out.

Movement by the pallets caught my eye.

Yep, I'd recognize that silhouette anywhere.

Fucking hell. Well, I got myself into this mess. Maybe I can get us out of it?

I wasn't holding my breath. Still, I crawled until I was able to grab Ulysses's ankle.

He spun and nearly hit me.

Only at the last minute did he pull his punch. "Fucking hell."

"Did you say something?" Chief. Bellowing.

"Nope. I didn't say anything." Ulysses angled himself toward the house—obviously where he thought—or knew—Gerard to be. "Just thinking I'm a damn fool idiot for coming out here. I'd have been better staying home."

"With O'Sullivan? Don't worry—he's next."

Just in case I hadn't figured out just how fucked we truly were.

"I'd like to think he's smarter than you." Ulysses held my gaze. "But I'm questioning that assertion."

"Kid's too damn trusting for his own good."

Ulysses arched an eyebrow.

I shrugged as I tried to play the odds in my mind. Us getting out of here alive. Whether keeping my presence a surprise was a good idea or not. If I could save Ulysses—even if that meant sacrificing myself. Finally knowing, in my heart of hearts, that kind of thinking would piss him off even more than me showing up unannounced. Nope. Either we were both surviving or we were both dying.

"How, precisely, did we get into this mess?" Ulysses poked his head over our parapet of pallets.

"Jesus, don't do that." He might have dark skin, but the light from the fire could easily glint off his head and make us a target.

Make him a target.

"We got into this mess because you came here without me." *We got into this mess because I love you and no way was I letting you confront my chief alone.* "We have to do...something."

Ulysses sighed. "He's got a gun. I don't need to remind you that we came unarmed. At least I assume you don't have a gun in your jacket."

"I don't." Said churlishly.

He yanked his phone out of his back pocket. "I need to call Colton."

"I've already called emergency."

"Right."

The heat from the fire was intense. I worried embers would land on the pallets protecting us and catch them on fire. I'd deal with that when it happened. Right now, gun trumped everything. Then I did precisely what I'd admonished Ulysses for doing—I looked.

Gerard got off a shot.

It whizzed past my head.

Ulysses yanked me down. "I know I say you're naïve, but did you think he wouldn't shoot at you?"

"We have a bigger problem."

He snickered. "If he decides to try to shoot through the pallets then I suspect we're dead." He held my gaze. His dark-brown eyes were nearly black in this light.

"There's a propane tank."

He blinked. Then, his eyes widened. "And you think—"

"Even if it's empty, there'll be residual gas. So yeah, it's going to burst and become a projectile."

"It could come this way."

"It could take out the chief."

"Again, Finn, I don't give a shit about him. I just want us to get out of this alive."

A thunderous crack came from the burning house.

Second floor caving in. Thank Christ we weren't in there.

"Finnegan O'Sullivan." Chief's voice bellowed. Even over the roaring fire, his words were clear. "I saw you. I know you're out there."

"We're not coming out." Ulysses shouted back. He glared at me.

Another gunshot rang out. This one entirely too close for comfort as it splintered the wood above our heads.

"Fuck." Ulysses spat the word.

"Sliver?"

"Nope. Just thinking what a fuckwit he is. And that you're going to try to save him."

"Yeah. I am." I raised my hands and, slowly, stood.

"For fuck's sake." Ulysses spat out the curse. And then followed my lead.

"Uh, Chief." I cleared my throat.

Gerard swung the gun back and forth between Ulysses and me—clearly unable to decide who to shoot first. "What?" Another bellow.

"There's a propane tank behind you." With that, I dove for Ulysses, tackling him to the ground.

He landed with an *oof*.

Moments later, a deafening explosion rent the air and consumed the night.

A massive blast of hot air roared across my back, even as Ulysses struggled to get out from under me. "Stay the fuck down. That was the tank exploding. We're lucky it didn't land over here, but that fire just got major fuel."

"Your chief?"

My breath caught. I didn't want to look. No way he survived that blast. Hell, we shouldn't have survived it.

Sirens wailed in the distance.

My gaze clashed with Ulysses's.

"Colton."

We said the name at the same time.

Finally, I rolled off him. "We need to get out of here."

"To try to hide from the cops?"

I snickered. "Yeah, no. Colton's going to know we were here. He'll see my pickup truck and your SUV down the road."

"Fuck."

"Yep, pretty much. I don't know how I'm going to explain this to him." Even as I said the words, snow began to fall. "Colton needs to call the fire department."

"If he hasn't already. This blaze has got to be visible for at least a mile."

More embers fell.

"These pallets are going to catch fire. We need to move."

We ran.

When we were far enough away, Ulysses put his hands on his hips. "What the *hell* do you think you were doing at the scene of an active shooter? You could've gotten shot."

I blinked. "You were here!"

"And so were you!"

"So why are you upset that I was there when you were here?"

"Because I fucking love you and you scared me the fuck to death!"

"Yeah, well, I fucking love you too, so where does that leave us?"

We stared at each other as the snow began to fall in earnest.

"Hands up!" Colton's voice rang through the air.

"It's me. Finn. And Ulysses is here with me." We both raised our hands in the air and slowly turned toward the end of the driveway where Colton stood.

"Jesus, Finnegan. What the hell's going on?"

"You call in the fire?"

"Yeah, but I told them I had to secure the scene first. So...is the scene secure?"

"Chief's dead—if that's what you're asking. I think he was alone." I turned my attention to Ulysses.

He shrugged. "I think so. He said everyone else had been arrested."

"McInerny's here?" Colton advanced toward us.

I pointed to the massive inferno over my shoulder. "I think the fire got him. Which would be the height of irony."

More sirens sounded from the distance.

"Hall Three, right? They're going to need reinforcements."

Colton merely stared for a moment before heading back the way he'd come.

"What...?" Ulysses gestured.

"He's not in uniform. Probably doesn't have a radio."

"He's got a cell phone right, though?"

"Quicker to reach dispatch through his radio." I shrugged.

"You shouldn't be out in the cold."

"Uh, neither should you." I blinked. "You said you loved me."

"Love." He squinted. "I love you. I still think you're an idiot—"

"Hey, I saved your ass—"

"I would've found a way out." He appeared positively indignant.

"Well, now you don't have to. Uh, maybe we can go somewhere warmer?"

"You two can go sit in the back of the cruiser." Colton threw blankets at us.

That we deftly caught. I unfolded mine and wrapped it around my shoulders. Wasn't likely to keep the chill at bay—but it might keep the worst of the snow off my clothes. "Why do we have to sit in the back of the cruiser? We're not criminals." Now I was indignant.

Colton glared—his dark brown eyes nearly black in the night. "Because I have a dead body and arson. Technically, you two shouldn't even be in the same vehicle."

"We're not suspects." This seemed super obvious to me. Clearly Colton didn't agree.

"Finn has only been out of the hospital three days. He should be home. Or, even better, back at the hospital being checked out." Ulysses. Trying to plead my case.

"Being at the hospital is never better." I attempted to look serious. The shiver wracking me really didn't help make the argument.

"Cruiser. Now." Colton pointed.

With Ulysses beside me, I trudged that way. "In case I forget later, I really did mean that I love you."

He grasped my hand. "I know. Trust me, I know."

Chapter Thirty-One

Ulysses

I sat at my desk and eyed my phone as if it had all the answers.

—Can I ask you on a date?—

I held my breath after sending the text to Finn. At least Colton had located Finn's phone and returned it. Bruised, but still intact.

He replied immediately. *—You just want to get laid. —*

—Maybe. —

—There's no maybe about it. —

Before I could answer, my phone rang. 'Hey." I tried to inject as much softness as I could.

"Hello, yourself. I woke up alone this morning."

"Yeah." I winced. "You were sleeping so peacefully—and I had this press conference to get to." *All or nothing.* "Can I ask you on a third date? And fourth? How many dates do we have to count before we stop saying they're dates?"

A long silence ensued. Then some rustling. "This is beginning to sound like...well, a long-term relationship. Except you don't do relationships. Remember?"

"If you want to know the answer to that question, you'd better turn up to those dates. I'll pick you up at seven. Okay?"

"I can meet you there—wherever *there* is."

"Stavros's. Reservation for seven-thirty."

"Wow. Fancy."

I rolled my eyes. Stavros's Greek wasn't the fanciest in town...but the place was a step above what we normally did—which was fast food. "Would you prefer the Italian place?"

"And have you spend double the money? No, I'm good. You know me—I'm just as happy at Fifties as anywhere else."

"Would you prefer Fifties?" I'd grown quite fond of the place myself in my months living in Mission City.

"Stavros's is fine. I haven't been there in years. I'll be ready for you to pick me up at seven. For our *date*." He hung up.

I spent the next six hours fielding interviews from various news organizations across the spectrum. British Columbia, of course. A couple from around Canada. A few online and one from Australia because of course. Why the hell not? I was wondering about that call when I remembered we had a recent Aussie transplant. Whether Dean being in Mission City for just over a year had anything to do with the interest from the land down under, I had no idea. Something to ask, the next time I saw him.

"You look spent." Spring put another Timmie's coffee on my desk.

"Thank you. And I'm never going to sleep tonight."

"You've got your date with Finn tonight. I'm certain you'll find a bit of insomnia will be a small price to pay."

"How do you know about my date?"

"Because I was sitting at the desk next to you when you spoke to him. Sheesh, Boss. Get with the program." She chuckled. "You on speaking terms with Colton again?"

"I didn't realize we were ever not on speaking terms." I chuckled. "He's still mad I didn't call. That said, one less bad guy to prosecute isn't necessarily a bad thing. Not that I wanted Gerard dead or anything."

"Or anything."

"But, still. Not a huge loss in the world."

"You know his wife's death was tragic."

"Yep." I clicked my pen closed.

"And Marlon's addiction to gambling started soon after that."

"Yep." I closed the lid of my laptop and secured it to the docking station. I was happy to leave it here tonight. Tomorrow would be soon enough to retrieve it.

"And Chief was at risk of losing the family home."

"Got all that. But a child died in the fire in February."

She bit her lower lip.

"And millions of dollars in insurance fraud hurts everyone. And selling drugs, Spring."

"Well—"

"And Marlon left Finn to die." To me, that was the end of any possible sympathy. A kid dying was bad enough. Truly. The family would be scarred for the rest of their lives—even though they hadn't done anything wrong. And poor David, ODed— another lost child.

Then leaving a fellow firefighter to die in a blaze? Yeah, that was right up there with unforgivable sins. "Plus, the dogs—" I swallowed. That part of the investigation was looking pretty gruesome as well. "They won't even be able to charge all the people who bet on those fights. Scum of the Earth."

"Yeah. How's Yanna holding up? You believe she didn't know what was going on?"

"She's got a sick child at home. Yes, she's the manager for Hearts & Paws—so the proverbial buck stops with her. But Meyer and Selah were good at covering their tracks. Finn only figured out the false paperwork because he knows the numbers of the streets so well. That kind of knowledge is certainly something I don't possess."

"How many dogs were saved?"

"The cops found five. Three had to be euthanized because they'd been used for fighting repeatedly."

"Oh my God." Spring blinked several times. "That's horrible."

"The other two need homes. We can run a feature on them—"

"I'll do it. And ensure folks know Yanna and the shelter aren't to blame. That they'll need our help more than ever."

I nodded as I rose. "I'll make a donation. Finn said last night he'd put in a bit of extra time while he's on leave. The doctor said light exercise as he gets his equilibrium back might be a good thing. He just can't overdo it." I put my coat on. Overdo it *again*.

The overnight snow had mostly melted—but my bike was done for the season. *Maybe forever. Finn really doesn't like you riding that thing. He appreciates the leather—but not the risk.* "You can close up?"

She waved me off. "Have a good date. Lock him in for a solid relationship—if that's what you both want."

I held my wool scarf in my hands. "I don't want to get ahead of myself. Or of him."

"He's smitten. You're smitten. You'll figure it out." She turned her attention back to her laptop. "Oh, another story just hit. I'll forward you the link—but promise me you won't look until tomorrow?"

"But if I'm the story—"

"I know where you are." She made a shooing motion.

On that note, I headed out. As I drove to Finn's, I reflected on the—so far three—stories published in other papers that had discussed my previous *situation.* None had made it the focus of the story, though, so I was grateful for that. I'd seriously considered giving Spring the byline for this story. Except she just didn't know it as well as I did. So she couldn't have bluffed the shoe-leather reporting. Well, maybe she could've—the woman was damn smart. Still, if things had gone south, I needed to be the one to take the flak. Whatever that looked like.

I kept my speed at the limit as I headed to Finn's. The road were slick, as the snow had turned to a cold, heavy rain. Perhaps a night to spend at home by the fire. Still, I had dinner reservations.

And a plan.

Finn emerged from his cabin as I pulled up. He hopped in and leaned over for a peck. A kiss that came as naturally as breathing. "I'm ready." His boyish smile emerged.

"How's your head?" I turned my SUV around and had us heading back down the driveway.

"Mom says it's okay for me to go out tonight."

"Oh? I didn't see her car." I'd only spotted Finn's pickup truck.

"Nothing like that. She came to visit."

"And to check up on you, I'm quite certain."

"You would be certainly correct."

"I can't blame her. Less than twenty-four hours ago, you were being shot at." I pulled onto his road.

"Not sure what that has to do with a concussion."

I chuckled. "Maybe that you need your head examined? Following me like that?"

This time, he laughed. "I saved your life."

I chanced the quickest of glances toward him. "How do you figure that?"

"If I hadn't been there, then you wouldn't have known about the propane tank. If you hadn't known about the—"

"Okay, I get it." I laughed as I pulled on the street that would take us back to Mission City's downtown. "I'll grant you that much. I'd also appreciate if you didn't stick your neck out like that again." I cast another quick glance. "Profession aside. I'd never ask you not to be a firefighter."

"Oh, phew. Because that would be a deal-breaker."

I smiled. Yeah, I'd known that. To Finn, being a firefighter was his raison d'être.

Like, for me, reporting was in my blood. "I suppose I could've been a detective?"

"You planning to join the RCMP?"

I barked out a laugh at Finn's question. 'Uh, no. I was just thinking that if I wasn't a reporter, I wouldn't make a bad detective. Private, of course. I'm not meant for law enforcement."

"No, too conformist for you. Too many rules." No missing the smile in his words.

"Hey."

"Just keeping it real." He placed his hand on my thigh. "Thank you for coming to get me."

"My pleasure. Truly. Now, when was the last time you went to Stavros's?"

He regaled me with the few times he'd gone over the years. Usually with his mother. He also made it clear calamari was a hard no, and I wasn't allowed to have it either.

Since that particular food wasn't my favorite, I didn't have a problem with that edict.

By the time we were seated, and Stavros's niece Timothea had taken our order, my nerves were ratcheted up to maximum.

Finn held his hand out.

I grasped it.

"Unless you're planning to tell me that you never want to see me again, then there's no reason to be nervous."

"How do you know I'm nervous?"

"Oh Jesus, Ulysses. I know you by now."

"How did you know to follow me? Where I was headed?"

"An unlocked phone screen. You might want to be more careful in the future."

I considered. "If I didn't have confidential information on it—although deeply layered under encryption—then I could just give you my password."

"Like I gave you the spare key to my place?"

"Oh yeah. I used that this morning when I left. I should give it back to you."

He waved me off.

I didn't argue.

"Two colas." Timothea put the glasses on the table and grinned. Her blue eyes sparkled. "And your meals should be up shortly."

Finn squeezed my hand. "No rush."

She glanced down. "Yeah, I figured as much. Oh, new customers. I have to go." With that, she headed toward the door and the new arrivals.

I followed her with my gaze and cocked my head.

Finn turned—obviously to see what had caught my attention. He chuckled. "That would be Stanley and Justin. Must be date night because they don't have their two kids." He pivoted his attention back to me. "Justin's one of the handsome gingers I mentioned all those months ago. I warned you Mission City has several very attractive gay redheads. Fun fact—Justin looks nearly identical to Stanley's ex-boyfriend, Maddox. We all thought Stanley getting together with Justin was a hoot—because obviously the guy has a type."

"Stanley?"

"Yep. Although, to be fair, Justin sort of got thrown in his path." He sobered. "Stanley's younger brother died, leaving his beloved son behind. Stanley stepped up to take care of the boy. Justin happened to be Angus's counselor and, well—" He shrugged. "Sometimes we don't see love coming, and it catches us off guard. Later, after the men formally adopted Angus, they adopted a little girl—Opal. They now have this amazing life that came out of a profound tragedy."

I held his gaze.

"I responded to the call from Angus about his dad." He tightened his grip on my fingers. "The man was dead, but Angus kept begging us to do something. Those calls—" He swallowed. "I hate when nothing can be done. Won't stop me from doing my job, though. I want back out into the field. Real bad."

Taking in the story proved tough. "Family's what we make of it, right?"

He blinked. "Uh, yeah."

"Do you want kids?"

He stilled. Slowly, he shook his head. "I love working with the kids at the high school. I love volunteering at the shelter. I'm not one of those guys who feels his life isn't complete without having a legacy to leave. I worried about my mom wanting grandkids, but we had that conversation. She understands. She's also the first to admit being a parent—especially a single parent—is really hard. Now—" He drew in a breath and let it out. "If I met someone who knew they wanted to become a parent—that their lives wouldn't be complete without that—I'd reconsider."

"You shouldn't have to." I continued to hold his hand.

"Life is about compromises."

"That's a lifelong commitment. That's more than a compromise. That's—" I floundered.

"So how about you?"

"Nope. Kids are great. Someone else's, though. I had a shitty childhood, and I worry I'd be a bad parent. And, frankly, it's just not for me."

"Knowing yourself is important. I love that gay people have choices."

"Yeah. I'm old enough to remember when they didn't. I'm happy to never go back to that time."

"One moussaka and one chicken souvlaki." Timothea waited until we pulled our hands apart before putting the plates of heavenly smelling food before us. "Anything else?"

We shook our heads.

"Bon appetit." With that, she left us.

Finn held my gaze. "Was the *kids* discussion the hardest part of the evening?"

"Christ, I hope so."

"Great. Let's eat."

Chapter Thirty-Two

Finn

The chicken souvlaki was delicious. The restaurant was amazing. My date was finally calmer as he devoured his moussaka. I sipped my cola. "I feel like my world has tilted, you know?"

"Is you head bothering you? I should've brought food to your cabin instead of bringing you out." He scanned the restaurant—likely looking for Timothea.

"Ulysses." I waved my hand.

His attention snapped to me. "Huh?"

"I'm fine. Mild headache, no vertigo. Mom took me to see Doctor Raymond today. She trusts the neurologist, but wanted me to see my family doctor. To touch base, she said."

"Your mother is a force of nature."

"I believe she would see that as a compliment."

"I mean it as such."

"Yeah." I sipped my drink again. "I talked to her about Giancarlo. She thinks I should consider getting counseling. Maybe up at Healing Horses Ranch. Maybe with someone like Justin."

Ulysses cocked his head. "How do you feel about that?"

"About Giancarlo or about seeing a therapist? I'm really okay. I mean, I feel betrayed by a bunch of people—some of whom I trusted and some of whom I knew would screw me over eventually. Whether I should be surprised or just resigned now it's happened is an open debate. One I'd rather not have."

He squinted.

"Gerard and Marlon are fuckwits. Giancarlo has my number, and I won't refuse to take his call. Does anything else really matter? I see the neurologist in two weeks, and as long as there haven't been any setbacks, I should be cleared to return to light duties with a goal to be back to fighting fires in about a month. Don't worry—I'm going to be honest with the doctor. I don't want to go back before I'm fit for duty."

"That sounds too easy."

"Like I'm too accepting?" I ran my finger up and down my glass of cola. "I've always known Marlon was a jerk, He was my nemesis in school. Everyone knew he got his job because of his dad...and his dad wasn't a great chief."

Ulysses snickered.

I offered a small smile. "Yeah. So I think I've just been waiting for something bad to happen. I just held my breath and hoped that whatever happened didn't cost someone their life." I rubbed my forehead. "But a child died, and David. And all those dogs—" I swallowed. Hard. "So yeah, I'm upset. Me being upset doesn't change things. That's why I said I feel like my world is tilted."

"You consider applying for the job as chief?"

"What?" I eyed him. "I'm too young."

"You're good with people. You're organized. You keep your head in a crisis."

"I want to fight fires while I'm still healthy enough to do it. Maybe when I retire from firefighting, then I'll look at some kind of administrative job." He leaned closer. "The truth? I like our current mayor, but the last one was an idiot. So do I want to spend all my time embroiled in dealing with politics? Hell no."

Ulysses smiled. "See? Just like I'd never want to be on the inside of law enforcement."

I held out my glass.

He clinked his to mine and we both sipped our drinks.

Finally, he put his glass back down. "I have news."

I held his gaze. "Yeah?"

"The Vancouver Sun called—they've offered me my old job back."

My gut clenched. This was everything he'd wanted—and they were offering it to him. "Oh?" Casual.

"Yeah."

"But what about what happened before?"

"According to the editor, I've done my penance and most people will forget about the entire thing."

"Do you believe that?"

He closed his eyes for a moment. "Well, my part in the *incident* has been addressed several times in the last twenty-four hours and no one's come after me with a pitchfork."

"Did you expect them to?"

"Truthfully? Anything was possible."

"So you're going back to Vancouver?" *That's not so bad. It's only an hour away. Maybe he can come out on weekends...or I can go in on my days off. Or—*

"Uh, no." He offered a smile. "That's not the life I want anymore."

This time, I blinked. "I don't understand."

"I also got offers from papers in Calgary and Toronto. Which is crazy because I don't know those cities. I guess they figure I can adapt."

"You can. And if that's what you want, then you should definitely go for it. Grab that chance."

"Like I said, though...that's not the life I envision for myself. I like the slower pace of a small town. And I know this might be all the excitement I ever see in Mission City. I'm okay with that. I can nurture talent here. I can encourage kids who are interested to pursue journalism. Hell, I've been offered a chance to do a lecture at the university in Abbotsford. And UBC called as well. They want to do a feature about me as an alumnus. I said sure—as long as I could be a cautionary tale."

"Yeah, I can see that about you. But Mission City? Aren't you going to get bored?"

"With Spring Dixon as my protégé? No, not likely. More like I've got to stay sharp and on my toes. Plus, I like Mission City. I like my boyfriend."

I sipped my drink again as I tried to gather my thoughts. "So where does that leave us?" Heat raced to my cheeks.

He grinned. "I love when you blush."

By now, I was certain my cheeks matched the red of my hair.

"I plan to keep working at the paper. I like what I've helped build with Spring." Ulysses shrugged. "I'm going to finish the edits on the novel manuscript and I'll consider—after a lot of soul-searching and deliberation—whether or not I'll unveil myself."

"You don't have to. I shouldn't have reacted the way I did."

He shrugged. "You were right—I hadn't been honest with you. And that was my bad. You got me thinking—what if kids who look like me knew that being a novelist was possible? What if the literary world, who already *know* me, get to see the real me?"

"You're not worried?"

"If someone isn't going to buy my book because I'm Black, then I probably wasn't who they thought I was anyway. I can take a hit to my sales. Now, my publisher might not like that."

"Or your sales might increase, and they might be glad."

"No way to know. This new book is one of my best—at least that's what my editor says. If sales drop off, then we'll have an inkling. I'm hoping readers won't choose to read my books differently if they know what I look like."

I sure as shit hoped they didn't either. "So, no Vancouver, Toronto, or Calgary?"

He shook his head.

"Just small-town living?"

He nodded. "Oh, and I'm going to give you a month or two of getting used to me before I move into your place."

"Oh?" I chuckled. "Why my place?"

"It's bigger, of course. That loft looks perfect for writing."

"I write poetry up there."

"I know."

"I could add a second desk. Hell, I might even give you the window."

He waggled his eyebrows.

"You'll be giving up your view of Mount Baker."

He shrugged. "To be in your bed every night? Small sacrifice. Truly—I won't miss the condo. It's never felt like home."

"Oh?"

"Home is with you—if you'll have me."

My heart skipped a beat. "That easy?"

"Well, I have bad habits. Oh, and we're getting a dog. I've always wanted a dog, and since I'm the boss, I can bring one to the office with me." He grinned.

My chest expanded. "I've wanted a dog since my last one died."

"I know. So we'll be doggy daddies."

I rolled my eyes. "That sounds so bad."

"Do you object?"

"Hell, no." I held his gaze—getting lost in those dark-brown irises. "This still counts as a first date, though. And I'm not putting out. No matter how much you make my dreams come true." I extended my hand.

Ulysses grasped it. "Bribery first—dog and all. The rest will come later."

Should I be worried that he hasn't spoken about love? Well, we'd sort of yelled that we loved each other after Gerard died. If we never said those words again, I was really okay with it. "Two months?"

"Give or take."

"Yeah. Okay. Give or take." I squeezed his hand.

He squeezed back.

Epilogue

Ulysses

Two months. Give or take.

The give had been all of two weeks and the take had been even less than that.

As we stood in the lobby Hearts and Paws, Finn vibrated with excitement.

I nudged my boyfriend. "Do you know that guy?" I pointed toward the Black gentleman who stood by the billboard of pets available for rescue. The guy was about my height. His bald pate shone in the sunlight coming in from the window. His beard was overgrown and his eyebrows were a little bushy. I didn't want to say unkempt—but definitely not someone I would think of as a corporate type. Of course, the flannel shirt and dirty jeans also leant themselves more to lumberjack than boardroom. And the dude was built. Solid muscle—visible even under the clothes.

Finn shook his head. Then, in true Finn fashion, he stepped toward the man and extended his hand. "Finn O'Sullivan. I volunteer here, but I'm picking up my rescue dog today."

Slowly, the man reciprocated. "Carver. I'm also here picking up a rescue. Well, a pair."

"Oh? That's great! Is Carver your first name or your last name? Oh, this is my boyfriend, Ulysses. He's the editor of the Mission City Gazette. You might already know that. I'm a firefighter."

"I read the newspaper. So I know who you both are." He cleared his throat. "It's just Carver." He caught my gaze.

I nodded back. Might've been my imagination, but I detected a guy who just wanted to be left alone.

Finn could be...a little much. Enthusiasm in spades and a man who wore his heart on his sleeve. A damn easy man to love.

Yanna entered the lobby. She had one small dog in her arms and another on a leash. "Okay, Carver. You remember Walter." She rubbed the ears of the dog in her arms. The older mutt with mobility issues. "And Poppin is sure glad to see you."

The dog was pulling her way toward the guy.

Carver stepped forward, and dropped to his haunches. "Hello, Poppin. Are you looking forward to coming home with me?" He held out his hand.

She licked it with great enthusiasm.

Walter yipped.

Carver stuck out his hand for Walter to sniff. "I'm right here. I have two hands, so I promise you'll each always get lots of pets and love." He cast a glance over his shoulder to meet my gaze. "I read the profiles you wrote in the paper, and when Yanna said they could go together, I knew this was meant to be."

"Oh God, that's so lovely." Finn pressed a hand to his chest. "I wanted to take all of them, but Ulysses can only take one dog to work with him and Thelma will be harder to place because she's a pittie mix although, let's be honest, she's just a big mush pot."

"I considered Thelma...but I think I like little dogs who get overlooked." He gave Poppin scritches behind her ear. "We're going to be a family."

Finn sighed. "We are too. I mean, Ulysses is moving in with me, and we're rescuing Thelma, so that's a sort of family."

I put my arm around Finn's waist and drew him close. "I think Carver understands."

"That family comes in all shapes and sizes? Yes, I get that. Congratulations on moving in together. That's a big step." The man offered a warm smile that lit his eyes.

Still, I sensed an underlying sadness.

"Do you need help with the harnesses and tethers? You've got your SUV set up, right?" Yanna handed Walter to Carver.

"Yes, I do." He nodded. "Gallia at Wags and Love helped me set everything up. Everything is ready at home. This is the last stop."

Walter licked his chin.

"Thank you, buddy. I think we're going to do just fine." To Yanna, he said, "And we've got appointments with Dr. Dixon tomorrow to get them checked."

"Dr. Zephyra has their records." Yanna handed him a cloth bag with the shelter's logo on it. "Poppin's meds are in there. Make certain you take them with you to the appointment tomorrow."

"I will." Carver grasped the bag with the hand holding Poppin's leash.

"Oh, can I say *goodbye*?" Finn blinked.

"Of course." Carver advanced toward my boyfriend with his new brood.

As Finn said his farewells, I moved toward the counter where Yanna stood. "Busy day."

She grinned. "The best. Thank you for the stories. Especially the one about how I didn't know."

Before she could start again, I waved her off. "You're good. Hopefully more volunteers will come. I know Finn plans to keep coming by."

"That's good of him."

"He's the best."

"Yes, he truly is." She smiled. 'Let me go get Thelma. I'll be right back." With that, she was gone.

"Let me grab the door." Finn opened the door and held it as Carver and the two dogs departed. When the door was closed, he made his way over to me. "Oh God, wasn't that the sweetest ever? I was so worried about those two—and they've gone together!"

I pulled him in for a long hug. "You're a good man."

He eyed me. "So are you, you know. Inviting Mom over tonight even though it's your first official night living with me."

"Well, you're a mama's boy in the best possible way. And your mom knows someone interested in buying my condo. So, uh, win/win."

"You're so cute."

"And here we are." Yanna emerged with a very excited Thelma.

Finn and I both dropped to our haunches as the pittie mix launched herself at us. Somehow, she managed to lick both of us pretty much at the same time.

We all laughed.

Yanna handed me the leash. "I assume you've visited Gallia as well?"

"Yep. Everything's arranged at home." My smile was about a mile wide.

"We even fixed up the old dog run so she'll be able to go outside safely." Finn grinned. "She's going to have the best life ever."

"She'll have the two of you—she's very lucky. I'll see you next week, right?" Yanna held Finn's gaze.

"Of course. Thelma will be with Ulysses that day, so I can come around and hang out with the cats."

"Oh, we have a new bonded pair of seniors who arrived yesterday. Tragic story. Kirk and Spock. If they're still here, maybe you can spend some time with them?"

Finn caught my gaze.

I tilted my head. "Let's get Thelma settled first. We don't even know if she likes cats—"

"She loves cats. Used to live with one." Yanna tried for innocent.

I wasn't buying it for a moment. "Kirk and Spock, eh?"

"Yep."

"We'll get back to you."

Finn grinned. He took Thelma's leash, we waved goodbye to Yanna, and we headed out to my SUV. After he secured her in the back seat, we got into the front.

"Hey, Finn. There's one more thing I need to tell you."

He leaned back so Thelma could lick his ear. "Oh yeah, what's that?"

"Well first, that I'm okay if we rescue a pair of senior cats."

"Really? You wouldn't mind?"

"If Thelma is as good with them as Yanna seems to think she will be? Sure...why not?"

He pecked my cheek. "I promise to stop at three."

Given I'd half expected to be coming home with Walter and Poppin, I was already impressed by his restraint.

"There's something else."

"Oh?" He arched an eyebrow.

I swallowed. "I love you."

His eyes widened. "Can you repeat that?"

"I love you. I'm ready to tell you now. I knew a while ago. For sure at the fire, but really the night you took me to the basketball game. But—" I swallowed. "I couldn't trust myself. Couldn't trust us. I wanted to be certain...that I was good enough for you."

He cocked his head. "Ulysses? I love you too. I'm happy we finally figured it out. Together."

"I'm glad I stopped my motorcycle for you."

"Well, I think Rodney Saunders stopped it for you. Damn kid. Still, if he hadn't been joyriding, we might not have wound up together. Although, I have to say, even if you hadn't stopped, I would've found you anyway. We were meant to be together, and I really love you too."

I leaned over.

He met me halfway.

We kissed.

Thelma nuzzled us.

Yep, our own family.

My found family.

Forever.

Want to know more about Carver? Check out Styx's Storm!

Want more Gabbi Grey?

Check out her Love in Mission City series, set in beautiful British Columbia.

The first book is
Ginger Snapping All the Way (Love in Mission City Book 1)

Also available:
Ginger Snapping All the Way(Love in Mission City Book 1)
Stanley's Christmas Redemption (Love in Mission City Book 2)
The Beauty of the Beast (Love in Mission City Book 2.5)
Sleigh Bells and Second Chances (Love in Mission City Book 3)
A Daddy for Christmas 2: Foster (Love in Mission City Book 3.5)
Rayne's Return (Love in Mission City Book 4)
Gideon's Gratitude (Love in Mission City Book 5)
Quinton's Quest (Love in Mission City Book 6)
Ulysses's Ultimatum (Love in Mission City Book 7)
Love in Mission City: The Boyfriend Gamble
Love in Mission City: The Four Seasons
Love in Mission City: The Boyfriends Duet
Love in Mission City: The Shorts
Love in Mission City: The Wedding Duet
A Daddy for Christmas 3: Lorcan
Pup, Pup, and Away
A Daddy for Christmas 4: Raphael
Anderson's Reinvention
Rayne Check
Archer's Awakening
Leo's Lust

Finn's Find

Styx's Storm

Love Without Reservations

Page Against The Machine

The Lightkeeper's Love Affair

Ace's Place

Marcus's Cadence

Not in it for the Money

Also:

Edging Coach (co-written with L.A. Witt)

Hugh (Single Dads of Gaynor Beach)

Anthony (Single Dads of Gaynor Beach)

Xavier (Single Dads of Gaynor Beach)

Love Furever (Friends of Gaynor Beach Animal Rescue)

Husky Love (Friends of Gaynor Beach Animal Rescue)

Yorkie to My Heart (Friends of Gaynor Beach Animal Rescue)

A Furever Home (co-written with Kaje Harper – Friends of Gaynor Beach Animal Rescue)

Axe to Grind (Road to Rocktoberfest 2023)

Grindstone's Edge (Road to Rocktoberfest 2024)

Voice to Raise (Road to Rocktoberfest 2025)

Drums and Lullabies (Road to Rocktoberfest 2026)

My Past, Your Future

If Only for Today

Catch a Tiger by the Tail

Solstice Surprise

Valentino in Vancouver

You See Me

Sun, Surf, and Surprises

Ginger in the City

Caressa's Homecoming (Bound by Love Book 1)

Cole's Reckoning (Bound by Love Book 2)

A Little Christmas: Tobias

An Uncommon Gentleman

A Sensible Gentleman

A Wounded Gentleman

Finding Noah (Foggy Basin Season 2)

Noah's Holiday (A Foggy Basin Short Story)

Dancing Through Pride (A Foggy Basin Short Story)

Keystrokes and Kittens (Foggy Basin Season 3)

Hot Rucking Canadian

Big Rucking Disaster

Didn't See You Coming

Unlocked and Unlost

Audiobooks

Ginger Snapping All the Way

Stanley's Christmas Redemption

Sleigh Bells and Second Chances

Rayne's Return

Gideon's Gratitude

Quinton's Quest

Ulysses's Ultimatum

Rayne Check

Archer's Awakening

Leo's Lust

Finn's Find

A Daddy for Christmas 2: Foster

A Daddy for Christmas 3: Lorcan

Puppy Pride

Thought You Were the One

Love in Mission City: The Shorts

Page Against the Machine

The Lightkeeper's Love Affair

Ace's Place

Marcus's Cadence

Not in it for the Money

Hugh (Single Dads of Gaynor Beach)

Anthony (Single Dads of Gaynor Beach)

Love Furever (Friends of Gaynor Beach Animal Rescue)

Husky Love (Friends of Gaynor Beach Animal Rescue)

A Furever Home (co-written with Kaje Harper – Friends of Gaynor Beach Animal Rescue)

My Past, Your Future

If Only for Today

Catch a Tiger by the Tail

Solstice Surprise

An Uncommon Gentleman

A Sensible Gentleman

A Wounded Gentleman

Didn't See You Coming

Unlocked and Unlost

Want a free short story? The story is set in Gaynor Beach, California where there are plenty of single dads and puppy rescues! You can sign up for my newsletter so you can keep up with all the great stuff I'm doing as well as pictures of my own pooches, Ally and Finnegan.

Hemingway's Happy Day

Love contemporary MF romances? What's better than love in the beautiful Cedar Valley in British Columbia, Canada? Find small town romances with a touch of angst, a bit of heat, and a lot of heart...

The Absolution of Abigail Reardon (prequel)
The Luminosity of Loriana Harper (Book 1)
The Making of Marnie Jones (Book 2)
The Redemption of Remy St. Claire (Book 3)

Interested in knowing more about Gabbi?

Sign up for her newsletter

Follow her on Bookbub

Follow her on Instagram

USA Today Bestselling author Gabbi Grey lives in beautiful British Columbia where her fur baby chin-poo keeps her safe from the nasty neighborhood squirrels. Working for the government by day, she spends her early mornings writing contemporary, gay, sweet, and dark erotic BDSM romances. While she firmly believes in happy endings, she also believes in making her characters suffer before finding their true love. She also writes m/f romances as Gabbi Black and Gabbi Powell.

www.ingramcontent.com/pod-product-compliance
Lightning Source LLC
LaVergne TN
LVHW091033080826
845145LV00002B/471

* 9 7 8 1 9 9 7 9 0 4 1 9 9 *